"Let's go upstairs, then."

"You certainly don't waste any time," Gable remarked dryly.

"It's all your fault, Mr. McCrea," Annabel answered lightly. Her voice held a throaty quality, and it made Gable look up from the bill as a strange pulse began to beat somewhere inside him.

"You've gotten me all worked up over dinner. Now it's time to deliver." Giving him a slow, devastating smile that made him drop his pen, she turned and headed out of the restaurant toward the elevator.

Gable was stunned. Had Annabel Porter just flirted with him?

Dear Reader,

Spellbinders! That's what we're striving for. The editors at Silhouette are determined to capture your imagination and win your heart with every single book we publish. Each month, six Special Editions are chosen with *you* in mind.

Our authors are our inspiration. Writers such as Nora Roberts, Tracy Sinclair, Kathleen Eagle, Carole Halston and Linda Howard—to name but a few—are masters at creating endearing characters and heartrending love stories. Their characters are everyday people—just like you and me—whose lives have been touched by love, whose dreams and desires suddenly come true!

So find a cozy, quiet place to read, and create your own special moment with a Silhouette Special Edition.

Sincerely,

The Editors
SILHOUETTE BOOKS

JUDE O'NEILL
A Family of Two

Silhouette Special Edition

Published by Silhouette Books New York

America's Publisher of Contemporary Romance

For Patti,
who lends me courage from her inexhaustible supply

SILHOUETTE BOOKS
300 East 42nd St., New York, N.Y. 10017

Copyright © 1987 by Judy Blundell

ISBN: 0-373-09408-6

First Silhouette Books printing September 1987

America's Publisher of Contemporary Romance

Printed in the U.S.A.

Books by Jude O'Neill

Silhouette Romance
Just One Look #464

Silhouette Special Edition
The Midnight Hour #387
A Family of Two #408

JUDE O'NEILL

tossed aside the glamorous life of an underpaid editor
in Manhattan to become a full-time writer. Since then
she has penned everything from radio commercials
and book jackets to film reviews and novels. Married
to an artist, she divides her time between California
and New York.

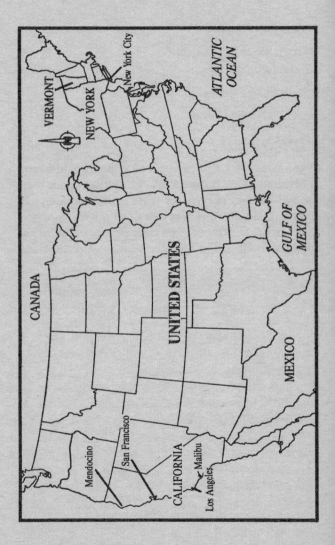

Chapter One

The red light on the answering machine was blinking again when she came out of the shower. Annabel threw her wadded-up wet towel at it. It missed the machine and hit her coffee cup, which promptly tipped over and spilled its cold, muddy contents onto the arm of the couch. Then the cup rolled placidly off the cushion and landed on the carpet, spilling a few more drops.

"That was your fault, Gable McCrea," Annabel said aloud. "Will you stop calling me!"

She wiped up the coffee with the towel, then hurled the sodden mass across the living room to the hamper by the bathroom door. Living in a studio apartment had its advantages; you could clean up easily if you were blessed with good aim at wastebaskets and hampers. Once a junior high basketball champ, Annabel had refined her natural talent for the hook shot to a fine art.

She sat on her heels and regarded the blinking red light for a moment. Then she sighed and pushed the Play button on her machine. She steeled herself for the sound of the voice she'd gotten to know so well over the past three days.

"Gable McCrea again. I'm now at 555-5242. I'll be here until four-thirty."

"Mr. McCrea," Annabel told the machine mildly, "surely it must be obvious to you by this time that I am not going to return your call. This week, anyway." In answer, the machine clicked and rewound to await another call, and Annabel sighed and stood up again. What was she doing trying to reason with an answering machine? That's what seven days spent cooped up in your apartment could do to you.

Why she hadn't taken everyone's advice and gone away to some nice warm island for her vacation, she had no idea. Instead, she had obstinately insisted that a week in her apartment with nothing to do was exactly what she was longing for.

She must have been insane. If there was a more dismal place than New York City during a cold, rainy week in February, Annabel didn't know where it could be, and she certainly never wanted to find out. The weather was too biting for her to wander around the city, as she'd planned; all her friends were busy with work, as she should have realized; and her adventuresome parents had fled freezing New Jersey for a golf tournament in Malaysia.

Annabel had thought she'd need at least a week off to recuperate from directing and editing her second film, *Writing Off Craig*. She was thrilled that it had turned out to be a hit, but after a year of raising the money for it, another year in preproduction and then shooting and editing it, and six months promoting it to any journalist who would listen to her, she was exhausted. She had felt as though she never wanted to look at another script again; certainly she wasn't ready to tackle the piles she kept receiving from her agent, friends of friends and what must be the entire graduating class from her alma mater, New York University's film school. She felt curiously directionless from having no idea what her next project would be, but that was a feeling she should savor. Who said, Annabel had told herself stoutly, that she had to jump straight from one grueling project to another?

That rational course of inaction had lasted exactly three days.

She'd started innocently enough with just one script, picking it up idly as she was soaking in the tub. Before she knew it, she'd gone through the short pile in the bathroom, and, fueling herself with pots of coffee, she'd tackled the medium-sized pile by her bed. Now she was working on the towering mountain on one side of the couch. The short stack on the kitchen table still beckoned. The constant hope that the next script would be the perfect one for her to do spurred her on.

She should have gone to Bermuda. Or at least to her parents' home in Teaneck. She should have known she wouldn't be able to relax and ignore the scripts clumped around her apartment. At least on a distant island she could get away from the telephone.

Although, Annabel decided with another glance at the answering machine, with Gable McCrea's persistence, he would have tracked her down in the middle of the Sahara. Or even in New Jersey.

She knew who he was, of course. He was A Famous Hollywood Producer. Not that she held it against him;

she even admired some of the films he'd done. But she and he were two very different styles of film people, and she didn't mean simply a director versus a producer.

Annabel was one of the new breed of independent filmmakers who scorned the notion that they needed to reside in Hollywood to do important work. She had managed to make her films outside the aegis of a major studio or producer, and she intended to keep it that way. Gable McCrea was pure Hollywood. He was exactly the kind of producer she tended to avoid: a throwback to the old days of the studio system, when the producer had a personal stamp on a film and was better known than the director or the writer. Annabel didn't want to work with a savvy Hollywood producer; she just might get eaten alive.

She frowned, puzzled. To the best of her knowledge, it had been several years since Gable McCrea had produced a film, and she had a feeling his last one hadn't done too well. She wondered how old he was; he'd certainly been around for a while. Maybe he was losing his drive as he aged.

But now apparently he had a property he wanted her to look at. She supposed she was flattered a bit, since she wasn't exactly a heavy hitter in the film industry—yet. Her first film, a low-budget dramatic comedy, had garnered praise, but it certainly hadn't raked in profits that Hollywood would be impressed by. Even the success of *Writing Off Craig* was modest by Hollywood standards.

Well, no matter what, she wasn't interested in doing Gable McCrea's type of film. Besides, the man was unpardonably rude. Her agent had told him that she was on vacation and wasn't taking any calls, yet for three days now he had badgered her machine with a succession of numbers he could be reached at in Manhattan. So if he could ignore her wish to be left alone, she could ignore his requests to return his calls.

Annabel sighed and stretched and considered ordering in some food. The night was far too wet and icy to venture out in. She pulled a slouchy gray cardigan on over her pullover and put on a thicker pair of socks. She felt cozy and snug in her small apartment, with the icy rain beating against the window panes.

She was heading for the kitchen area, lost in thoughts of spicy Szechuan chicken, when three heavy knocks resounded through the apartment. She stopped in the middle of the room, her heart thumping in her chest.

Visitors had to be buzzed in from downstairs, and even her next-door neighbor strictly adhered to the Manhattan etiquette of never coming over without calling first. Even though she was protected by several strong locks, Annabel couldn't repress a twinge of uneasy fear. She should have listened to her mother and moved into an apartment building that boasted a doorman.

She tiptoed to the door and looked through the peephole. The distorted image of an unfamiliar and very wet man confronted her. He spoke.

"I know you're looking at me, in there. Can you possibly overcome your New York paranoia and let me in?"

"Why should I? Who are you?"

"I'm Gable McCrea," the man said matter-of-factly, as if she should have known.

Annabel slumped against the door. He was right: she *should* have known. That strong, compelling voice on her machine certainly wouldn't stop at hounding her from a distance. The fear that had coiled inside her body dissolved and anger took its place. With shaking fingers she undid the triple bolts and opened the door.

He was wet, all right. He should have looked bedraggled and cold, but he didn't. He looked as though he'd just taken an invigorating swim; the glistening raindrops seemed only an athletic addition to the glossy image of an extremely fit man. His dark hair was slicked back off his forehead, throwing the lean lines of his face into high relief. His cheekbones were slashes in a taut face, his nose high-bridged and aquiline. His eyes were the color of steel.

The strange thing was that she couldn't say if he was handsome. His appeal had nothing to do with something so mundane as a pleasing arrangement of features. His was simply and purely a sensual impact, an impact so strong that she had to consciously avoid looking directly into his silver-gray eyes or at his long-fingered hands or his mouth. Unfortunately, that didn't leave her many other places to look. For lack of any other choice, Annabel decided to concentrate on his forehead.

"How did you get up here?" she asked. One long line creased his high brow. It was a line of irritation, and it looked well-worn. Even so, Gable McCrea was certainly younger than he had any right to be.

"I was about to ring from downstairs, when a very nice woman let me in as she was leaving. I guess I must look trustworthy." He smiled briefly but as punctuation to his statement, not out of genuine warmth. The smile never reached his eyes.

Annabel decided then and there that she didn't like him. She tended to steer clear of people without a sense of humor. In her opinion, the lack of one, especially in a film producer, was a serious shortcoming.

"I see." Her voice was low and quiet, as it usually was when she was struggling to hold on to her temper. "Mr. McCrea, the buzzer is there for a purpose: so vistors can be screened. In New York, when a person comes up to an apartment without buzzing, it is not only inconsiderate, it is dangerous. It can give an apartment dweller a heart attack. Now," she concluded, beginning to shut the door, "it's been delightful, but if you don't mind—"

His eyes flickered over her. "You can't possibly be Annabel Porter."

Her body froze into a stance of excruciating self-control. Her hand tightened on the doorknob. "I'm Annabel Porter," she said, her voice as cutting as the icy February wind outside. She was tired of men's surprise when they discovered who she was. She was a small-boned woman with a too-round face and a cupid's-bow mouth that led people to describe her as adorable. She was also thirty-four years old, and she was beginning to wonder if she'd ever outgrow the label. It didn't help that she was struggling to make it in what was still very much a male-dominated profession. Why did everyone expect a female director to be an Amazon?

Gable McCrea's eyes narrowed as he carefully considered her frothy ponytail of wavy, light brown hair, her double layer of sweaters and her fuzzily stockinged feet. Suddenly, Annabel was uncomfortably aware that she wasn't exactly at her professional best. She always preferred to meet casual Hollywood types in an impeccably tailored gray flannel suit. For meetings with stuffy New York backers, she broke out her black leather skirt. She always believed in unsettling the opposition. But even she had yet to conduct a meeting in sweatpants.

She braced herself for the comment he was surely forming, something along the lines of how a tiny thing like her could wield any clout on a movie set. Surely she was too young or too cute or too short to have achieved her reputation.

He didn't say a word, but he took advantage of her distraction by walking past her into her apartment.

"Mr. McCrea—"

He was already standing by the couch, looking down at her answering machine.

"Can I help you, Mr. McCrea?"

He spun around. "I'm wondering why you aren't courteous enough to answer your messages, Ms. Porter."

"And I'm wondering," she snapped, "why you aren't courteous enough to refrain from calling when you're asked to, and why you don't call before coming to a person's home and why you don't wait for an invitation before walking in."

"I have to talk to you, and I have no time to waste with silly power games. I don't play them, and I don't appreciate some snot-nosed youngster playing them on me."

"Excuse me, but I couldn't have heard you correctly," she said icily. "Did you call me a snot-nosed youngster? Mr. McCrea, I am over thirty. And my mother *has* taught me how to use a handkerchief."

He didn't have either of the two reactions she expected: he didn't smile, and he didn't look annoyed. He was still gazing at her with the same serious frown. "Look, I came here to talk about a project with you. I don't want to alienate you."

"Well, you certainly know how to ingratiate yourself."

He walked to the window and looked out onto the dark street. "How old are you, anyway?"

"How old are you?" she snapped back.

He turned around. "Fair enough. I'm forty."

"Thirty-four." The beginnings of a smile teased her mouth. "I guess that means we're both grown-ups."

This time his smile was genuine. Not very big, but genuine. "I haven't been acting much like one, have I?"

His indirect apology disarmed her, but she wasn't giving an inch.

"No."

"It's been a tough week. Look, I apologize for barging in like this. I have to put together this deal, and I had to see you before I went back to L.A. It was driving me crazy that you were right here in your apartment and I couldn't get to you. I want you for this film."

"Mr. McCrea, before you go any further, I have to tell you that I'm not interested. I'm sorry you came all this way for nothing."

"I'm not asking you for a commitment, Ms. Porter. I'm asking you to listen."

Annabel hesitated. She couldn't possibly tell this powerful man standing dripping on her carpet that she didn't want to work with him because she suspected he could step all over her. If she revealed that piece of information, it would be all over Hollywood by tomorrow afternoon—even by morning, considering the time difference.

Gable was watching her carefully, as if measuring the extent of her hesitation. "I have the rights to *A Family of Two*," he said softly.

Annabel slowly sank down into the couch. He couldn't have gotten her attention more completely if he had set off a bomb. The book had been a sensation even before it was printed and bound. Written by Delia Worthington-Crane, the illegitimate daughter of the world-famous painter Josiah Crane and his mistress, Melinda Silver, it not only told the story of Delia's fight for her inheritance but went back thirty years to the very beginning of the famous love affair of the artist and the beautiful, aristocratic rebel.

The case had made headlines just two years before. Josiah Crane, one of the most lyrical and powerful of the twentieth-century American painters, had died at the age of seventy-nine, leaving his entire estate to a foundation. Delia had appeared out of the blue, claiming to be his daughter by his mistress of fifteen years, Melinda Silver, who had died in 1952 at the age of thirty-seven. Delia had been adopted as an infant, and only after Josiah Crane had died and his life had been splashed across magazines and television did her adoptive mother, Giselle Worthington, recognize the man and woman who had been at the same French clinic as she to have their baby. Melinda had delivered her child, but Giselle's had been stillborn, and the couple had arranged to give their baby to her. Fragile and emotionally devastated by the experience, Melinda had returned to the States and suffered a nervous breakdown. Not long afterward, she had committed suicide.

It had been easy for Josiah and Melinda to keep her pregnancy a secret; they lived on Josiah's secluded estate near Mendocino in California. The lovers had considered it a necessary deception; a doctor had warned Melinda that she would have difficulty bringing the baby to term, and they could not jeopardize the pending annulment of her unhappy marriage on the grounds that she was barren. Perhaps that was the reason they had ultimately decided to give up the child. No one really knew for sure. But thirty-two years later, through painstaking detective work, Delia had traced the facts of her birth. Then she had gone to the authorities with her discoveries and sued for the bulk of the vast Crane estate.

It had been a celebrated legal battle. At first Delia's claim had seemed to be nothing but a giant hoax, but slowly, with her quiet sincerity and a haunting dark resemblance to Melinda, she had begun to elicit sympathy. Investigators had crawled over the Crane mansion searching for clues. Then the startling discovery of Melinda Silver's diary had proved that she had, indeed, borne a daughter in secret. The entire estate had gone to Delia, and she had promptly made a sizable donation to the Crane foundation.

The media had taken the beautiful woman with the regal bearing to their hearts. With the help of a ghost writer, she had published her story. Since Delia had used Melinda's diary for research, it had been the most intimate glimpse of the reclusive Josiah Crane ever given.

The book could make a blockbuster film, Annabel knew. She also knew how many studios had gone after it. All the elements for a great film were there: the doomed love of Melinda and Josiah, Melinda's inability to get a divorce from her husband, their years of attempting an annulment, Melinda's tragic breakdown after bearing the child she could not keep and her anger at Josiah for talking her into giving up the child—the anger that had destroyed their love and driven her mad. Framing the story and giving it focus was the child, grown up into a raven-haired beauty like her mother, bravely facing a storm of disbelief to claim her birthright. And best of all, weaving through the story with a purity of color and line that dazzled and astounded still, were the glorious paintings of Josiah Crane, celebrating his passion for one woman he had loved and never forgotten, the great tragedy of his life.

And Gable McCrea had the rights and wanted her to direct it.

"Let me get you a towel," Annabel said weakly.

Gable was too smart to let his relief show. "I'd appreciate it."

"Have you had dinner?" she asked as she emerged from the bathroom and tossed a towel at him.

"No."

"I was just about to have something," she said, heading for the kitchen. "Care to join me?"

"Sure." He leaned over the counter that separated the tiny kitchen from the rest of the apartment and watched Annabel as she opened the refrigerator. "I haven't had home cooking in a—" He stopped as she reached in and came back with a handful of paper. "You're going to cook that?"

"Take-out menus," Annabel said. "I've got pizza, Chinese, deli, Cajun or Thai."

"You keep them in the refrigerator?"

"Where else? What would you like?"

"I'd like a decent meal."

"Hey, this is *gourmet* take-out."

He took the menus from her hands. "I'll take you out to dinner. In a good restaurant." When she hesitated, he said gravely, "Please. I've been eating on the run all week. I need a civilized meal. I'm told that my hotel has an excellent restaurant. Then, if you like the idea over dinner, I can run upstairs and get the script for you."

That sounded reasonable. And Annabel had to admit that, even though she'd had some time to adjust to Gable McCrea's presence in her apartment, she was far from comfortable with him there. He seemed far too powerful, almost overbearing, in the small space. Perhaps a more impersonal arena would be better. Besides, somehow it didn't seem appropriate to duel over his project in plain view of her socks drying on the radiator.

On her way to the closet, she hesitated. "Mr. McCrea, can you answer me one thing first?"

"What?"

"Why me?" she asked simply. Gable would know what she meant. She had gotten a lot of publicity, but she still had only two films under her belt. Small-scale, low-budget dramatic productions about everyday relationships, they hardly qualified her to make what surely must be a sweeping epic about a legendary love affair and the spectacular emergence of an heir to a legacy of art and deception.

"Because you come in on time and on budget. Because you're good with actors. Because you're good with relationships between men and women. Because you're good, period. And because of *Writing Off Craig*."

"What about it?"

"That subplot about Janine and Charlie—how they gradually do everything take-out and mail order and never leave their apartment? I liked it. It was funny and pathetic, but there was something there in the relationship, how obsessive it was, that makes me think you could handle Josiah and Melinda without losing the audience's sympathy for them."

"Oh. Is that how you see Josiah and Melinda? Obsessive?"

He nodded.

"I've done small films with low budgets, you know."

"Of course I know. That's why I need you—you'd be surprised what the budget is on this. And I want a small, independent film. The only difference is that it's a period piece with more scope than you're used to. You think you can't handle that?"

"Of course I can handle it. I don't know if I want to."

"It's going to be a high-profile project. I don't have to tell you that as a female director, you'd be breaking new ground."

"Mr. McCrea, I can't say I don't feel a responsibility to other female directors, but I will not make a film I don't believe in," she returned sharply.

"I didn't mean to suggest that you would," he answered calmly. "But you can't know whether you believe in it or not until we've discussed it, can you?"

Annabel headed for the closet again but stopped and turned to deliver one last warning. "I don't make Hollywood movies."

"I don't want a Hollywood movie, Ms. Porter," Gable said impatiently. "That's why I am in some benighted section of Manhattan in the middle of a rainstorm trying to woo a stubborn director who won't agree to a free meal. Now, get your coat."

Chapter Two

Gable preferred blondes. Tall, cool women with impeccable grooming. Women with angles, not curves. Women who were fit and muscular from their daily workout in the gym. Well dressed, intelligent and able to choose which wine to have with the *suprêmes de pigeon et foie gras*.

He certainly wasn't interested in this tiny, curvaceous pocket of energy with an outrageous head of wild brown hair who kept take-out menus instead of endive in her refrigerator and who, when invited out to dinner, barely looked in the mirror but simply fluffed out that fountain of a ponytail, pulled on absurd, shiny rubber boots, preposterously paired them with a luxurious cashmere coat and cheerfully led the way to the street.

It was good that he wasn't interested in the least, he congratulated himself. He never mixed business with pleasure, and he would have to work closely with this director he had known he'd wanted to hire, sight unseen, since he'd come out of a screening of *Writing Off Craig*. A little investigation into her background and a screening of her earlier film had been almost unnecessary to seal his resolve. He wasn't going to let Annabel Porter say no, no matter how warily she was looking at him with those huge cat eyes of hers.

Yes, he was very glad he wasn't interested. In the least. But he had to admit he was amused. He could see why Annabel Porter was a good director. She had certainly taken charge of the evening with a kind of aplomb he had to admire. She had done the impossible and conjured up a cab on this miserable night, dashing across the street to hail one zooming in the opposite direction, giving the driver no choice but to stop. Wearing those silly rubber boots, she had strolled into the very chic French restaurant in his hotel as if she belonged there. In fact, she did, Gable now realized. The stylish New Yorkers in their furs didn't look at her at all patronizingly. Her style was unique and self-assured, and suddenly Gable saw that somehow the crazy combination of sweaters and fleecy pants didn't look in the least out of place.

It had just taken him a little while to realize it. He wondered why he was so slow on the uptake this evening. Ever since she'd opened her door and inexplicably trained her gaze on his forehead, he'd felt as though he'd been walking through cotton.

He'd ordered the steak *au poivre* and been surprised when Annabel asked if he'd mind if she chose the wine, saying with charming honesty that she didn't often get to order from such an excellent list. When he'd nodded politely, she perused the wine list and came up with an unfamiliar Bordeaux that caused the waiter to beam approvingly in that very French way.

The vintage turned out to be excellent.

Gable swirled the red wine in his glass, inhaling the rich fumes approvingly. Rule number one, he told himself sternly: don't underestimate her.

"Don't you like the wine?" Annabel asked.

He roused himself and looked up at her. The candlelight illuminated an extraordinary pair of green eyes. They were shot through with amber, and one had a tiny triangle of deep blue in the lower left corner. They were shrewd eyes, but so surprisingly warm....

Gable took a huge, and distinctly gauche, gulp of wine. Rarely did he find himself off balance, and he hated it when he did. "Yes, it's excellent. Good choice."

"You're surprised." It was a statement.

He wasn't used to being read so easily. "You seem more like the diet cola type," he said before he could stop himself.

What had he just said? Gable was rarely ungracious, but tonight outrageous things were slipping out of him, as though some other person, some very callow, foolish person, had said them. Somewhere he had lost his manners as well as his reflexes. The easy flattery so prevalent in Hollywood was suddenly beyond him. He was, uncharacteristically, saying what was on his mind. When it came to cajoling a reluctant director to take on his project, that could be dangerous, he realized.

Annabel hadn't even bristled at his comment; she merely studied him thoughtfully. "That surprises me," she said.

"What's that?"

She took a sip of wine and fixed those eyes on him again, tipping him back off balance. He almost felt as though the chair were heeling over. "I didn't think you would underestimate anyone. Even someone in red rubber boots who knows good Bordeaux.''

"I have a feeling you're used to being underestimated, Ms. Porter.''

"You're right. I don't like it very much.''

He carefully put his wine down on the table. "I won't do it again.'' He meant it.

"Good. Tell me about your film. Do you have a script?''

"I have a wonderful script. You'll like it.''

She cocked an eyebrow at him and then gave her attention to her salad. "Have you thought about casting?''

"I haven't a notion about who I'd like for Delia or Melinda yet, but I think Benjamin Hall would be perfect for Josiah Crane. He's shown some interest. He's a big star, of course, but I don't think he'd overpower the film, and we need at least one big draw. I know you've worked with him before.''

An expression he couldn't define crossed Annabel's face. It was gone before he could decipher it, and he shrugged it off. She would tell him soon enough if she objected to his ideas; he had no doubt that Annabel Porter would always speak her mind. Tonight he had to concentrate on wooing her—in a professional sense, of course.

Gable had long been amused by how similar his job was to romantic seduction, and he mentally used those images when swaying a talent to his film. It was ironic, since he never played the role of the seducer in real life; if he was interested in a woman, he didn't play any games. But the tools of seduction were there in his business—the wine, the flattery, the intimate restaurant, the total absorption in the person sitting across the table. He stopped short of diamonds from Tiffany's, however—though he had been known to send flowers on occasion.

But tonight he was careful. He didn't flatter Annabel; she didn't need it. He told her, simply and seriously, what he saw in the film and why he wanted her to direct it. He forgot himself and let her intent expression lead him on to expose his earnest enthusiasm for this project. Annabel let him talk, interrupting only to ask an occasional incisive question.

By the end of dinner, he could tell she was intrigued. She hadn't said more than a couple of words, but she was thinking, at least. Gable stopped talking and sipped his coffee. He sensed she needed some time. After a moment, she spoke.

"I'd like to see the script."

Relief rushed through him. "Fine."

She pushed her chair back immediately and stood up. "Let's go upstairs, then."

"You certainly don't waste any time," Gable remarked dryly as he signed for the check.

"It's all your fault, Mr. McCrea," she answered lightly. Her voice had taken on a sudden surprising lilt, as if the tension had dissolved with her decision. It also held a throaty quality, purring like a sleek, expensive car, and it made Gable look up from the bill as a strange pulse began to beat somewhere inside him.

"You've gotten me all worked up over dinner," Annabel went on. "Now it's time to deliver." Giving him a slow, devastating smile that made him drop his pen, she turned and headed out of the restaurant and toward the elevator.

Gable let out a long breath. Had her remark been deliberately suggestive, or was he crazy? Had Annabel Porter just flirted with him? He didn't think she was the type, but then again, she'd been surprising him all evening.

He followed her to the elevator with an idiotic grin on his face, which he immediately wiped off when she turned. This woman was some potent combination. Her face had an old-fashioned sweetness that led him to think of high lace collars and long white dresses on green lawns in someplace like Newport. But her arch manner and her razor-sharp mind honed her beauty and made it undeniably sensual; he'd never known intelligence could be so sexy. And then there was her very womanly body. Maybe, Gable decided grudgingly, it was time he rediscovered curves.

As soon as the elevator doors closed, Annabel immediately began talking about the project, about financial backing and deadlines and casting. The woman who had thrown him that suggestive smile in the dining room might well have disappeared. Gable wondered if he had imagined her. Maybe he just *wanted* Annabel to flirt with him. Somehow, she made him feel like a stodgy old producer. He almost felt he should light up a big, fat cigar.

When they entered his suite, he immediately switched on all the lights to defuse any intimate stirrings in the air—he was sure they were all in his imagination, anyway—and headed for the script and the copy of Melinda's diary he'd gotten from Delia. He handed them to her.

"What a view," Annabel said, crossing to the window. "It must be spectacular when it's clear. You can even see the Chrysler Building. Isn't it beautiful?"

Gable came up behind her to look out at the lights of Manhattan visible through the rain. The truth was that he'd been too exhausted every night to appreciate the view. But now he admired the way the soft gray mist blurred the sharp edges; the glorious lights looked soft and dreamy tonight.

"It's lovely," he said. Annabel turned around, and suddenly they were very close. Some scent rose from her hair or her skin—he wasn't sure which, or what it was—baby powder? roses? violets? Whatever it was, it was fresher than the exotic perfumes he was used to smelling on women. A flare of excitement roared up inside him, and he immediately strained to clamp it down.

She stepped away, back toward the center of the room. "Have you thought about locations yet?" she asked.

"I've gotten permission from Delia to shoot at Josiah's estate in Mendocino. Do you know the town? It's about a three-hour drive north of San Francisco. Beautiful coastline. It looks very much like New England. It's strange—Josiah totally rejected his past once he and Melinda left Boston, but he picked this place because it reminded him so much of his home. The house is an incredible place."

"Is it as beautiful as they say?"

"Beautiful and bizarre. It's barely accessible—we're going to have a hell of a time getting equipment trucks in there. The road is carved into a steep incline, and the house looks rather like a Victorian mansion gone askew. The layout is a bit crazy. Rumor has it that there are even secret passages and secret rooms buried in it somewhere, though no one's ever found them. Josiah was quite a character."

"Sounds like a difficult place to shoot in," Annabel observed, thumbing through the diary.

"It's not so bad. Crane knocked down walls and put in skylights to let in the light."

Gable watched as she frowned over the diary. Her mouth was incredibly lush, the upper lip an inviting, furling curve, the lower full, almost pouting. He'd forgotten women could have mouths like that. Her skin was unbelievable; it was smooth and pale, but it seemed to catch the light and glow from within.

He stopped himself. *I'm developing a crush on my director,* he thought, amazed.

"I'm not sure how soon I can get back to you on this," Annabel said. "Definitely by Friday, though. Is that okay with you?"

"Fine. But I'll be back in L.A. by then. Here." He fished a pen out of his jacket pocket and scrawled a number on the script. "That's my home number."

He looked up. Her face was close again, too close. It was tilted up so that she could look at him, and he could see the flawless, creamy perfection of her skin. He smelled that elusive scent again. Her teeth caught her lower lip, and he felt the barest hint of a sigh against his face. Her slanted eyes were glinting green in the soft light. They were grave but somehow so warm, almost expectant....

And before he could stop himself, he was kissing her.

Annabel's head swam. Gable McCrea was kissing her. Hard.

And she was kissing him back. Harder. Deeper. More intensely, she thought dizzily, than she'd ever kissed a man in her life.

She didn't even know him, really. She wasn't even sure if she *liked* him.

But she didn't want to stop kissing him. She supposed she'd wanted to from the moment she'd seen him. For a woman not given to impulsive romanticism, this was nothing less than shocking. Shocking but ... very nice.

Somehow the script and the diary had dropped from her hands and landed with a thud on the carpet. With those barriers gone, their bodies pressed together, and he was bending over her, his long fingers cupping her face, sliding around her jaw, down her neck.

His lips were cool against hers, but inside his mouth all was warm and sweet, velvet and sleek. The feel of him excited her as she'd never dreamed she could be excited. He kissed her as though there were no world but her mouth and the peculiar way it fitted against his own. It was an extraordinary sensation, to be kissed so thoroughly and with such concentration, and Annabel marveled at the poverty of her existence before it.

Her fingers curled into his shoulders, gripping him tightly. Gable groaned against her, and a fresh arousal ripped through her. She never, ever, wanted to stop doing this.

Then his fingers tightened on her shoulders, and he paused, his lips still against hers but now unmoving. Her eyes flew open and caught him gazing at her. She had a confused impression of mercury-colored eyes, cool, almost assessing, staring into her widened ones. She flushed and pulled away.

Her breathing was ragged as she bent to retrieve the script. Had his eyes been open, staring at her levelly, while she'd been sighing into his mouth like a teenager, her eyes closed with bliss?

"I'm sorry," Gable said, bending down to help her. "That shouldn't have happened."

She raised her eyes to his as they crouched, their hands meeting on the script, but she remained quiet, watchful.

"What I mean is, we might be working together." They rose slowly together, hands still gripping the script. Gable dropped his hand and passed it through his hair.

"Hell, you're not even my type," he said suddenly. Then he cursed and turned away.

"You've really been a ten on the debonair scale tonight, Gable."

He looked back at her. His dark expression didn't change. "Annabel, I didn't mean that the way it sounded. I keep saying things tonight..." He shook his head and took a deep breath. "Look, I think you're very attractive, but—"

"Don't get carried away with the compliments here, Gabe. Next you're going to be telling me I'm swell, and I don't know if I can take it."

"Annabel, I—"

She waved a hand to silence him. "Don't bother. I know what you're going to say. We might be working together, we both know how intense a movie set can get and what a small world it is and neither of us wants to do anything to jeopardize this film. Is that what you were going to say?"

"Yes."

"All right, then. We kissed. Big deal. It's over. From now on, it's strictly business." Where did this tough-girl act come from? Annabel wondered. She felt like a punctured set of water wings.

Was that relief in those light eyes? The least the man could do was look a bit regretful for appearances' sake, she thought, gritting her teeth. She wondered if the script was heavy enough to inflict damage if she cracked it down on his head with all the force in her body. Probably not. If only it were a mini-series.

Anyway, it was too early to antagonize a possible producer. That could come later. Not that she had any intention of making a movie with this impossible man.

"I'll just say good-night," she said crisply.

"Let me put you into a cab."

She put a hand on his chest to stop him. He looked down at it, and she quickly snatched it away. "Please don't. They have very solicitous doormen downstairs. That's why you pay the big money."

Wrapping her coat around her with a flourish, she headed for the door. She flung it open, then paused on the threshold and spun around.

"By the way, Mr. McCrea—"

"Yes?"

"I think you're very attractive, too. But don't worry—you're not my type, either."

And then she slipped out, closing the door softly behind her. She stalked down the hallway and was relieved when the elevator arrived immediately. She practically leaped into it, then stabbed at the lobby button.

The elevator slid downward without any perceptible movement, so unlike the creaking, jerking lift she always avoided in her apartment building. She hung on to a convenient railing anyway, feeling slightly dizzy. As she dropped away from Gable McCrea's room in the sky toward the lobby below, Annabel felt as though she were slowly waking up from a trance that had begun the moment she'd opened her door to him earlier that evening.

She'd never had such an experience in her life. All during dinner, as he had talked, she'd been listening intently while inwardly marveling at how strangely familiar he seemed. Even his face, the way it changed like quicksilver, one expression stealing over it almost before the other left, seemed so well-known, so dear. The way his mobile mouth formed around words, twisted with irony, curled into a half-smile. The patrician nose. The way his dusky hair looked—dark, with one wide streak of silver on the left side. It was as if she knew how it felt without touching it, knew how his mouth would feel against her own. Surely she had known this man before. Surely she had sat with him over other candlelit tables, perhaps in another lifetime, another world.

The sensation had made her giddy. She'd felt warm and expectant, dizzy with longing. She'd even flirted with him after the meal. Annabel winced at the memory. She never flirted. She wasn't the type. Then she'd been so unsettled by her uncharacteristic behavior and by the heady knowledge that she was on her way to his room that she'd immediately spoken crisply about business to defuse the atmosphere. But nothing had worked. She had been lost, and she'd known it.

Moments before he'd reached for her she had known with absolute certainty that he was going to, and she had also known, amid her fear, that she would respond as she had. It had seemed as inevitable as the whole night had been for this woman and this man to come together, as if every movement had been choreographed centuries before.

Annabel rubbed her icy hands. She must be crazy. She'd just met the man, and she was spiraling off into flights of fancy about fate and cosmic attraction like some poor witless soul muttering to himself on the street. What was the matter with her?

Wise up, Annabel, she told herself grimly as the elevator arrived at the sleek marble lobby. What was truly inevitable was that they would both back off. They were a Producer and a Director, not a Man and a Woman. There was too much riding on the film for both of them. Gable McCrea was shrewd enough to realize that an affair with his director could undermine his power. Not that any woman could really have power over him, Annabel guessed, no matter what happened in their private hours.

The man was positively dangerous. She tucked the script under her arm, where it seemed to burn through her overcoat.

The doorman magically whistled up a cab, and Annabel slipped into it gratefully. She'd wait a few days before she read the script, she decided. She wanted to be free of the spell of Gable McCrea before she plunged into it. Too bad if he was in a hurry; he deserved to wait.

"Yes?"

"Good morning, Gable. Listen, who is this screenwriter? The script is incredible. I mean, there's hardly anything I want to change, just a few—"

"Who *is* this?"

"It's Annabel Porter."

"Annabel? What the—what time is it?"

"It's seven o'clock. Are you awake?"

Gable sat back against the pillows. "Now I am."

"Oh, I'm sorry—did I wake you? I guess I didn't notice the time."

"It's quite all right Annabel. Do you always have script conferences this early?"

"Well, no. I was just lying here with the script, and—"

"You're still in bed, too?"

"I've been reading all night."

He had her, then. She had read all night. She was still in bed. Gable chased away the irrelevant thought of what Annabel might be wearing. "You were saying?" He reached for a pack of cigarettes on the night table and then remembered he'd quit ten years ago. Her voice was cool and fresh, spilling through the telephone with a rushing enthusiasm that made the sluggish morning blood in his veins begin to move. Suddenly, she sounded very young.

Gable caught a glimpse of himself in the mirror across from the bed. His face was creased from sleep, and the gray streak in his hair mocked him with the strain of the past four years. He felt old.

Annabel was crisply dissecting the scene on page twenty-seven; then she moved on to the scene on page thirty-two. "The thing is, Gable, all the stuff about Delia is great, which is lucky, since she's the focus of the script. She's an incredible character. Is she really like this?"

He grimaced. "Not really. You might say the writer took a few liberties necessary for the script. But she's already approved it."

"Anyway, once we go into the flashback, well...there's a great deal I can do with this, which is wonderful for a director, but it seems to me that you're relying on me to make Josiah and Melinda sympathetic in their seclusion, and there's only so much I can do. Let's face it, Melinda needs work. And Josiah—he can be too overbearing, and—"

"But, Annabel, Benjamin Hall will be playing him. That alone will make the character likable. Who can resist those green eyes?"

Who indeed? Annabel wondered wryly. But she didn't want to think about her past with Benjamin Hall right now. She reached over to her night table for her cup of coffee. "I'd still like to talk about it with the writer," she continued. "So who is this guy, anyway?" She glanced down at the title page. "What kind of a name is A. Fortuna Iuvat?"

"That's pronounced Yoo-vat. He's from one of the Eastern Bloc countries originally, I think, though he's pretty mysterious about it. Been living in the United States for years, but he's a bit of a recluse. He's a neighbor of mine. Fascinating character—you'll have to meet him. This is his first script."

"It's very good. I'm surprised you went without a Hollywood screenwriter."

"Annabel, I'm not wedded to Hollywood. I'm looking for a fresh approach," Gable said tiredly.

Gable's voice still sounded thick from sleep, and Annabel supposed she should have waited before calling him, but she'd been afraid of missing him. He looked like the type to rise at six and go for a ten-mile run.

But he was still in bed. She tried to picture that long, powerful body on smooth white sheets.

"Annabel? Did you hear me?"

She started. Had he been saying something? "What?" she barked into the receiver. She hadn't meant to be gruff, but she was embarrassed about the turn her thoughts had taken.

"Does this mean you'll do the film?"

She stared down at the script in her lap. Funny, she hadn't even put her decision into words. After trying desperately to ignore the script while she tossed and turned in bed, she'd finally gotten up, made a pot of tea and curled up in bed to read. She had ten pages of notes in her tiny handwriting, she had laughed and cried and spoken out loud to the characters, yet she'd never said to herself that she would do it. But somewhere around four o'clock in the morning, the decision had been made.

"I think we should talk about the problems I see—" she began.

"We'll work it out. Are you in?"

She took a deep breath and closed her eyes against the image of Gable McCrea, brown and lithe against the white sheets. She'd have to exorcise this impossible, unfamiliar lust. She couldn't admit one ounce of softness in her attitude toward him. She'd have to be at her strongest if she was to work with him and retain control of her film.

Her film. She looked down at the script again and felt a fierce possessiveness sweep over her. It could be her film. She could do it. Even if she had to remind herself every damn day that she had to follow her best professional instincts and never, ever, get involved with her overbearing producer, she would do it.

"I'm in so far," she said. "But we do need to talk."

"Of course."

"And there's one crucial thing I have to get straight before we start."

"Okay," Gable said cautiously.

"Were your parents big movie fans?"

"What?"

"Your name."

"Oh. They were both actors."

Annabel waited, but no other information was forthcoming. She swung her legs out of bed, ready to head for the shower and the start of what would surely be a very busy day.

"Actors, huh?" she said. "That's okay, Gable—I won't hold it against you. So how do you feel about breakfast?"

"I like it. As long as I don't have to leave my hotel. I can meet you downstairs in an hour."

"Fine. As long as you're paying."

"Fine. As long as you like cold cereal and coffee. I told you this was a low-budget production."

Chapter Three

The short flight from San Francisco to Mendocino was horrendous, bumpy and foggy. The pilot's cheerful admonitions not to be nervous hadn't helped the planeful of startled passengers, who had found their morning coffee suddenly sloshing into their laps as the small plane pitched and bucked its way through unusual turbulence. Annabel alternately gripped the arms of her seat and wiped her damp palms with a sodden handkerchief. Not fond of flying in the best of conditions, she was frankly terrified.

But she really couldn't complain; this was the first bumpy weather she'd had to fly through, literally and figuratively, since she'd started work on *A Family of Two* four months ago. Never before had she seen preproduction wrapped up faster or more smoothly. And that was thanks to the tireless Gable McCrea, who, she'd discovered, could be amazingly charming when it suited him.

He could crisply bark an order and then smoothly sweet-talk a reluctant actress. He could knock back a beer with the stunt coordinator and select the perfect champagne for a studio president. He was so supremely capable that he was terrifying.

That first breakfast at the Meridien—they'd had eggs Benedict, not cold cereal, in spite of Gable's warning—had extended into a working lunch, and then into a blur of meetings extending over the next several months, in New York and California, where they'd met with actors and actresses and lined up locations and had script conferences and more breakfasts and lunches and dinners, until Annabel had begun to think about dieting. Gable was inordinately fond of centering meetings around food.

They had even flown down to an island in the Caribbean, where they'd met with Benjamin Hall, had a quick piña colada at the airport and not gotten one spare moment to step out onto the beckoning pink beaches.

Annabel had flown back and forth between the coasts and back and forth between Mendocino and Los Angeles so often that every single one of her plants had died, which was something of a relief, since she'd never cared for them properly anyway. Their demise had prompted the only joke she'd heard Gable make during the whole proceeding. He had walked in, gazed around at the trailing brown stems of her spider plant and the pitiful state of the philodendrons and the ferns, and looked at her, deadpan. "We should probably be relieved," he'd remarked, "that you don't own a dog."

The process of hammering out the details of a film was just as important as the eventual filming, but it was always the most frustrating period for Annabel. Though she thrived on the set, she still felt unsteady in the tricky shifting sands of Hollywood politics. Thank goodness for

Gable. He'd already been working on the film for six months before she signed on, and he hustled frantically, pushing things along, making it happen, arranging meetings and distribution deals and financing, and juggling schedules and commitments from the crew and cast.

The rewrites she'd asked for had been impeccable, with the reclusive and eccentric Fortuna Iuvat mailing them to her as he finished them. It was an unusual way to work, but Annabel had to admit it had turned out well. She was looking forward to meeting him on the set.

So it had all come together somehow; the cast and crew were set for the first day of principal photography on the last Monday in June. This morning she had packed up a few more sweaters in the eighty-degree New York heat for the foggy summer climate of Mendocino and boarded a plane for the coast on what would be the final trip for the nine weeks the shooting of the film would involve.

She had the whole weekend ahead to prepare for that first day of shooting, and she could feel the energy coiled expectantly in her stomach. It felt rather like sitting on a bronco at a rodeo, Annabel reflected, waiting for the gate to be lifted and the animal to be propelled out into the wild arena, where it would pitch and buck to try to shake her off and trample her underfoot.

It was a particularly apt analogy at the moment, she decided grimly as the plane lurched, making her stomach feel as though it were hanging a good six inches above the rest of her. The dizzy feeling reminded her of how she still felt around Gable, though she didn't like to admit it. Staring out with unseeing eyes at the fog, Annabel wondered what it would be like to be with Gable for the next nine weeks in the small, totally exclusive world a movie set could become. She knew he'd be the kind of producer who would remain a part of the filming. He wouldn't, now that principal photography was about to begin, fly back to Hollywood and turn his back on the set. He was totally, single-mindedly committed to this project.

But what was the use of wondering about it? *You know what it will be like,* she told herself sourly, staring out the window. Like the past months—strictly rated G.

It was as though the kiss had never happened. Perhaps she had dreamed that stunning, earthshaking embrace. Gable treated her with cool detachment. They hardly even argued. They were disgustingly of one mind when it came to what would be good for the film. So far.

The airport runway suddenly loomed up out of the fog, making Annabel jump. She hadn't realized they were that low. She barely had time to be terrified before the plane was bumping down on the ground. The relieved passengers burst into applause. Annabel would have initiated a standing ovation had she been at all certain her legs would work. She carefully pried her fingers off the armrests, then used the balled-up handkerchief in her lap to wipe her palms. She'd made it.

Now for the hard part: seeing Gable again. It had been almost a month since they'd shaken hands in Los Angeles over the completion of the final details. They'd spoken on the phone a thousand times but hadn't seen each other. She'd been spending most of her time in Mendocino, preparing for the shoot.

The plane taxied to a stop, and Annabel rose weakly, reached for her bag, and followed the rest of the passengers off the plane. When she felt the fresh air on her face she began to cheer up. Now she blessed the cool vapor of the fog as it caressed her cheeks. The concrete under her feet felt wonderful. Mendocino was wonderful. She was sure it was, even though she couldn't see it. How would she ever find Gable in all this fog?

"Annie!"

There was only one person who called her that. Annabel's steps slowed. Benjamin Hall materialized out of the mist, looking like a friendly brown bear.

The famous green eyes shone at her. "God, Annie, it's good to see you."

"It's good to see you, too, Ben." He looked tanned and healthy; he was starting this film only three days after wrapping up the one in the Caribbean.

He held her at arm's length. "You look adorable—whoops, sorry. You look—gorgeous. Sophisticated. Cool. Lovely. Everything. Tall, even."

"Okay, okay, enough," Annabel said, laughing.

"Good flight?"

"Oh, terrific, if you like bucking broncos."

"Hmm. You'll probably remember it as an oasis of calm after you've been on the set a few weeks."

"Probably." They laughed and walked together toward the baggage claim. "Where's Gable?"

"He got hung up with some problem or other. Nothing serious—don't frown at me. You'll be on the set soon enough. Anyway, I volunteered to come get you. I wanted to see you alone, anyway."

"Oh?" Annabel asked cautiously.

"Don't be nervous. Gable was at our meetings, after all, and I just wanted to make sure you didn't hate me."

She looked up at him, genuinely surprised. "Why would I hate you, Ben?"

"You know why. Darling, I can be such a bastard."

"I won't argue with that," Annabel said mildly. Benjamin Hall had been the first and last mistake she'd made in mixing business and romance. It was typical of both his charm and his carelessness that he could greet her so warmly after not speaking to her for four years, except for the meetings they'd had for the film, where they'd pretended, for Gable's sake and their own, that nothing personal had ever existed between them.

It had been a stroke of blinding good fortune four years ago when she had managed to persuade him to be in *Conjugal Rights*, her first film. He'd been the hottest television star in the country because of his show *Montana Smith*, but he was longing to break into features. She'd been lucky enough to convince him to take a chance on a low-budget domestic comedy rather than go with the offers he'd had from major studios. It was a role totally different from the detective he played on TV and the action-oriented scripts that came his way as a result, and it had frightened him as much as it intrigued him. Ben had agreed to work for scale for a hefty percentage of the profits, and the gamble had paid off. His performance had earned him an Academy Award nomination and propelled him into the film career he'd always wanted.

But that was later. During the filming, Annabel had been touched by the star who had been called the sexiest man in America but who was so uncertain of his performance that he sweated his way through the rushes every day. The fact that Ben's image as a sex symbol secretly mystified him had been exactly what Annabel had been looking for—for her film. It gave him an appealing edge that other macho actors, though they were twice as good-looking, simply didn't have. He had been perfect as the hero of her film, handsome and masculine but continually dazed at the misfortunes that were befalling him. The audience had taken him to their hearts.

And Annabel had as well. She had made a mistake so naive that it still had the power to surprise her today: she had fallen in love with the character in the film, and she had transferred his qualities to the actor. She had imagined herself as falling in love with Ben. But she hadn't shown it during all the weeks of shooting, concentrating instead on getting through the film. She'd scurried away from the wrap party, relieved it was all over. Ben would never know about her silly infatuation.

But then, later that night, Ben had appeared at her door with a bottle of champagne and white roses and the confession that he'd been falling in love with her, too. He had sensed her old-fashioned nature and courted her gently. He had even, one night after a long dinner with his favorite champagne, mentioned marriage.

So it had been something of a shock a few weeks later when Ben had flown to Los Angeles for two weeks and she read in *Time* magazine that he was engaged to the actress Lily Macklin. She'd left two messages with his secretary in L.A., but he had never returned her calls. Annabel hadn't bothered to call again.

She had been hurt, but after a month she had woken up one morning and realized it was the first time she'd been able to relax in months. Ben had been all-consuming, demanding, childlike in his exuberance and his need, both as an actor and a suitor. He had been exciting and infuriating all at once. And the constant strain of his fame was wearying. Annabel had leapt out of bed that day with the realization that she had liked and admired an actor but had fallen in love with a character. She was, she realized, simply relieved it was over.

Six months later Ben had been nominated for Best Actor for his role in *Conjugal Rights*. On the morning it was announced, three dozen white roses had been delivered to her apartment with a note. "I will love you forever," it had said.

Ben had never married the actress, and as the years went on Annabel had read of his involvements with one woman after another. Now, sneaking a sidelong look at him, Annabel realized that he was nervous. Poor Ben. He couldn't bear not to be liked. How could she tell him that she'd been relieved when he'd left her high and dry? Annabel was aware of his fragile ego, and in this film the character of Josiah had to be supremely confident of his masculinity, a sensual, dynamic man. She couldn't let Ben know exactly how little she'd been destroyed by his desertion.

"Oh, Ben," she said carefully, "you know how it is. You go on after something like that happens. You take it day by day. Anyway, it was a long time ago." She reached for her bag and swung it over her arm. "I'm delighted you're playing Josiah."

Ben's green eyes cleared, and he no longer looked like a puppy begging forgiveness for messing on the rug. He grinned. "I'm so relieved," he said. "You can't imagine. I hate it when my past catches up with me. You know, I've wanted to call you so many times, but I was such a coward. It's these women, though, Annabel—I get myself into these impossible situations. It's awful. I hate it."

"Then maybe you could change," Annabel suggested logically.

"I do want to," Ben said. "The act *is* getting old. Or maybe I am."

"Never," Annabel said warmly as they headed toward the exit from the terminal.

Ben led her to a Jeep and threw her bags into the back. "I must admit," he said as he helped her inside, "I did have a mild anxiety attack when Gable told me you were the director. But when he told me I was your first choice for Josiah, I knew you must have forgiven me. Annabel, I do thank you for that." He shut the door and walked around to the driver's side.

Annabel grinned. Gable was quite an operator, all right. He must have fed Ben that false piece of information before he'd even approached her with the project. As Ben wheeled out of the parking lot and headed west for the rugged coastline, she sent a silent salute to Gable's audacity.

Benjamin kept up a steady stream of conversation, shouting over the noise of the rattling Jeep during the lurching ride. He gave her a blow-by-blow account of his experience filming in Eleuthera, and it wasn't until they reached the coast road that she was able to get a word in edgewise.

"What are you doing here so early, Ben? I would think you'd be taking it easy in L.A. for the weekend."

"Wanted to get a feel for the atmosphere again. I've got a great suite, and Gable's hired some fabulous caterer from San Francisco. You've got to try the vegetable frittatas. I've been wandering about the grounds, and it could all be very nice if my illustrious co-star hadn't decided to show up as well." Ben wheeled around a curve, sending Annabel against her door.

"Can you slow down a bit? So Sasha Durant is here, too?"

"She wants to commune with the spirit of Melinda," Ben said with a curled lip.

Annabel scented trouble. "How do you like her?" she asked carefully. "Ben, watch that curve—"

"I see it—no problem. Like her? I don't. She's one of those intelligent actresses. I can't stand them."

"What a liar you are. You loved Claire Potts. Can you slow down, Ben?"

"Claire was *nice*. Sasha is a tiger. She'll probably demand fifty takes of every scene. She's been a star on Broadway, for heaven's sake. A New York actress. What does she know about movies?

"She's made a film already, and you know it. She's supposed to be very professional. Watch that car—"

"No problem—I see it. I mean, for crying out loud, Annie, she went to the Yale School of Drama. I can't stand it. I was doing carpentry while she was doing Molière."

"She's very nice. And she's very beautiful. Ben, you're tailgating—"

He eased on the brakes, but a rear tire hit a soft shoulder. The wheels spun for a moment, then recovered. Annabel closed her eyes against the sheer cliff to the right of them.

"Annabel," he went on unconcernedly, "I live in Beverly Hills. Beautiful women are everywhere. The cashier at the darn Mini-Mart looks like Bo Derek. I'm immune, believe me. Wow, look at this road. Gorgeous coastline. The drop must be a couple of thousand feet right here."

"Great," Annabel said weakly. Her handkerchief had barely had a chance to dry out. It was now a twisted rope in her lap. "Ben," she said tightly, "could you do me a favor and please slow down? I'd like to stay alive to make this movie."

He looked over at her. "You nervous?" he yelled.

"Could you watch the road, please? Yes, I am a bit."

"No problem." To Annabel's great relief, he slowed down. "So how do you like our producer?" he asked.

"He might be crazy, but he's thorough. He certainly believes in getting involved on the set."

Only the exuberant Ben could think of Gable's methodical personality as crazy. "Yes, he's very dedicated," she said noncommittally. In Hollywood language, Ben had also just told her that Gable could turn out to be a pain in the neck. Somehow that didn't surprise her. "Ben, it would be nice if you'd slow down on the curves instead of speeding up. If you don't mind."

"No problem."

"Uh, Ben, don't you have to turn—"

Annabel was interrupted by a squeal of tires as Ben suddenly jammed on the brakes to negotiate a sharp right turn to a road that was almost hidden from the main highway. The tires skidded and spun, and the Jeep bumped onto the tiny road, kicking a shower of small rocks and dirt behind it.

"Ben!" Annabel shouted above the noise. "For heaven's sake—"

"Sorry, I always almost miss that turn," Ben yelled back placidly, speeding up again. They jounced up the steep incline for several minutes while Annabel finger-combed her hair and tried to relax. She wanted to look cool and collected when she saw Gable again. She found that her heart was tripping at the mere thought of him, tall and implacable, with that slight smile he allowed himself when he greeted her. Or maybe her heart was just beating so fast because she'd barely made it here alive.

"So will you have a little chat with Sasha for me?" Ben asked lightly.

"What?"

He squealed around a hairpin turn. "You know, make sure she won't do a million takes. And—oh, yes—there's some nonsense she's talking about changes in the first scene we're shooting. Nothing important, I'm sure.''

"What do you mean?"

"She muttered something about some lines she wanted to change. You know how difficult it is to understand the diction of those Method actors. I don't know."

As Ben zoomed around the last blind curve and skidded to a stop next to a production van, a glimmer of revelation began to dawn in Annabel's mind.

"Ben," she asked carefully, "did you come and pick me up so that you could get me on your side in this dispute?"

"Annie! I'm shocked that you could—"

"Come on, Ben. The truth, please."

"Well, maybe a little. But I just thought you should know that Sasha was talking to Gable about changing the first scene we're shooting. She's out to get me—I know it. And Gable's on her side."

"Actors," Annabel grumbled under her breath.

"What?"

"Nothing." She eased out of her seat and stretched her shaky legs. A bumpy flight and a hair-raising ride could be nothing compared to a power struggle between her two stars. Things had certainly taken off with a jolt.

Ben came around the side of the Jeep and looked at her, deflated.

"You're angry with me."

"No, I'm not." Annabel realized suddenly what she should have known all along: Ben was afraid of Sasha Durant. He was scared the classically trained beauty would act him off the screen. She put a hand on his arm. "Don't worry, Ben. I'm not going to let her steal the show. We need two strong characters on the screen. So I'll take care of you. Okay?"

"Annie, you're the greatest." Ben threw his arms around her in an exuberant hug. "I'm so glad you're here."

Surprised but touched, Annabel hugged him back. But her whole body stiffened and her heart began to race when she heard the voice behind her.

"Well, well, *Annie*," Gable said, his voice mocking. "I'm glad you're here, too. We have a few things to straighten out. Not that I want to intrude on this, uh, touching interlude. But do you think you could tear yourself away and take care of some business?"

She would not feel uncomfortable, Annabel thought determinedly before she turned around. It was a perfectly innocent hug.

She gently pulled away from Ben. "Hello, Gable. Nice to see you, too."

"I see you've already met up with Ben," Gable said colorlessly.

Sasha Durant, tall and lovely in a long white dress, came up from behind Gable and smiled at Annabel. "Hi. Did you have a good flight?"

"Hello, Sasha. It was fine."

Gable waited politely until they finished exchanging pleasantries, then went on as though he hadn't been interrupted. "Ben might have told you about the crisis we had this morning—you don't have to worry about it. I straightened everything out with Sasha. We're going to change the dialogue in the first scene."

So it was war, then.

Gable had just signaled the start of hostilities. He knew exactly what he was doing. He was as smooth as butter, but his thrust was deadly. He was undermining her authority in front of the actors. It was the worst thing a producer could do to a director, and it announced to all concerned who was boss on this film. It would be all over the set within the hour, and she would be lost.

She was outwardly calm, but inside she was a roiling mass of confusion. Adrenaline was pumping from the sudden attack on her blind side. Annabel considered her opponent and her strategy. All three of them were watching her with seeming casualness, but she knew she was on trial. She kept her eyes on Gable. His gray eyes were cool and confident, and that confidence shook her as nothing else could. He wasn't nervous in the least. *He expects to control this film,* Annabel realized with cold dread.

With that sudden knowledge, her chin lifted and her eyes narrowed. Nobody got away with undermining her authority on a set. Nobody. Not even Gable McCrea. And that smug man smiling patronizingly at her was about to find that out. The battle was about to commence, and she had no intention of losing an inch of territory.

The others must have seen something in her face, for Sasha shifted nervously. Ben coughed and squinted at the misty Pacific. Gable didn't move.

"Sasha," Annabel said in a friendly tone, "why don't you let me unpack and settle in a bit, and then we can go over your problems with the scene."

"Oh, that's not necessary—really, Annabel," Sasha said. "I'm fine now. It's all taken care of."

"I don't think so." Annabel's tone was quiet, but the three heads jerked toward her. She had achieved the desired effect. It was what she thought of as her director's voice—crisp, low-pitched, perfectly controlled, but absolutely deadly. It was known to make grown men quail.

Now it made even the perfectly poised Sasha Durant back away a step. Ben turned to fumble with Annabel's luggage. Gable's eyebrow shot up.

"Of course, Annabel," Sasha said in a rush. "How rude of me to bring this up before you had a chance to settle in. I'll just go over my notes and wait for you."

"Thank you," Annabel said crisply. "I'm going to have a talk with Gable. Ben, would you mind bringing my bag up to the house? I can take it upstairs."

"No problem." Ben beat a hasty retreat, but he still allowed Sasha to remain ahead of him up the drive to the house. He seemed in no mood for a confrontation.

Neither was Gable, apparently. He didn't say a word as they turned up the drive together. Annabel didn't speak either. Her strategy called for him to be the one to begin. Anything he said would be spoken in his defense, and she wanted him on the defensive.

She tried to concentrate on the setting in front of her. She'd been here many times for preproduction duties, but the sight of the rambling gray mansion still gave her a pleasant shock. There seemed to be an almost palpable tension between its classic lines and its occasional quirky angles, its false towers and the one long addition that had housed Josiah's studio. The darkness of the day and the swirling fog made it look as though it were crouching on the hill, sunk in its melancholy and its secrets. Annabel knew it would look terrific on film.

They entered the house, still silent, their footsteps echoing on the hardwood floor. The flat illumination from the skylights gave an even, luminous tone to Gable's skin. His expression was set and closed, his eyes cool.

"I thought Sasha's objections made sense," he said finally. "She's an intelligent actress, and she came up with some good ideas."

Annabel said nothing. She proceeded to the staircase.

"She's afraid of looking ridiculous in that first scene, where Josiah is showing her the house and she's babbling about the kitchen utensils. You're the one who wanted Melinda to be a strong character. We can talk to Fortuna about coming up with a new angle for the scene. He works fast."

Annabel waited until she was on the second step before she turned around. It had been a calculated move; for their first confrontation, she didn't want to be looking up at Gable. Now their eyes were dead level.

Her voice was low and even. "We can discuss Sasha's objections to the scene. That's not the problem, and you know it. I don't like power games, Gable, but I didn't get here by refusing to play them. If this is going to get ugly, I'll be in there swinging. If you want a director you can push around, then you're going to have to get on the plane to L.A. and find one."

"Are you saying you'd break your contract?" Gable asked coolly. "I could sue you."

"Go ahead." Annabel stared him down just as coolly, but her knuckles were white as she gripped the oak banister behind her.

Gable's skin seemed like paper stretched over the bones of his face, so thin and tight was his expression. She could see a muscle working in the line of his jaw, but he still said nothing. She didn't flinch; she wouldn't allow herself even one tiny movement.

Finally, he walked casually past her until he was standing on her stair and she had to look up at him again. "Calm down, Annabel," he said. "Talk to Sasha, and let me know what you think about the scene." He smiled that dry, detached smile that was just a movement of facial muscles—the humorless smile she hated, the one that made her wonder who he really was. "You can be pretty nasty, you know that?"

Annabel's eyebrow quirked upward. She smiled sweetly at him. "I think I should let you in on something, Gable. I didn't get to where I am by being a nice guy." Then she swept past him to continue up the stairs to her room.

Gable leaned against the banister and watched Annabel mount the stairs. Her spine was perfectly erect, as if she were giving a posture lesson to a group of debutantes. Her legs seemed to move independently of the rest of her body as they smoothly took each step with no energy wasted, no feminine, alluring swing of hips.

He'd underestimated her again, dammit. By the end of the day the whole crew would know about the scene outside. And she'd done it so easily, he marveled. She'd said four words. *"I don't think so."* But her tone had let them each know in no uncertain terms where they stood. He was beginning to see how Annabel Porter had earned her reputation.

It was not what he'd imagined when he'd hired her. Sure, he'd heard that she was strong-minded and tough, but Hollywood said that, along with more uncomplimentary adjectives, about any woman who had the nerve and courage and wits to tackle the monumental task of making it as a director. He'd thought he'd be able to control her. Preproduction had gone smoothly because they'd agreed so surprisingly often. He'd known things might go differently on the set; she had a strong personal vision, but he'd thought he could bend it to his own will. He might have made a very big mistake, Gable realized now. But he had no intention of letting the reins of the picture slip from his hands.

He heard the catering crew rattling through the hall on their way to the kitchens and realized that he was staring at empty air, air that was still electrified by her brief presence in it. She did have a way of shaking things up. And here, on the set, she would really begin to wield her power. He would just have to be right beside her, directing her, like a father teaching a child to drive, one hand poised to grab the wheel.

If Annabel knew his thoughts, she would think he was being patronizing, Gable mused, grimacing. He wasn't at all. He was being careful.

Because if there was one thing Gable hated, it was surprises. Even tantalizing ones in small packages.

Annabel quickly passed the caterers unpacking in the kitchen and slipped out the door. She headed across the back lawn toward the bluff overlooking the ocean. She had gone straight up the front stairs and through the hall to the back stairs and down again. She felt a sudden longing to be outside, but she didn't want to pass Gable again.

The Pacific was a calm gray-green that flashed an occasional lacy frill as it swirled around glistening rocks the color of sable. The mist was heavier now but so fine that Annabel could barely feel it. Yet when she touched her hair it was damp with minuscule droplets of moisture.

She sat cross-legged on the grass, not minding the wet, trying to calm herself with the beautiful scene before her. She would have to talk to Sasha soon, she knew, but the confrontation with Gable had shaken her more than she cared to admit, and she needed time to recover. She *had* gone a little overboard; it was foolish to give Gable an ultimatum after their first disagreement. But there had been something about the look in his eyes that had provoked her past the point of discretion.

She had to be logical about this, get it into some kind of order. There were two problems, Annabel decided, hugging her knees and resting her chin on them. The first was that there was a natural antagonism between the two of them. So far, perhaps because they needed to assert their professionalism after that shaky start in Gable's hotel room, they'd managed to avoid any major confrontations. But had his conciliatory nature concealed some sort of secret machinations to undermine her power? He was a Hollywood producer, after all.

Annabel sighed. If that were true, she would have a battle on her hands. She supposed she could handle that. No matter how wealthy or powerful Gable-the-Hollywood-producer was, she wasn't intimidated by him. But then there was Gable-the-man—which, Annabel reflected glumly, brought her smack up against problem number two.

She hadn't gotten over the kiss. They may have acted as though it had never happened, but it hadn't helped. It had been *months*, and she hadn't gotten over it. She remembered his mouth, so cool and hard against hers, so hungry, searching, touching something inside her, some urgent place she hadn't even known was there. It had been frightening to feel all that power inside her, straining against him, wanting him, feeling him straining against her, too. What, Annabel wondered again and again during the nights spent awake in her bed, would happen if they ever let go?

"Annabel?"

She turned. Sasha was standing hesitantly behind her. She had changed from the long white dress into a navy-blue sweater and jeans, and, if anything, she looked more striking. Annabel could see now why she and Gable had instinctively zeroed in on Sasha instead of the dozens of actresses they'd considered. Though she looked nothing like Melinda, there was an elusive quality about her that called the doomed woman to mind. Perhaps it was the simplicity of her face and her carriage; it was the same presence that Melinda had in such artless abundance, the woman who had gradually shed her couture clothes and elaborate hairstyles to become the simple beauty she'd been born to be.

"I hate to interrupt you," Sasha said when Annabel continued to stare at her.

"You're not. I'm sorry—I was thinking of how similar you can look to those portraits of Melinda sometimes. Please sit down with me—that is, if you don't mind getting a little wet."

"I don't mind. I love this mist. It feels so clean somehow. Before I came here I thought that California just meant L.A. and all that brown smog." Sasha smiled and plopped down with an appealing lack of grace next to Annabel.

"Look," she said, tucking her legs up under her chin like Annabel's, "I've been a stage actress mostly—you know that. I live in New York. Hollywood is somewhat of a mystery to me, though my agent tries to educate me. I can't begin to figure out all those Byzantine levels of power."

Annabel laughed. "I know just what you mean. I always have to get a lecture on which restaurants I absolutely shouldn't go to in L.A., and where to sit in the ones I *should* go to. I can never remember, though. Ben nearly passed out when he heard I ate in the *front* room of Spago.''

Sasha grimaced. "He would. Anyway, what I'm trying to do here is apologize about this morning. I should have waited for you to get here. I don't want to get off on the wrong foot, Annabel. I don't want to alienate you. I've really been looking forward to working with you."

"Me, too. Don't worry about this morning. Tell me, what's the problem with the scene?"

"I just feel so stupid saying that dialogue. I thought I could, but—" She shrugged. "Melinda needs to be a strong character. I don't want her to get overshadowed by Josiah's personality. I'm afraid of her sounding like a fool, babbling away about the kitchen while Josiah's talking about love and eternity. It's early in the film, and it could prejudice the audience against her."

"But I think the audience will get the subtext, that you're really terrified but determined to make a home with this man. I'm afraid sometimes of the film being too somber—you know, the great tragic love and all that. We want Melinda to be human and real—and occasionally funny."

Sasha shuddered. "I can't be funny. I've never been funny. My teacher at Yale told me to stick with drama."

"Sasha, that was *years* ago."

"Hey, thanks a lot."

Annabel laughed. "See? You were funny just then. So did you respect this teacher's opinion so much that you'd continue to follow it for years?"

Sasha grinned. "He also told me to stay away from Shakespeare."

Annabel grinned back. Sasha Durant had won a Tony award for her portrayal of Cordelia in an imaginatively staged *King Lear* on Broadway, a performance so stunning that it had catapulted her into the front ranks of theater actresses.

"I can see why you're still following this guy's advice," Annabel said dryly. "Look, Sasha, I do like the dialogue in that scene. I like the contrast between Josiah and Melinda, how they each deal with the fact that they've turned their backs on the world." She thought for a moment. "Hey, I've got an idea. Why don't we do this—let's rehearse it two ways. We'll do the original, and then we'll try switching that dialogue from Melinda to Josiah."

"You mean I would get Josiah's speech? And he'll get mine about the kitchen?"

"Maybe. It might work."

Sasha nodded slowly. "It might."

"Then again, you might be pleasantly surprised if you try the original."

"I don't know—"

"Sasha, we're not talking the Marx Brothers here. No belly laughs—just a soft chuckle now and then. You can handle it—I promise. I won't let you look stupid."

"All right. You know, I've been so nervous about this project, for so many reasons. My agent didn't want me to do it—he was hesitant about Gable, of course. I'm sure we all were."

"Hmm," Annabel said noncommittally. She had no idea what Sasha was talking about.

"Not that breakdowns are at all unusual in this business. Though when it comes to a producer, you really want someone stable. But it was at least three years ago, and I was so impressed with Gable when I finally met him."

"What did you hear about the breakdown?" Annabel asked, her heart pounding. How could she not have known about this?

"Just the dirt everyone else knew. After *Nightfall* was such a bomb—though I hear that he gave away the final cut to the director, who was having an affair with the editor, and it was butchered behind his back—he went crazy or something. Adelaide Anders, who was the editor on *Nightfall*, left him flat and—"

"Adelaide Anders?" For some reason, Annabel's heart sank. She had met the editor. Adelaide Anders was the type of tall, leggy blonde who could rattle a queen with her perfect composure. She was the exact opposite of the short, brunette, excitable Annabel. Not that it was relevant, she scolded herself. She forced her attention back to Sasha.

"Oh, yes, they were together for years. Then he went to live in the desert, or the mountains—I forget where—and dropped out for a while. Everyone said he was finished, that he couldn't raise money if he were making *Gone with the Wind*. That's why everyone's waiting to see how *A Family of Two* turns out. He's sunk every penny into this thing. They say—whoever 'they' are—if this one doesn't make it, he's finished. I don't know how he beat out everyone for the rights to the story, but I hear he's got something going with Delia Worthington-Crane."

Sasha extended her legs and unconcernedly examined her sneakers. Annabel stared at the ground between her knees. She had just learned several very important facts, and she was struggling to assimilate them. If she hadn't been such a complete idiot, she would have learned them months ago. That's what she got for not living in L.A. like any self-respecting director. She was out of the gossip pipeline, and this wasn't the first time that had worked against her. Annabel instantly decided that if she wanted to make it in this business, she had to do something about that. Or at least start listening to her agent.

She tried to picture the tall, cool man she'd just left having an emotional collapse. She supposed many strong people did—it wasn't that unusual in the stress-filled modern world—but Gable McCrea? It just didn't fit, somehow. And she was shocked to find out that Gable was broke. How could he be? She'd ridden in his Ferrari, for heaven's sake.

But the worst part was that the one thing that was bothering her the most was the irrelevant information that he was having an affair with Delia Worthington-Crane. The woman was gorgeous.

Sasha sighed and stood up. "Well, I'll give you some privacy, Annabel. Look, it's all gossip about Gable. Who knows the real story? In Hollywood they think you're having a breakdown if your tan fades. Anyway," she said, shrugging, "I don't care if the guy is on Thorazine. He's gotten us this far. The script is great, you're the best there is, Ben is an impossible human being but a great actor, so I think we'll all do just fine. I'll see you inside, okay?"

"Okay. I'll be in soon." Annabel heard the whisper of Sasha's footsteps retreat across the grass. She flopped onto her back and stared up at the pearly pewter sky, as opalescent as Gable's strange, unreadable eyes. Now she itched to know what really lay behind that inscrutable expression. He was certainly turning out to be a man of mystery.

But it wasn't her mystery to solve. She flipped over abruptly, jumped up and headed to the house. She had enough problems without trying to untangle the complexities of Gable McCrea. This was certainly turning out to be no ordinary film shoot. She'd be lucky if she made it through the first week without having a breakdown of her own.

Chapter Four

"Cut and print," Annabel said. She sprang out of her chair. "Sasha, that was great! You're the best!"

Gable watched her dash through the cameras and cables and spin Sasha around in an exuberant hug. Sasha hugged her back, glowing. Annabel didn't give compliments easily, but when she did, she lavished them.

"Thanks for reading the lines, Ben," she said, turning to him. "I appreciate it."

Annabel had earlier made an unprecedented request of Sasha and Ben; she had asked that in important scenes each of them remain on the set to feed the lines to the one getting a close-up. Often during the filming the major stars went off to relax in their dressing rooms while the script girl fed the other star the lines. To keep things humming at an emotional pitch, Annabel had asked if the actors would help each other out.

Somehow, Gable hadn't been surprised when they'd agreed. Already, after only a week on the set, they would go to any lengths for Annabel. He had a feeling she had an ulterior motive for her request, as well. Surely if Sasha and Ben went out of their way for each other, it would soften the atmosphere between them.

He had to admire her, Gable thought, watching the crew shut down for the day as Annabel thanked each of them in turn, her hands gesticulating wildly as she talked about how pleased she was with the first week's shoot. She had solved the problem of Sasha's reluctance to play the first scene with seeming ease.

Somehow her crazy suggestion to switch the dialogue had worked. It had given Ben and Sasha an opportunity to play with their roles and loosen up with each other. And when Sasha had seen Ben say her lines, she had been struck by the competitive urge to do it better, and she had turned in a flawless, light reading for the cameras. Suddenly Melinda had emerged before their eyes, not just a beautiful woman but a rounded human being, touchingly vulnerable. The straightforward scene had become a tiny perfect crystal of shimmering emotional facets, the kind of scene that would evoke laughter with a lump in the throat.

Perhaps he'd been a little hasty in interfering that first day after all. Annabel hadn't said a word of reproach since, however, and Gable had to admit he was a little surprised at her restraint. Somehow he'd expected that she would knock him down and jump on his chest at the first opportunity.

He chuckled at the thought. Maybe it wouldn't be so terrible to be underneath the delectable Annabel. Then, when he realized he was chuckling to himself like a madman, he cleared his throat and quickly exited the set. All he needed was to have the crew see him laughing all by himself. They'd really think he was nuts. He wasn't oblivious to the gossip about his recent past.

He made his usual long list of phone calls and had a solitary dinner in his room, but he couldn't stop thinking about Annabel. An image of her as he'd seen her this morning wouldn't go away. It had been in the chill dawn, and she had pounced on her first cup of coffee gratefully, warming her cold hands on the cup. Her face had been rosy with sleep and cold, yet her orders to the crew were crisp and commanding. She was such an intriguing bundle of contradictions, Gable mused, her childlike appreciation of the hot drink vying with her professional role, never compromising it, always enhancing her essential lovableness.

Lovableness? Where had that word come from? He had formerly applied it solely to dogs or occasionally to small children. He shook his head and frowned down at the script he was trying to concentrate on. But the image of her face rose up from the page.

She was so close now, just down the hall. As he'd passed her door he'd seen the light, so he knew she was probably still awake, despite her early call, going over the next day's shooting. The sliver of light underneath her door had seemed to beckon to him with a promise of enfolding warmth.

He had tried so damned hard to put the kiss out of his mind. Instead it had lingered, teasing him insistently with its seductive, tantalizing whisper of a promise he couldn't ignore. *You want her,* Gable told himself grimly. *Admit it.*

So what? a rational voice answered, calming him. *You've wanted many women, and you haven't taken them all to bed.*

Bolstered by that bracing reminder, Gable decided he really should, just as a gesture to smooth away any lingering animosity between them, drop in on her to say how pleased he'd been with the first week's shooting. He'd be leaving for Los Angeles soon on business, so it might be his last opportunity. He got up with a satisfied grunt and headed down the hall toward her room.

He was almost at her door when it opened suddenly, sending a ray of light out into the dark hall. Gable stepped back instinctively into the shadows and saw Benjamin Hall emerge, yawn and amble down the hall in the opposite direction.

Gable found that both his hands were clenched into fists by his sides. He'd heard the stories about Annabel's affair with Ben. After he'd broken in on the hug the first day, he wondered if it had been renewed. The thought made his muscles tighten. Without stopping to think, he crossed the hall and rapped smartly on her door.

It was flung open almost instantly. "Now what?" Annabel asked, her expression amused. It tightened when she saw him.

"Expecting someone?" Gable asked curtly, striding past her.

"Something wrong?" she asked mildly.

Gable stopped in the middle of the room and turned back to look at her. She was dressed in a football jersey and white leggings with thick yellow socks, and her hair was down for a change, curling wildly to her shoulders. Behind tortoiseshell glasses, the ones that always reminded Gable of an English schoolgirl, her expression was puzzled.

He turned away again, thrust his hands into his pockets and watched the breeze stir the white curtains. He'd been surprised when Annabel had picked this room for her stay. It was tiny, but she'd said it reminded her of her apartment in New York. And she had loved the plain lines of the Shaker furniture, the pristine snowy white coverlet, the headboard Josiah Crane had carved himself. Gable would have thought she'd have chosen the suite of rooms painted in robin's egg blue that Josiah had furnished for Melinda, though Melinda had never really used it. The diary had made very clear that she preferred to be with Josiah—until the last troubled months of her life. But Annabel had insisted that Sasha be the one to enjoy the blue suite. She'd said she felt Melinda's presence more keenly in the small white room anyway.

"Gable? Is something wrong?"

He spun around. She had closed the door and was leaning against it, her arms folded, watching him warily.

"Your personal life is your own business," he said tersely. "I don't want to interfere with that. But in the interests of the film, I do feel an obligation to issue a warning—just for everyone's good, you understand."

She pushed off the door and walked slowly across the room. Through the thin leggings he could see the muscles of her calves, the suggestion of the curves of her bottom. "And that is?" she asked.

"Your relationship with Benjamin Hall is hardly a secret, Annabel."

"Oh?" Annabel asked coolly, sitting cross-legged on the bed.

"Obviously."

"Oh. And?"

"And?"

"And what is this warning you're issuing me?"

"Well," Gable said, irritated somehow at Annabel's calm reaction, "we should be careful that it doesn't affect the film. For example, we wouldn't want to weigh the film unfairly in terms of the character of Josiah.''

He saw color rise to her cheeks, but she didn't move. When she spoke he heard the low, even tone he'd learned to recognize as Annabel's version of fury. It could be downright unnerving, and he suddenly wished he had kept his mouth shut.

"Gable," she said quietly, "we are not getting off to a good start here. You have done nothing but undermine my professionalism since I arrived on the set. I also feel an obligation to issue a warning—just for everyone's good, you understand." Her mocking tone lashed across the room at him. "Grow up."

"What?"

"I didn't think you'd turn out to be one of that breed of men I keep running into—the ones who just can't accept the fact that there should be such a thing as a female director."

"That's ridiculous. I hired you, didn't I?"

She nodded gravely. "And I'm beginning to wonder why. You haven't treated me like a professional. You've treated me like a lackey."

"Did anyone ever tell you that you have a chip on your shoulder the size of a small moraine?"

"No," she said quietly. "Has anyone ever told you that you can be unforgivably insulting?"

He decided to be conciliatory. "Look, Annabel, I don't want you to be afraid that I don't respect your abilities—" he began.

"I hate to inform you," Annabel broke in icily, "but worrying about whether or not you respect me doesn't keep me up nights, Gable. I'm not here to prove myself to you. I've dealt with my share of prejudices, and I don't have the time or inclination to cajole you into believing that I'm competent.''

"I didn't mean that!" Gable snapped.

She uncoiled herself from the bed and rose in a fluid movement he admired in spite of himself. "Well, well," she murmured, crossing to the window and looking out. "I think I just heard the cool Gable McCrea actually raise his voice. I'm surprised the mirrors didn't crack."

Gable took a deep breath and moved closer to her. "Annabel," he said soberly, looking out the window with her, "this film is important to me for many reasons, and I tend to get single-minded about it. I was out of line about Ben. I'm sorry."

She turned to stare at him quizzically. "Did you just apologize?"

"Is that so unbelievable?"

Annabel sighed and took off her glasses. She rubbed her eyes tiredly. "No. Yes. I don't know. You have a tendency to surprise me."

"Maybe you don't know me as well as you think you do."

Annabel stared up at him, her eyes frankly speculative. Green glinted out at him through the lush forest of dark lashes.

"Maybe I don't," she said. "And maybe you don't know me as well as you think you do, either. I'm not having an affair with Ben, Gable."

He was suddenly, acutely aware of her nearness. His senses felt swamped with her scent, with the fresh clarity of her skin, the curling riot of her hair. How easy it would be to reach over and tilt her chin to allow him access to her sweetly humorous mouth. It seemed as though the world had ceased to exist outside this prim white room, a room suddenly charged with her sensual presence.

Annabel looked away from him and out the window again. Her voice was hushed and grave. "Don't kiss me," she said.

It took a moment for Gable to register her words. "What?"

She looked up at him. "Don't kiss me."

"I wasn't going to kiss you," he said.

"Yes, you were."

"How do you know?"

"I can tell."

"How do you know you weren't going to kiss me?"

"I wouldn't."

"You did once."

"No, I didn't. I kissed you *back*. That's different."

"Semantics," Gable said. He put his hand on the back of her neck.

She stayed rigid. "No. I don't want this."

"I don't either," Gable said, his fingers lightly running over the soft skin of her neck. "But it's here, isn't it, Annabel?" He felt her quick, involuntary shiver. "So what can we possibly do about it?"

"Not this," Annabel whispered as her eyes closed in response to his touch. She gave a closemouthed sound of longing, of need, and it was then that his control unraveled.

He tipped her chin up and grabbed fistfuls of her hair as he pulled her closer, wanting to luxuriate in its weight and scent. The intoxicating, liberating flood of pure sensation rushed through him as her mouth opened against his.

He felt that peculiar drowning sensation again that claimed him when he was close to her. Her body was still beneath his hands, rigid, as if one tiny movement would send her out of control, but her skin was warm where his lips and his hands touched it.

She pulled away breathlessly. "Gable—"

"Annabel—"

They spoke at the same time, a question, a plea. Their eyes met. Gable could see everything, then; her hesitancy and her need shone out at him like a beacon, drawing him to her in ways he couldn't begin to untangle.

Their faces drew closer again in an excruciatingly slow movement, their gazes locked with every millimeter gained, waiting for the other to draw away, to speak, to stop. But neither could stop, could speak. Their lips met again, gentler this time, and Annabel's eyes fluttered closed.

She sighed into his mouth as if she had come home. Gable's arms slid around her, and his heart thumped like a thousand thundering hooves in his chest. Never had he felt so vulnerable, never so strong. His hands traced her spine, smoothed her hips, then brought her up against him with sudden, surprising force as his desire escalated with the fresh sensation of having her so close and so willing.

Annabel moaned when she felt him against her. She was torn between exploring every sweet, provocative caress to the fullest and running away from him as fast she could. His face was rough with stubble, but her fingers rubbed over it wonderingly. She brought them to the corners of his mouth so that she could feel it against hers, try to capture the mystery of how perfectly it fit over hers.

It was as though she were on a rocking, pitching ship, leaning for balance on Gable, whose legs were now spread to grasp her more firmly. He was holding her against his body, but the action had nothing to do with protectiveness; it was hunger, it was need. There was a roaring in her ears, a trembling in her limbs, and Annabel could only wonder dazedly how she would ever have the strength to break this contact.

He was relentless, and she was spinning over the edge. She'd never known she could be this excited without actually fainting, unable to contain all the sensations ripping through her body. His mouth was so hard, so cool, so soft, so yielding. His hands were moving over her body now, caressing it with a heat that made her own hands move to the same sweet, desperate compulsion.

Perhaps they wouldn't have stopped if they hadn't heard the noise. It was only a loud bang from the downstairs hall, but it recalled the outside world and gave Annabel the strength to pull away.

"No," she said, trying to regain her breath. "No, Gable. We can't—"

"Why not?" he asked urgently. "Is there a rule book for this somewhere?" He grasped her fiercely. "Annabel, we can handle it. What happens in this room can be totally separate from what happens out there."

She gazed at him, wide-eyed. "What are you talking about? I can't make love with you and have that not affect how I work with you."

"I can."

The words, spoken so calmly, brought Annabel under control as nothing else could. She could see, looking at the granite of his gaze, that he was serious, that he could separate the nights from the days with no effort at all. The knowledge frightened her; she recognized with a cold, dead certainty that standing in front of her was a man who knew everything about desire and nothing about love. She felt her own desire ebb away from her body, leaving her weak, numb. She turned away.

"If that's true, Gable, you're no temptation at all."

"Oh, no?" He reached over and caressed her cheek, ran his thumb over the curve of her lips. This time he felt no quickening of her pulse, no reluctant yielding. He knew if he tried to kiss her again, she would not respond.

"Dammit, Annabel," he said, "tell me what's wrong."

She looked at him wonderingly. "You really don't know, do you?"

"No," he spit out through clenched teeth.

"Gable, I can't divide up my feelings as you can. I can't separate what happens in here from the rest of my life. It will change me. It will change *us*. But if you feel differently, it would be a disaster, for both of us, if we got involved."

"I don't understand you."

"Then that's your misfortune. I'm sorry for you."

Her wide green eyes did indeed hold a kind of sorrow in them, Gable saw, and he knew with a sickening feeling that he couldn't fight her certainty, couldn't seduce her resolve. Fury ripped through him, and he cursed, bringing his fist crashing down on the headboard of the bed.

"Gable, for heaven's sake—" Annabel began. But she stopped, staring at the front of the headboard. A small drawer concealed in the intricate carving there had popped open.

They stared at it, transfixed, their reaction time slowed by the emotions still churning inside them. Annabel reached over slowly and felt inside. Her fingers explored the drawer and found a carefully folded packet of paper wedged inside. She pulled it out.

In the silence, they could hear the clock by Annabel's bed ticking insistently. Together they looked down at the small bundle and back up at each other.

The dried paper crackled as Annabel began, with fingers that trembled slightly, to open its folds. They both jumped when there was a sharp knock at her door. They had time only to look up again in surprise as Delia Worthington-Crane swept in.

Delia's dark eyes flicked over them. "Hello."

Annabel had to admire both her beauty and her bearing. She stood in the doorway like a Roman general with her gray cape pushed back off her shoulders to flow behind her, her strong, angular face smooth as marble. Thick dark eyebrows arched impressively above deep blue eyes. Impeccably poised, she waited.

Then from behind her came a slight scurrying, and Delia was suddenly propelled forward into the room. Her gray high-heeled pumps slid on the small hooked rug, and she pitched forward for an instant. But even gravity couldn't fell Delia Worthington-Crane. She recovered and whirled around to confront a smaller woman with an identically moussed and groomed haircut. "Really, Mother!" she hissed fiercely.

"Oh, I'm sorry, honey. You were charging up the stairs at such a clip that I thought I'd lose you. I guess I came around that corner a little too fast." The woman smiled apologetically at her daughter and then beamed at Annabel and Gable amiably. "Hi, Gable. You must be Annabel. I'm Giselle. And this is Delia."

"I'm very happy to meet you." So this was Giselle Worthington, the woman who had raised the child of one of the most famous painters of the century. She looked younger somehow, Annabel thought, since the trial. She had dyed her hair a color very much like Delia's, and she was certainly dressing differently.

Gable spoke up. "Hello, Giselle. Delia, I didn't know you were coming up tonight."

"Obviously," Delia drawled. She had a flat voice without much range to it. Annabel wondered if that was why she was so rarely seen interviewed on television. She was much more effective in print. She turned to Annabel. "Are you working on the film, uh—?"

"This is Annabel Porter. The director," Gable said pointedly.

"Of course we know she's the director, Gable," Giselle chided him good-naturedly. She turned to Annabel. "I'm very pleased to meet you," she said warmly. "I loved *Writing Off Craig*. I couldn't be happier that you're doing Delia's story."

"Well, thank you. I'm glad to meet you, too."

"I know I look a sight," Giselle said confidingly. "The trip took three hours, and I'm exhausted. We were going to go straight to the hotel, but Delia wanted to stop and see Gable, so we did. We saw you at the window."

"Yes," Delia said as she walked farther into the room and looked around. "You looked quite . . . cozy."

"As a matter of fact," Annabel said, feeling that it was a good time to change the subject, "we had just made a rather startling discovery when you came in."

"Oh?" Delia asked, bored.

Annabel stepped away to reveal the tiny drawer in the headboard. "We found this—" she held out the paper "—in there." She pointed to the drawer. "We were just about to read it."

A small "Oh, dear!" came from Giselle.

Delia was across the room in a few quick strides. "How exciting!" she breathed, her voice suddenly full of excitement. "Let me see."

Before Annabel knew quite what had happened, Delia had unfolded the papers and was reading them rapaciously. "Well, well," she said when she'd finished, "it appears as though my mother wrote poetry. Not very good, I'm afraid. No wonder she hid it."

"May I have it back?" Annabel asked politely.

She shrugged. "Sure." She handed the papers to Annabel as she went by, heading for Gable. She kissed him on the cheek. "Hello, darling."

"Hello, Delia." Gable walked over to Giselle. "And here's a proper hello for you, too," he said, kissing her.

"Oh, thank you, Gable. You're sweet. We should go back downstairs, though. Monte is tired, I'm sure. We had such a long drive," Giselle fretted.

"Monte?"

"The chauffeur," Delia explained. "Mother treats him like a son. How's the filming going, Gable?"

While Gable spoke to Delia, Giselle turned to Annabel. "Well, it *was* a long ride. I must look a sight," she repeated, looking in the mirror and smoothing her hair.

"You look fine," Annabel assured her. "As a matter of fact, I was just thinking how terrific you look. Different from the trial, somehow—"

She paused awkwardly, suddenly realizing that it had been a rather tactless thing to say. But Giselle didn't seem to mind. "You're not kidding," she said with laugh. "I was a wreck. All that publicity—I nearly had a nervous breakdown. I probably would have, if it hadn't been for Delia. Anyway, after all that I went all out at the beauty place Delia goes to in Beverly Hills. I got the works," she confided. "Do you like the hair?"

Annabel had to marvel at the crazy conversation she was having with Giselle. They'd just met, and here they were, chatting away about hairstyles.

"You look beautiful," Annabel said sincerely.

"Antoine is a genius," Giselle began, but her daughter interrupted.

Delia's voice was clipped and cold. "Let's go, Mother. We should check into the hotel."

"All right. It was lovely meeting you, Annabel. Good night, Gable."

Delia turned to Gable. "I'll be here about eleven tomorrow. Maybe we can have breakfast together."

"I don't think so. I'll be breakfasting about six."

She shuddered. "Brunch, then." Then she suddenly appeared to regret her clipped tone. "Listen, I don't mean to run off. Do you both want to join us for a drink at the hotel?"

"Thanks, but I'll have to pass," Annabel said. "I've got to be up before dawn. It's time I was in bed."

"Gable? Surely you'll come."

"I'm afraid not," Gable said. "It's been a long day. Good night, Delia. Night, Giselle."

Delia stood her ground. "Aren't you going to walk us outside?" she asked Gable pointedly. "It's rather late."

"Of course," he returned smoothly. He turned to Annabel, his gaze opaque, holding no hint of his feelings. "Good night, Annabel," he said.

"Good night." Annabel watched him escort Delia and Giselle out the door. He closed it softly behind him without a word, without even a significant glance or a more private goodbye, even though five minutes before he'd been sliding his hands along every part of her body he could reach. Again, it was as though they'd had no personal contact at all.

Annabel felt suddenly cold. She switched off the over-head light, leaving only the small light on at her bedside. Hugging herself for warmth, she went back to the bed and crawled under the covers. Her body still felt as though there were a galvanizing current running through it from his touch. His cool, long fingers had branded her skin. Strange how he could warm her when his face, his heart, his soul, were so closed to her. She had seen that tonight, as fleeting as the glimpse into the real Gable had been.

She sighed and smoothed open the papers Delia had given back to her. She recognized the tiny black hand-writing as Melinda's immediately.

She turned them over in her hands. She thought of Melinda retreating to this small white room, near the end of her life, and hiding the poems away. Had she hoped someone would find them one day?

The well-worn path leads downward
to the iron sea, the rocks
impale;
they stifle sound.
Oh, the soundless spiraling cry I cry
I cry...

Annabel read the poems slowly, turning the pages with care as she went back to reread them again and again. Some broke off abruptly. Some were streams of images flowing without meter—images of water, tears, loss, a void. All the colors were gray. Annabel thought of Josiah, downstairs in his studio painting with his brilliant, shimmering palette of extraordinary color, while Melinda sat upstairs writing, with her images of a complete absence of any vivid hue. It was as though all color had been bleached out of her world.

Annabel switched off the light, but she didn't sleep. She stared up at the ceiling, wondering why a woman so tortured by guilt never thought of trying to get her baby back. And what horrible circumstance had forced her into giving her away. What had happened in those two weeks after Melinda and Josiah left for France that had led them to give up their child? That mystery added a poignant note to the ending of the film. But in real life it was tantalizing, infuriating.

"The loss, the loss..." Melinda had written. The tone in the poems was vastly different from the rushed, excited, tender tone of the diary. It was abrupt, shuttered, bleak with a hurt so deep and wide that all light had fled.

"The loss, the loss," Annabel whispered into the darkness. Why did the words call to mind an image of a tall man with eyes the color of winter moonlight, striding out her door without a backward glance of regret?

Restless nights were dangerous for a director. Most people, watching tanned and fit directors plug their films on morning talk shows, didn't realize that the profession was, quite simply, physically arduous. Annabel usually went into training months before a shoot, building up her strength and stamina. Working sixteen-hour days required a great deal of mental and physical discipline, and never had Annabel needed it more than she did now.

On an average day they filmed from six in the morning to six at night, during and after which she conferred with the cinematographer and wardrobe people and set designers and actors until she saw the rushes, ate a hasty dinner and retired to her bedroom at ten with the pages

and notes for the next day's shooting. Then
at dawn again the next day, facing a million
sions that could make or break the film. The on..
that kept her going were sheer terror that the whol..
would tumble down like a house of cards and occasional
exhilaration when it miraculously managed to go well
that day.

So she really couldn't congratulate herself too much
for managing to banish hazardous thoughts of Gable
McCrea's smooth expertise with kisses and caresses; she
was too tired to think about anything more pleasurable
than a stolen hour in the bathtub. Most of the time.

Thankfully, Gable was a great help with her program
for self-discipline; he obligingly disappeared into the
wilds of Hollywood a few days after Delia arrived.

And it turned out that Delia Worthington-Crane had
arrived with a vengeance. She had decided that she
couldn't tolerate the hotel in town, she liked the caterers
Gable had hired and she wanted to keep an eye on things
for "authenticity," she said, so she simply moved in.
Since she had the title of story consultant, Annabel really
couldn't object. Not to mention that Delia happened to
own the house they were staying in. She moved into a
suite on the third floor, with Giselle in the adjoining one.
Delia had tried to talk her mother into going back to
L.A., where they now lived, but Giselle was having too
much of a ball to heed her daughter's barbed hints.

Annabel didn't mind Giselle's presence. She was actually a cheerful addition to the set, with her enthusiasm
for every detail of the filmmaking. She was perfect for
the actors; vain as they were, they were delighted to have
her discuss their unhappy childhoods or their hair or their
makeup for hours.

Gable had left so soon after Delia's arrival that Annabel hadn't had much chance to observe them together. But the possessive look in Delia's gaze when it rested on Gable made Annabel feel curiously homicidal. It was undoubtedly lucky for all concerned, then, that Gable showed no sign of returning to Mendocino.

The lights came up, accompanied by Ben Hall's groan.

"That was the worst torture ever devised by man," he said.

"You don't have to attend the rushes, Ben," Annabel said mildly. "I'll let you know how you're doing."

"I can't help it—I have to come. It's like biting down on an aching tooth."

"Masochist," Sasha said, leaning over the back of his chair.

"But you know, Annabel," Ben went on, "I must admit, I'm beginning to think this film might not stink after all."

"Gee, thanks."

"I wasn't too bad in that scene."

"Come on, Ben," Sasha said, standing up and yawning. "Let's get a nip of brandy for an anesthetic, and I'll walk you to your room. It's past our bedtime. It's almost nine-thirty, after all."

Annabel watched them stroll off together, still chatting amiably. She didn't know how it happened, but somewhere along the way the two stars had become friends. She'd actually seen them having lunch together on the lawn yesterday. Sasha had been throwing back her head with uproarious laughter at something Ben had said.

Then she sat stock still as a new thought struck her. Could it be that they were more than friends? Hadn't Ben looked extra terrified lately? That could only mean that he was falling in love. Annabel tried the idea on for size and felt distinctly uneasy. She had gotten fond of the wry and sharp Sasha, and she suspected that the actress was more tender underneath than she let on. But perhaps she was just the woman who could handle Ben Hall.

The room had emptied out quickly, most people heading for a late dinner or the hotel in town, where most of the crew was staying. Annabel remained in her chair a few moments, thinking about the footage she had just seen. It was a crucial scene for Ben—it was when Josiah learns that Melinda is pregnant. Joy and fear battle in his face as he thinks through the implications of her news. The miracle to come is tempered by both the doctor's warning that she may not bring the baby to term and the agonizing knowledge that this will put an end to their hope for an annulment. Despite her rebellious nature, Melinda had desperately wanted to be Josiah's legal mate.

Annabel had been pleased with the sizzle between Ben and Sasha on screen, and it seemed to point to the truth of her earlier supposition. There was a new, quiet power to Ben's acting, and Sasha matched him inch for inch, making the scenes crackle with that special electricity between the leads a director always hopes for.

Annabel picked up her notes and stood to head for the door. She jumped with surprise when she saw Gable leaning against the back wall. She hadn't seen him in several weeks, and she was furious with herself for the excited thrill that ran through her.

"You startled me. When did you get back?"

"Just in time for the rushes." Gable looked grim.

Annabel gripped her notebook. "So what do you think?" she asked, trying to sound casual.

"I think, Annabel, that we've got serious problems with this film. We need to talk."

Chapter Five

"Okay," Annabel said calmly, leaning back to rest against the chair behind her. "Shoot."

"I'm afraid you're losing it, Annabel," Gable said.

"I beg your pardon?"

"You're losing the focus of the script. I'm seeing a sunny love story up there, with none of the dark overtones."

"Gable," Annabel said quietly, "I'm shooting the script as written."

"I know that. I'm talking about the tone. I'm not getting the real story of Josiah and Melinda. I'm not getting the neurotic obsession they had with each other."

"Gable, no matter how hard you try, you can't get away from the fact that this is a love story. It's not constant Sturm und Drang, you know."

"If you disagreed with the script, you should have discussed it before this point."

"First of all, I'm not disagreeing with the script. I'm shooting the dialogue as written. And I *did* discuss how I felt, Gable. I guess you weren't listening. That must have been why preproduction went so smoothly."

"I think," Gable went on doggedly, "you're telling a lyrical love story that has nothing to do with the script."

"Maybe I should talk to the elusive Fortuna Iuvat about it. I still don't understand why he isn't on the set, like most writers."

"I told you, he's reclusive. But I agree. I think he needs to be here."

"Well, at last. I want to talk to him about some things."

"Like what?"

Annabel waved her bundle of papers. "I want to show him Melinda's poetry and some passages in her diary. I have so many questions, Gable. Melinda describes a nursery in great detail. Josiah was painting murals for it, she said. What happened to it? Why didn't Fortuna include it in the script?"

"Because we don't think it existed. Nobody ever saw it. No visitors or servants then, no investigators since. It was Melinda's fantasy about what she *wanted* Josiah to feel. She was emotionally fragile, neurotic."

"I don't believe that. She wasn't unbalanced. Not then."

"According to her family—"

"Her family," Annabel pointed out acidly, "thought she was crazy for not living with a husband who didn't love her. They disowned her for living with Josiah. She was dead to them." She turned the pages of the diary. "Listen to this passage about the nursery: 'How like him to want to embrace the child so close to his heart by having him or her so near. It is the one time I have seen something take precedence over his work. Even I am banished to the other wing during the day if I'm not modeling for him.' "

"Annabel," Gable said patiently, "maybe the nursery did exist for a time. We don't know. But there's no evidence that Josiah really wanted the child in the first place. If he had, why didn't he ever try to contact Delia? He lived another thirty years."

"That's precisely what I've been wondering," she mused. "Why? The more I read this, the more questions I have. You know what's strange? The diary's most erotic passages are all during Melinda's pregnancy. It's as if she and Josiah experienced a fresh passion then. How could a man who was fascinated by the sight of his child growing inside Melinda every day, who used to caress it as they made love, not want it?"

"Annabel, what are you getting at?"

"I'm not sure. I have this feeling that something doesn't fit. Something had to have happened in those last two weeks not covered by the diary. Something to make them give up that child."

"We know why it happened. Melinda was sure she was close to an annulment on the grounds that she was barren."

"That's why they kept the pregnancy a secret. But why give away the child? They were so in love."

"That's it precisely, Annabel. Their relationship was too intense to support another person. They were still hoping for an annulment." Gable's voice was strained, and she looked at him sharply. "Only their love was important. Nothing else mattered," he went on, his voice charged with some emotion she couldn't understand. "For God's sake, can't you understand that?"

Suddenly there was anguish in his face, in his bleak gaze, and Annabel let the diary fall to her side. She had never seen such pure emotion in his eyes.

As she stared at him, she saw the shuttered gaze return. In a flash the emotion was gone, the smooth, imperturbable mask was back, and she was left wondering what secret inroad to his soul she had glimpsed.

She tried to keep her voice neutral, knowing that Gable would dodge any attempt to question him. "Well, I just wish the pieces would fit together better."

"They won't," he said curtly. "We'll never know. We can just do the best we can with what we have. Which brings me back to the original subject."

"Which is?"

Gable smiled his mirthless half smile. "Which is, if we're fundamentally disagreeing about the film, how is it going to turn out? I don't want a muddy film. It's got to have movement, thrust. We can't work at cross-purposes, or the film will be a mess. After all, you'll be editing it, too."

"We're not going to have that argument again, are we? You know I edit all my pictures. I agreed to have a coeditor. And Gable, I do remember your saying that we could work out our differences. I still believe that."

"That was before I found out you had a mind of your own."

She glanced at him sharply, but he was grinning at her. Her stomach lurched, a feeling she blamed on not having dinner yet, and she gave him a grudging grin. "Don't be charming at this late date, Gable. I don't think my heart could stand it."

His smile grew broader, and then they were standing there, not moving, absurdly grinning at each other. Annabel's heart did a quick back flip. The man could look as handsome as the devil—there was no doubt about it. No wonder she had to struggle to resist him.

"I should let you get your dinner," Gable said abruptly, breaking the eye contact and pushing away from the wall. "Look, let me think about what I saw today. The lyrical quality I see might not hurt the film. We don't have to worry until you start shooting the later scenes."

"Why don't we have a meeting with Fortuna?"

"Okay. It would be good to have his input. He's a very smart man. I'll let you know when." He started out.

"Gable!" she called. He turned and looked at her questioningly. "Would you do me one favor?"

"Maybe."

She walked quickly toward him, holding out the diary and Melinda's poetry. "Read these."

He took them gingerly, almost with distaste. "I don't think it will make a difference, Annabel. Anyway, I've already read the diary."

"Read it again. Please."

He nodded slowly, looking at her. "All right. Good night, Annabel." His voice softened suddenly as his eyes traced her features. "I'm sorry to have kept you. You look tired."

Unaccountable sadness filled her as she watched him walk away. Why was he fighting so hard against the love of their two characters? Why was he driven to tell such a dark tale, with no hint of the light that love could bring?

And why, Annabel wondered as she headed for the kitchen for some badly needed dinner, did she feel the insistent, inconvenient compulsion to figure him out?

When Annabel emerged from the kitchen, the lights along the stairs were already out. They were extinguished early, since everyone was usually in bed by now. There was only a faint light from the hallway above, and Annabel wished she had the flashlight she usually carried for these late-night excursions. Shrouded in darkness, the old house could be very eerie. She felt her way up the stairs cautiously.

She started when she saw someone break away from the shadows at the top of the stairs, and it took her a minute to recognize the elegant figure.

She sighed in relief. "Oh, hello, Delia. You startled me."

The figure stepped farther into the light, heading for the stairs. "It's Giselle, Annabel."

"Oh, sorry. Hi."

"I was heading down to the kitchen to snitch something to eat. I'm actually starting to like the food here. After a lifetime of cooking pot roast, this is interesting stuff. Is there any raspberry chicken left? Or should I have the black-bean chili?"

Annabel laughed. "They're both good. I just had a sandwich. I think it was a sun-dried tomato, goat cheese and basil. Interesting."

"No!" Giselle giggled and started down the stairs. "By the way, Gable looked like a thundercloud when I saw him before. I hope everything is all right."

"Everything's fine. Careful on those stairs."

As Giselle passed her, she put her hand on her arm. "I sneaked in to see the rushes tonight, Annabel—I hope you don't mind. I know I don't know anything about film, but I just wanted to tell you that I was really moved. I think it's going to be a great movie. But I'm sure you don't need me to tell you that."

Annabel was touched. "Oh, yes, I do. Thank you, Giselle."

"I mean," she continued, "I'm glad that you're showing how they cared for each other. They did, you know. I could tell."

"Giselle," Annabel said suddenly, "why do you think they gave the baby away? At the trial you said that you didn't know who they were, but you guessed they weren't married."

"Yes. You have to remember that this was the fifties. People just didn't have illegitimate children then. I mean, they did, of course, but adoption was the usual route. I just figured that was the case. I was only too glad to have a baby to replace my own. It gave me something to live for. And Delia has been such a good daughter. Perfect."

"Of course."

Giselle started down the stairs again. "Anyway, Annabel, I'm glad that something good is coming out of the story. For you, I mean. And Gable. You're making a work of art. Good can spring from tragedy, from wrong decisions and all the terrible things people can do to one another."

Giselle turned and faced her, and Annabel was struck by how different she looked. She looked her age, suddenly, and her face looked unexpectedly incongruous below the youthful hairstyle. The constant smile that so animated her expression was gone, and she looked, Annabel realized slowly, ravaged.

"Can't it?" Giselle asked her. Her voice was urgent.

"Of course it can," Annabel said automatically, wanting to reassure her without knowing why.

"Mother! What are you doing?" Delia's sharp tone broke in on them. Annabel looked up and saw her standing at the head of the stairs, dressed in a long silky robe.

"I was chatting with Annabel."

"Really, Mom, you shouldn't keep her. She has such an early call."

"That's okay," Annabel said.

"I'm sorry. I shouldn't have said a word," Giselle murmured nervously. Then she shook off her mood like a shower of raindrops. "I'd better get to that kitchen," she said gaily. "Pleasant dreams, Annabel."

"You, too," Annabel said, watching her navigate down the stairs. "That is, if you can after a bowl of that black-bean chili."

Hearing Giselle's laughter ringing in her ears, Annabel turned back toward Delia, but she had disappeared. She slowly felt her way to her room. Something was bothering Giselle, that was for sure. Some dark secret from her past, perhaps? Or maybe the mood of the place was getting to her—the dim corners, the long shadows. . . .

Annabel shivered. There were mysteries here, and so many secrets—Melinda's, Giselle's, Gable's. . . .

She pushed open her door with relief. "If only I had time to figure it all out," she grumbled. Then she quickly climbed into her pajamas and tumbled into bed. Surprisingly, she fell asleep immediately.

Just when Annabel thought she couldn't stand one more complication, it began to rain. It didn't help that the locals assured them that steady rain was a rare occurrence in Mendocino's summers. It still threw everything out of whack. They had been scheduled to begin the exterior shooting, and the weather made it impossible.

After endless meetings over two days with the director of photography, Gable and various other members of the crew, they had managed to juggle the schedule and squeeze another two days out of interior shots. And by waiting around for long stretches for the weather to clear, they had managed to do a bit of exterior shooting. But as a week passed and the rain continued, tempers had gotten shorter and shorter. There was no worse place to be than a movie set when the weather wouldn't clear, Annabel knew.

The delays were getting too expensive. They were already running on an unusually tight schedule, and every day lost cost them heavily. And now Annabel was fully aware of what a disaster that could mean for Gable. His expression grew more and more grim as the wet days went on.

By Friday night she felt wound up tighter than her alarm clock. She felt the heavy weight of the film on her shoulders pinning her down as she tossed and turned for an hour, trying to sleep while the rain pattered mockingly on the roof. Finally she gave up. Unable to concentrate on a book, she pulled a warm robe on over her silk nightshirt and headed downstairs.

Maybe some brandy would help, she mused, heading for the kitchen. She poured herself one and then decided to sit in Josiah's studio for a bit.

With the exception of her small white bedroom, it had become her favorite room in the old house. Here she felt the power of the artist Josiah Crane had been. The space was mostly bare now, since they had already shot the studio scenes in which the room had really come alive. Gable had cajoled a major collector into lending Crane's work from the period of the film, and the studio had looked very much as it had thirty years before. But even without his work on the walls and stacked around the room, the room somehow held the lingering scent of genius and linseed oil.

Annabel sat on the old red couch that she now knew from several of his paintings and sipped her brandy. She had been tempted to go to Gable tonight, but she had resisted. Perhaps that was why she couldn't sleep. She felt the need to give him the reassurance she didn't feel herself that everything would turn out fine. But she knew that Gable neither wanted nor needed her brand of comfort. So far she'd successfully avoided being alone with him again.

Sunk deep in her thoughts, Annabel looked up and found him there, watching her from the doorway. He was wearing old jeans and a soft blue shirt, which was unbuttoned all the way down. His brown skin gleamed in the diffused light of the studio. "What are you doing awake?" he growled.

She pushed at the springy curls on her forehead. "Couldn't sleep."

Gable held up his own brandy snifter. "Me either." He ambled across the floor and sat down on the couch, stretching his long legs in front of him.

Together they listened to the soft sound of rain on the skylight.

"I wish it didn't sound so damn comforting," Gable observed.

"It'll stop," Annabel said confidently.

"It usually does. Sometime. Question is, will we have enough money to go on when it does?"

"Things that bad?"

"That bad." He took a long swig of brandy.

"I think the crew might mutiny if this downpour goes on much longer. And Ben and Sasha had a huge fight at lunch. I tried to talk to them, but . . ." Annabel turned toward him. "Would you?"

"Would I what? Talk to them?" Gable snorted. "Are you kidding? Sorry, Annabel, but you're going to have to handle that one yourself. I'm no good at patching up lovers' quarrels, believe me. My job is to worry about this rain."

She turned to face him. "Is there anything I can do?"

His expression softened as he looked at her. He reached out and stroked her cheek with one long finger. "You're rather irresistible at times, do you know that, Annabel?" His eyes held hers, liquid and bright, for a moment. Then he smiled—a genuine smile, the smile she had begun to look for, wait for. It made his harsh, sensual face suddenly handsome. "I have a feeling," he said, "that you've been hearing a few rumors."

"I've heard that you're broke," Annabel answered straightforwardly. "That you have everything riding on this film. Is it true?"

He nodded. "I had a little trouble raising the money. So I had to create a big investor: me."

"I see."

"And what other rumors have you heard about me?" This time, she was silent.

"Something about a breakdown?" he prodded.

She nodded. "Something like that. Is that true, too?"

He sighed and tipped his head back to look up at the drizzling rain on the skylight. "No. It's a misconception people in Hollywood hold on to because they don't understand what I did and I haven't bothered to correct them. It's no use trying to deny a breakdown in that town; it's too common a phenomenon, and denials are the way it's always handled anyway. Four years ago I decided to reshuffle my priorities. I started leaving Hollywood for long periods and going to Vermont. Finally I moved there completely for a few years."

"Vermont?" The surprise in her voice made him turn to her questioningly. "Someone told me you lived in the desert, or the mountains—they weren't sure."

He chuckled. "Well, I was in the mountains—the Green Mountains. I'd spent some time in Vermont when I was a boy."

"Funny, I always assumed you grew up in Hollywood."

"Oh, I did. I only spent a summer in Vermont. My father got a job directing summer stock at a small theater there. It was the most normal period of my childhood, and I never forgot it. One perfect summer. So, years later I bought some land. Then four years ago I went back there and built a house."

"And what else did you do there?"

"I cultivated my garden."

She peered at him, trying to decide if he was teasing her. "Really?"

"Really. I learned to cook. If you're nice to me, I might cook a meal for you sometime. I read a lot of books, got to know the neighbors. That's where I met Fortuna, actually. I didn't want to do anything that had to do with movies. I didn't even have a television or a VCR." He paused, reflecting. "I enjoyed it immensely."

"And then what?"

"And then one day I read about the Crane case. It was funny—the adrenaline just shot up, almost as though I had nothing to do with it. It was the first time a story had appealed to me in years. So I got in touch with Delia, and—" He shrugged. "Here we are."

She remained silent, absorbing his words. "Why did you feel a need to 'reshuffle your priorities' in the first place?"

"Ah," Gable said. "Funny how most people don't think of that question. But I think it's a story for another night." He turned to look at her. "I'm sure we have better things to do right now."

Annabel sat up, suddenly nervous. She didn't like that lazy, suggestive tone in his voice. "Yes, we should get to bed."

"My thoughts exactly. It's about time, don't you think?" One finger skated around the collar of her deep emerald robe. "This is pretty. Matches your eyes."

Annabel shifted away. "Where did Gable the charming seducer come from? You've never handed me a line like that before."

He shrugged, unconcerned. "Nothing else I do seems to work. I thought I'd try it."

She wasn't far enough away to evade his long arms. He could reach one wispy curl by her ear, and he managed to take full advantage of such an innocent conquest. Annabel shivered at the light touch.

"Annabel," he said huskily, winding the curl around his finger, "I'm in no mood tonight to play games. I can't deny what's between us anymore."

Her breathing seemed to stop. She tilted her head away from him, but that only left more of her neck bare, and his fingers were sliding over it, caressing it softly. And then he was beside her, pressing his mouth against the hollow of her throat. She felt the tip of his tongue, ever so lightly, flick against her skin. She didn't move.

How could this be happening? Annabel wondered dazedly. How could she be giving in to him again? She knew it was a mistake, she knew it, but she could not, for all her force of will, make herself get up and move out of his reach. She thought she would die if he didn't continue to touch her in the same deliberate way, his hands

sliding her robe down her arms and then gliding back up
to her shoulders, smoothing them through her nightshirt.

The arousal in his eyes as he looked at her, at her body
exposed in the thin silk, sent something incandescent
shooting through her, but she was still strangely passive,
able only to watch him.

She could see he was fascinated by what lay beneath
the silk, and she watched as his fingers roamed the con-
tours of her body, caressing the curve of her collarbone,
the soft tops of her breasts, her shoulders. Slowly and
with infinite care he unfastened the tiny buttons running
down the front of her nightshirt, all the way down to the
tops of her thighs.

Then his hands parted the soft material, still more
slowly, as though the spell might be broken with any ir-
reverent haste. Annabel looked down at her partial nu-
dity without shame. She felt as though she were entangled
in a transparent, shimmering web of her own desire, and
she ached for Gable to burn away the binding threads
with the fire of his hands, his mouth, his body. She
wanted all of him to cover her, all of him to be with her,
around her, in her, and now she moved with the same
slow deliberation to bring his mouth to her breast.

She arched back with the sudden, surprisingly fierce
feel of his mouth on her skin. She gasped. He was so
sure, so expert in what he wanted, in what he knew she
wanted as well.

Greedy soon for his mouth against hers, she pulled his
head up, and he gazed at her with burning eyes she no
longer recognized. Then they moved together to bring
their mouths into a furious kiss.

Gable's hands were in her hair, urging her lips and
tongue into a fiery, ravenous kiss. She was out of her

depth, drowning in a desire so pure and intense it was profoundly shocking.

His bare chest was against hers, and the contact of skin against skin luxurious and heady. Keeping her mouth against his, he brought her into his lap, where she felt him straining against his jeans.

I can't stop! Annabel thought crazily, holding him just as fiercely so that his mouth remained against hers. *I can't. I can't....*

And perhaps she wouldn't have if they hadn't heard tapping heels coming down the hall straight toward them.

Annabel scrambled off Gable's lap and got to her feet. She didn't have time to button the nightshirt, but she quickly slipped into her robe and knotted the sash.

Gable sighed. "Not again," he said. "It's only Delia, you know."

"Button your shirt," Annabel hissed.

"Why?" he asked. "Maybe she'll leave if she realizes she's intruding."

"How can you say that?" She gave him an assessing look, then quickly arranged a convenient newspaper to cover his lap. He grinned wickedly at her.

The door opened slowly, and Delia paused at the threshold. She took in Gable's tousled hair and irritated scowl and Annabel's attempt to look composed despite her swollen mouth and the wild disarray of her hair.

It didn't faze her a bit. "Well, well," she said, walking farther into the room. "You movie people sure know how to have a good time. Mind if I join you? I couldn't sleep, either."

"Annabel and I were having a private discussion, Delia," Gable said pointedly.

"I'll just stay a minute," she answered smoothly, and she sat down on the couch.

Annabel slowly sank into an armchair across from them. She'd already suspected that whatever was between Gable and Delia had ended some time ago. With all Gable's faults, she knew his sense of honor would not permit him to pursue her if he were still involved with Delia.

But Delia always seemed to turn up when they were alone, which seemed to indicate that she was still possessive. What was odd, Annabel reflected, was that she didn't seem emotionally affected. She had the composed air of someone simply staking out her territory.

Gable's eyebrows looked as threatening as thunderheads as he shot Delia a dark glare. Annabel shifted uneasily in her chair. "I should really—" she began.

"No." Gable's voice sliced through the air. Then he added more gently, "Please don't leave yet. I still want to talk to you." He gave Delia another significant look and sipped his brandy leisurely, with the air of a man who could outwait any opponent.

Delia was unmoved. She simply ignored his obvious desire to have her gone. "Gable, I did want to speak with you about the party tomorrow night."

"Why?"

"Well, we should make plans. We're both invited."

"And Giselle is, too. And Annabel," he said, turning to her. "I was about to invite you."

"What party?"

"I'm sure Annabel wouldn't want to leave the set."

"It's her day off. And that's her decision, don't you think?" Gable and Delia glared at each other.

Annabel tried again. "What party?"

"Saturday night. Frank and Joan Brill. All of Hollywood is going."

"The A list *and* the B list," Delia put in. "Frank and Joan are giving the best parties this year. Do you know them?"

"Not personally," Annabel answered. Everyone knew about the couple—they were the hottest young producing team in Hollywood. "It sounds very exciting, but I really don't think I can make it."

"Why not?" Gable asked.

"Gable, I can barely manage to crawl into bed by the time Saturday night rolls around."

"Nonsense. It will do you good to get out."

"And I really should be available to the crew."

"What are you talking about? Most of them are flying back down to L.A. for the weekend, anyway."

"Well, then there's Ben and Sasha—"

"They'll be at the party, too."

"And I don't want to impose—"

"I'm *taking* you, Annabel. Joan and Frank are good friends of mine. You're not imposing."

"I don't have anything to wear—"

"We'll find something."

"Gable, I hate parties," Annabel finally admitted in a rush.

"Parties are part of the business, Annabel."

"So my agent tells me," she said mournfully. "I just don't do very well at them."

He leaned over. "I promise you you'll have fun," he said softly. "And I want to introduce you to some people."

"I don't know—"

"Fortuna will be there. It will be good to meet him in a relaxed setting."

"A Hollywood party—A *and* B list—a relaxed setting? Are you kidding?" Annabel sighed. "Oh, all right. I do want to meet him."

"Good. You can stay at my house in Malibu."

"Wait a second, Gable." Delia, who had been growing more and more agitated as Gable had firmly stifled each of Annabel's objections, finally broke in. "I was counting on staying at your house."

"I have several guest rooms, Delia," Gable said smoothly, ever the gentleman despite his irritation. "I would be delighted to have all three of you."

"Three of us?" Delia demanded.

"And Giselle, of course."

She inclined her head. "Of course."

Annabel stood up. "I think it's time I got some sleep."

Gable stood up as well. "Me, too."

Delia slowly uncurled herself and rose. "I'll come up with you. I forgot my flashlight."

The three of them ascended the stairs by the glow of Annabel's small light. They were an odd trio, she reflected. It was obvious that Delia would stick around so that she and Gable couldn't be alone, and Annabel, though irritated, was grateful. Her resolve, ironclad as it was when she was alone, had a tendency to become about as substantial as a soap bubble when Gable touched her.

Her room was at the end of the hall, so she said a quick good-night to the other two and slipped inside. Her heart pounded from the glower Gable had sent her as she left him, and she lay awake wondering if he would come to her.

It was wrong of her, she knew, but she couldn't suppress a thrill of pleasure that she would finally see a more personal side of him. She would stay in his house, among his things; she could look at his books and observe his taste, and perhaps they'd offer some clues to his mysterious character. She would see him in the circles he traveled in, among his colleagues and friends. And, along with these intimate glimpses, she wouldn't have to worry about being too dangerously charmed by it all. She had a live-in chaperone, Delia, to make sure that she didn't see any more of Gable than was strictly proper. At least Giselle would be there to lighten the atmosphere. Annabel didn't know if the three of them would survive the weekend without her.

She heard the hallway clock strike two before she began to feel at all sleepy. She was relieved that Gable had apparently decided not to pursue any further what had passed between them downstairs. As a matter of fact, she was relieved that *she* hadn't been the one to sneak down the hall to his room.

As she drifted off, her mind left the intricacies of her developing relationship with Gable and occupied itself with that most crucial and feminine of concerns: she had absolutely nothing to wear to a party.

Chapter Six

Annabel lifted one soapy leg and regarded it contentedly. It had been such a long time since she'd pampered herself. Gable's bathtub was huge, and she had filled it to the brim with hot water and apricot bubble bath. She sipped appreciatively at her preparty glass of perfectly chilled champagne. She had to admit she was enjoying this. Especially since she knew Delia was waiting impatiently for her to get out.

And also waiting for her, laid out on her bed, was a deliciously filmy silver gown, sewn with tiny sequins, cut very low in back, and quite possibly the sexiest dress she'd ever seen. She didn't want to think what it must have cost.

Giselle had tapped on her door in Mendocino that afternoon as she was packing and still wondering frantically if she'd be able to find an outfit in an L.A. shop in the three hours or so she had before the party. Giselle had entered, holding this knockout of a dress, confessed sheepishly that she'd bought it even though it was really too small and totally inappropriate for her—"Who do I think I am, Joan Collins?" she had said ruefully—and that nothing in the world would give her greater pleasure than for Annabel to wear it to the party. She had looked so crestfallen at Annabel's reluctance that Annabel had obligingly taken it and tried it on. It had fit like a second skin.

"I knew it would be perfect for you," Giselle had said, meeting Annabel's flushed, pleased face in the mirror.

"What about Delia?"

"What about her?" The bitterness in Giselle's tone made Annabel look at her sharply. "She has a million gowns," Giselle said mildly, shrugging.

"Then thank you. I always knew you were a fairy godmother," she'd answered.

"I just wish I could see you walk into that party in it."

Annabel had sat down on the bed with her, concerned. "Aren't you coming with us?"

Giselle had shrugged. "Delia wants to go to this thing alone. I can't blame her. Who'd want her mother tagging after her all the time? She'll have a better time without me, and I'd like the weekend to hang around the Crane estate by myself."

Annabel remembered her words now, and realized she didn't believe them one bit. Giselle never "tagged after" Delia—she was very much her own person, attracting people by her genuine interest in them and her refusal to take herself seriously. She was the exact opposite of her daughter. Maybe it was starting to bother Delia that most people seemed to prefer her mother to herself. Whatever the reason, Delia and Giselle certainly had a complicated relationship.

She took another sip of champagne and decided it was time to rinse off. Staying too long in the bathtub before a party, no matter how little you cared for the person waiting to use it, was really hitting below the belt.

Besides, she decided, as she rinsed off in the shower and vigorously shampooed her hair, she was eager to get into that dress. There was something extremely unsatisfactory about the fact that nine times out of ten, Gable saw her in a ponytail, sneakers and jeans. It might be rather pleasant to demonstrate that she had a few more facets to her personality.

Gable pulled up in front of the Brills', handed the Ferrari keys to the parking attendant and didn't even wince when the boy screamed away from the curb and took the corner with an ear-piercing squeal of tires. Nothing had the power to faze him this evening, he reflected—not since Annabel had walked into the living room in that dress.

From the first night he'd met her, her individual, quirky style had grown on him, and he felt he'd become an expert on the extent of Annabel Porter's attraction. He thought he'd known every single permutation of her beauty. He'd come to know her tomboy appeal in jeans and a baseball cap on the set, her flushed and sleepy early-morning look, her delicate, valiant, touching fatigue at the end of a long day, her professional, elegant demeanor at meetings. He even knew how seductive she could look in a nightshirt, or curled up in a fleecy robe.

But then she had walked into the room tonight, and it was as though he'd never seen her before. His heart had seemed to stop beating at the sight of her, and he simply couldn't stop staring. He was confronted with a vision of a new Annabel, and it both seduced and unnerved him. When she'd turned for her wrap and he saw the creamy skin revealed by the plunging back of the dress, he'd lost the thread of what he'd been saying and had stammered like a teenager.

Delia had been furious, the kind of snappish, nasty anger that could spring only from hurt pride. The woman was difficult under the best of circumstances, but lately her behavior had been absolutely incomprehensible. He refused to believe she was jealous—she didn't have enough heart for that kind of emotion—but he couldn't imagine why she kept turning up when he was alone with Annabel. Tonight she had practically spit out her refusal to leave for the party with them. She'd insisted on more time to dress, and Gable had offered to leave her the limousine he'd ordered for the three of them. She'd agreed, and Gable had been delighted to be alone with Annabel. That, of course, had infuriated Delia further.

He'd forgotten Delia's anger as soon as he was in the small front seat of the Ferrari with Annabel. The subtle scent of her perfume and the angle of her beautiful white throat revealed by her upsweep of wild curls took all his attention. Then there was the sight of her unexpectedly lovely legs, carelessly crossed, to completely send him through the roof.

The butler opened the door to them, and Gable leaned to whisper in her ear. "Don't worry—I'll watch out for you."

"Thanks," she said, shooting him a grateful look. "I'll be okay once I get my bearings. Until then, I'll probably be the consummate wallflower."

"Not in that dress, you won't."

They were soon swept into the noise and light and confusion of a large party. Gable made the introductions to their hosts, and then, to his consternation, he discovered that Annabel seemed to be acquainted with half the people in the room, and the other half continually came up in order to get an introduction. Annabel, far from being a shrinking violet, was animated and charming. Gable felt himself getting more and more silent as she grew more and more confident.

"Is Fortuna here yet?" she managed to ask as a large group left them.

He scanned the crowd. "I don't see him."

"Annabel Porter!" A tall, handsome blond actor approached her with another equally ravishing creature of the opposite sex. "You look fabulous!"

"Absolutely gorgeous," his companion said matter-of-factly. "Tell me where you got that dress or I'll kill myself."

Gabel was temporarily separated from her, which gave him a moment to get his bearings. It was obvious that the grapevine was buzzing about *A Family of Two*; he was stopped every few feet to be congratulated. And everyone asked about Annabel.

It wasn't that he begrudged her her splashy success at the party, Gable told himself grudgingly, watching her get maneuvered into a corner by an important producer. He didn't know what it was, actually.

Yes, he did. He simply wanted to be the only one to appreciate her. They were isolated up in Mendocino, away from whatever "real life" was, and he'd had her all to himself, aside from the cast and crew. But here she was being monopolized by men who were obviously as enchanted with her as Gable was, and he felt sulky about it. His childishness surprised him. What was the matter with him? he wondered even as he strained over the heads in front of him for a glimpse of wild light brown curls.

The immense thought rolled over him like a large tank. *He wanted to be special in her life.*

The realization made him almost dizzy. He found her again, still in the corner, bantering with the producer, and the sight of her beautiful bare back made him ache. He imagined her, tousled and rosy, rising from his rumpled sheets in the morning. Now that same back was being admired, probably in a lecherous fashion, by strangers, and it killed him.

Gable backed away heedlessly, still transfixed by Annabel's back. He felt himself hit something and turned around. To his relief, it was the bar. "Scotch and soda," he said hoarsely.

He sipped his drink for a while, watching her, and got a perverse pleasure out of seeing her turn finally and scan the room for him anxiously. Their eyes met, and she smiled at him, that lush smile that was so damned inviting. She touched the producer's arm briefly in farewell and started across the room toward him.

Gable was unexpectedly filled with an irritation he knew quite well was childish and uncalled for. All he wanted to do was take her away from the party and get her alone. He wanted her so badly that before this evening he'd had no idea what desire could entail. It was now a living, throbbing, savage thing that built up behind his eyes and in his groin. She approached him slowly, as if in a dream, with all the vibrancy and warm, shimmering life he'd tried so hard to dismiss. He looked at her as if for the first time, and he wanted her more than he could ever imagine wanting any woman. And for the first time, he knew with swift sureness that he would never possess her. She was her own woman, she defied such notions as possession, and knowing that only made him want to possess her all the more.

* * *

Gable looked cranky, Annabel decided, eyeing him. He was leaning against the bar, drink in hand, waiting for her to approach. She wondered what had happened to upset him. She was having a surprisingly delightful time.

"You were right, Gable," she said as she came up. "This really is fun."

He gave her such an eloquent look of scorn that she had to laugh. "Not having a good time?"

"No."

"Don't mind Gable, he's just a grouch." A tall woman was standing behind him, smiling. She seemed to speak from an easy, intimate knowledge of him, Annabel noted with a twinge of uneasiness, taking in the beauty and grace in the woman's strong, intelligent face, her large gray eyes, her lovely hands.

Gable's face cleared as he heard the voice behind him, and he turned and immediately enveloped the woman in a huge hug. "Where have you been? I've been calling for days."

"Around," the woman said, still smiling affectionately at him.

"Who is he this time?"

The woman ignored his question. "Are you going to introduce me to Annabel Porter or do I have to introduce myself?"

"Annabel, this is Gish. My sister."

Relief coursed through Annabel. She found herself very glad that this formidable woman was Gable's sister, instead of yet another gorgeous creature from his past. "I'm very happy to meet you," she said, shaking her hand. "Gish?"

She nodded. "Gish and Gable. Disgustingly cute, isn't it? My mother named Gable, and my father named me. We had no choice but to go into show business."

"Gish is the best agent on the West Coast," Gable said.

Gish laughed. "As long as we're exaggerating, what about the East Coast?"

"That, too."

"Of course," Annabel said slowly. "Gish McCrea. Sorry I'm so slow on the uptake. Naturally, I've heard all about you. I had no idea you were related to Gable."

"Gish has such a strong maternal instinct that she can't expend it all on her baby brother," Gable said. "She has to torture actors, too."

"Gable, you know I hate being called maternal," Gish broke in, laughing. "It makes me want to wear an apron and start baking cookies and vacuuming. And you know how I feel about that."

"I'm not nervous. You will forever remain the least domesticated person I know. As a matter of fact, you'd get along fine with Annabel. She keeps take-out menus in her refrigerator instead of food."

"Mmm, that's what I love about New York," Gish said to Annabel. "It would take four hours in traffic to deliver a pizza in L.A."

"I have this deal with all my take-out restaurants," Annabel replied. "I give them tickets to screenings in exchange for preferential treatment. I usually get food in ten minutes—even less if it's summertime and all the big adventure movies are out. I suppose that's horribly unfair of me."

"Are you kidding? I call it genius."

They grinned at each other, and Gable looked pleased.

"Are you enjoying the party?" Gish asked her. "Do you know many people here?"

"She's like Scarlett O'Hara at the Twelve Oaks barbecue," Gable said grumpily, and Gish gave him a sudden interested look. He shifted uncomfortably.

"Tell me," he said gruffly to Gish, "who's your latest? Is he here? You see," he said gravely to Annabel, "my sister, I'm embarrassed to say, is the champion, hands down, at playing the field."

Gish shrugged. "I've been lonely since my dog died."

"And when was that?" Annabel asked, her eyes twinkling.

She got the answer she expected. "Ten years ago."

"Enough already," Gable groaned. "So which one is he?"

"Over there." Gish indicated a man across the room. He looked about forty-five, short and stocky, slightly rumpled, with a keen, amiable face enlivened by a large crooked nose.

"He looks okay," Gable admitted reluctantly. "A cut above the usual. At least he's not one of those cigarette ad men you usually favor. What does he do?"

"He's a lawyer."

"Oh, no. Someone stable. I definitely have to check him out. At least I can tell him where to have his suits pressed. Will you excuse me, ladies?"

Gable headed off purposefully into the crowd, and Annabel turned wonderingly to Gish. "He wasn't kidding."

"He feels he has to watch out for me. Actually, don't spread this around, but I don't really mind. When you spend so much time taking care of yourself and other people, it can be kind of nice." Gish looked affectionately after Gable and then turned back to Annabel. "So

I finally get to meet you. I've admired your work for so long. And Gable is ecstatic to have you on the film.''

"He is?"

"Oh, yes. He's had such a difficult time getting this together." She frowned. "He took so many risks. I was— I am—worried about him. But he'll never change, I guess. Somehow, he always manages to do shockingly well." She shrugged, and her expression cleared. "You know what they say: Fortune favors the daring."

"I've never heard that expression. I like it," Annabel said. "I suppose it's really true in our business. Fortune favors the daring. Who said it?"

"It's from Virgil, I believe."

"An agent who quotes Virgil—I'm definitely out of my league."

"I can even quote the Latin. Actually, I can't claim credit for my intellectual prowess—it's always been a favorite saying of Gable's. *Audentes Fortuna Iuvat.*''

Fortuna *what*? "Could you repeat that?" Annabel asked weakly.

"Audentes Fortuna Iuvat," Gish said dutifully. "Annabel, are you all right?"

"I'm fine," she answered, dazed. "Gish, will you excuse me?"

Anger mixed with puzzlement fueled her search through the party for Gable. What was going on? Who was the strange, elusive A. Fortuna Iuvat? Why had he and Gable conspired to make up a crazy name to shield him? "From one of the Eastern Bloc countries," Gable had said. The two of them had been laughing up their sleeves at their clever ruse, she was sure.

Was it so impossible for the man to trust her, to trust anybody? she wondered, angrily pushing through the crowd.

She found Gable on the terrace. She paused to watch him look out at the garden, trying to regain her breath and her temper. Silently, she glided up next to him and rested her icy hands on the rail next to his. She felt too ruled by her chaotic emotions to speak.

"He's a nice guy," Gable said without preliminaries.

She looked at him blankly.

"David Broder," he said, looking out at the garden. "Gish's boyfriend. I liked him." He shook his head, bemused. "I really did." He turned to her. "Did you like Gish?"

"Very much."

"I'm glad. I wanted you to meet her. It was one of the reasons I wanted you to come tonight."

Annabel clamped down her spurt of pleasure at his words. "And the other was to meet Fortuna?" she asked icily.

"Well, yes," he said hesitantly.

"Funny how he isn't around."

"Oh, he'll turn up."

"Gish is very smart," Annabel interrupted grimly. Gable looked puzzled. "She actually spoke to me in Latin. An interesting quotation, actually." Puzzlement changed to acute discomfort as Gable shifted slightly. "Translated, it means Fortune favors the daring. Ever hear of it?"

"Annabel—"

"Perhaps I can jog your memory. *Audentes Fortuna Iuvat*. Funny how those words ring a bell."

He sighed. "Now we've gotten to the second reason I wanted you to come tonight. I *did* want you to meet Fortuna."

"So you said. I hadn't realized he was from the pages of the *Aeneid*, though. That makes it a bit difficult, don't you think?'' Annabel dropped her mocking tone and turned to him. ''What's going on, Gable? Why have you cooked up this name, and who is this guy? Why haven't you told me? Don't you think I have a right to know?''

Gable sighed and looked back out at the garden. ''It's me.''

''What?''

''I wrote the screenplay.''

''You wrote . . . Then why—''

''Here you are! I've been looking all over for you!'' Delia walked across the wide terrace toward them.

''This is getting comical,'' Gable said, exasperated. ''How does she manage to do it?'' He raised his voice. ''Delia, I'm going to have to hang a little bell around your neck. Do remind me, will you?''

''What?'' Delia shrugged and ignored him. ''I just wanted to tell you that I won't be staying with you to-night after all. It's too far to drive back to Malibu, so I arranged for a room in a hotel. Besides, I don't think I could stand not having room service tomorrow morning.''

''Fine, Delia. We'll see you in Mendocino.''

''All right.'' A young actor whose perfectly chiseled face Annabel vaguely recognized from television beckoned across the terrace at Delia, and she smiled a Cheshire-cat smile. ''Don't worry if I'm not there tomorrow,'' she said.

''Fine,'' Gable answered, his eyes on Annabel. When Delia had disappeared, he took her arm. ''Let's get out of here, all right?'' His gaze brooked no argument.

''All right.''

They managed to slip out of the party unnoticed. Gable tore out of the driveway in the Ferrari, then collected himself and slowed down. He drove swiftly and silently down the dark streets. Annabel looked out the window with burning eyes. She felt betrayed, and she wasn't even sure why. But something had happened to spoil the easy camaraderie that had sprung up between them during this trip, and she felt hollow, as if she'd lost a well-loved old friend, instead of someone she'd just been getting to know.

Gable didn't speak until they were riding by the moonlit ocean.

"It's my first screenplay," he said suddenly, breaking the silence. "I wrote it in Vermont, after I'd gotten the rights to the book. I felt as if I had to write it."

"Does Delia know?" Annabel asked quietly.

Gable shook his head. "Nobody knows. Only you."

"Why?" Annabel asked, biting her lip so that she wouldn't cry out the question, letting him know how betrayed she felt. The question meant so many things. Why had he felt a need to write it? Why had he kept it a secret? And most important, her heart demanded, why hadn't he trusted her?

"It's a strange thing that happens when your stock goes down in Hollywood," he began. "Scary. Think of tonight, Annabel, at the party. Your stock is rising. Word is you'll be the next superstar director. They're already talking Oscars, and we haven't even finished the picture. That's how fast gossip moves—and how fast it can change your life. It's fun now, isn't it? But if your last two pictures didn't make any money and people thought that you'd just been through a severe breakdown, it would have been as if there were a wall of glass between you and everyone there. You're a beautiful, talented woman, and you would have been a pariah. Believe me," Gable said dryly, "I do not exaggerate."

He paused and slowed for a light, looked up at the moon with an abstracted air, then shifted smoothly and continued. "I don't mean to patronize you—I realize you know about the film business. But it's a whole different game when it happens to you. You become a cliché, and it's the most infuriating and terrifying thing. When I was in Vermont, I didn't care what anyone thought. I still don't give a damn, except for the reality of getting a picture made. A producer only has his good name. When I came around with *A Family of Two*, I realized what I was up against. You hear a lot about comebacks in this business, but you never really know what kind of gut-crunching hell you have to go through to make them. How could I sabotage the whole thing by admitting that I wrote the script? Nobody would have touched it. It would have had two strikes against it from the start, both of them mine. Can you see that?"

"Yes," she answered truthfully, but she still felt hollow inside. Although she had discovered one of Gable's secrets, she realized despairingly that she felt no closer to understanding him.

"I didn't enjoy deceiving you, Annabel," he said.

"No? What about your comments about what a smart guy old Fortuna was? You must have told me a dozen stories about how charming he was."

She could see his rueful grin by the dim light. "Well, I couldn't help having a bit of sport now and then. But please believe I was going to tell you tonight. It had gone on long enough." He turned into the winding driveway and stopped the car. "I hope," he said, still gripping the steering wheel, "that you'll accept my apology."

She paused. "I accept. But, oh, Gable," she burst out, "I wish you had trusted me!"

"No more than I, Annabel."

They walked to the house together, not touching. Gable didn't reach for her hand or tuck her arm underneath his own. He had drawn up inside himself again and become that cool, reserved enigma she was so familiar with.

He switched on one soft light in the living room. Out beyond the French doors at the end of the room Annabel could see the ocean, serene in the moonlight. The sand looked as silvered as the sea. The sky was a dark, deep cobalt with a sprinkling of hard white stars.

She paused at the entrance to the room. "I think I was a bit rude to Gish tonight. I left her rather abruptly."

"She doesn't bruise easily. But I'll make some kind of excuse for you."

Annabel started to turn away to go to her room, but she stopped. There was something she needed to know. She took a tentative step into the room. "Gable, you two seem so close. Why don't you tell Gish about the screenplay?"

Gable moved abruptly to the bar and poured two brandies. "Because she'd want to read it."

"Why don't you want her to?"

"I'm not quite sure. Maybe it's too personal for family to read. I don't know."

She took the offered snifter and crossed to the window to look out at the ocean. "I get the feeling that Gish is the only family you have," she said quietly, hoping it would be enough of an opening to get Gable to talk.

"Yes, she is." It was a typical Gable answer, only the information called for and no more, and Annabel had just decided to give up and retire to her room when he spoke again, haltingly. "Our parents are dead now, but even when they were alive Gish felt like the only family I had."

Annabel looked over at him. He appeared to be locked in a private struggle, half lost in memories and half lost in the reluctance to release them. "What are your parents like, Annabel?" he asked, his voice soft but vibrating with an intensity that carried it across the room.

She shrugged. "Pretty normal, I guess. I grew up in New Jersey. My father is retired—he used to head an advertising agency. My mother was a housewife who took classes on the side and to everyone's surprise got a graduate degree in business and became a stock analyst. Now they have a passion for golf. They go all over the world looking for the best courses. Ten years ago they couldn't find the time to go to Atlantic City."

"And when you were growing up? What was it like?"

"Oh, you know—dinner at six, pot roast or chicken, a starch and a vegetable, Little League for my brother, piano lessons for me. But when I started making films with my father's home movie camera, they encouraged that. Bought me equipment and books. And when I finished a film we would have a Friday night screening. My mother would make popcorn." She smiled, remembering. "They sat through some pretty awful stuff. You might say that was my first experience with rushes."

"That sounds nice."

"I suppose it was. It still is." She turned to him. "What were your parents like?"

"My parents met on the back lot at MGM. It was love at first sight, they said. They married three weeks later, and they never stopped being crazy about each other."

"That sounds nice, too. Romantic."

"I suppose it does. But do you know what it was like to live with that kind of romance when you're a kid? You're always in the way. It was clear to us early on that both Gish and I were unplanned. My parents were children themselves, really, and they were totally wrapped up in each other and themselves. They barely had time for us. When they'd concentrate their attention on us, it would be like a day at the fair. Their charm,'' Gable said with a tight smile, ''was considerable. But it didn't last. Their attention was like a spotlight, always sweeping on to something else. What was more important to them were their fights, their elaborate ways of making up, their second, third and fourth honeymoons, their blaming each other for the failure of their careers. Even amid all the bitterness, they couldn't stop loving. Even as they tore each other apart in front of their children, never noticing the children were there to watch, to hear—things they never should have heard or seen, things they couldn't possibly understand.''

Annabel stood paralyzed at the window, wanting to go to him but afraid he would draw away. ''Gable, I'm sorry,'' she whispered.

He shrugged. ''It wasn't all bad. Gish and I had each other. We used to go to the movies a lot. We used to cut school. It's a wonder we ever made anything of ourselves. Gish pulled herself out first, then grabbed me by the collar and dragged me along, kicking and screaming all the way. I was turning into a hellion, and she was determined I would make something of myself. She told me to grow up, that acting like a hoodlum wouldn't make my parents pay attention to me. She was right, of course.''

He walked across the room to her. ''You can see,'' he said lightly, ''why my sister and I have avoided marriage. We both know how disastrously engulfing love can be. It seems a terribly selfish emotion. I've seen it destroy lives.''

"That's why you wanted to write *A Family of Two*," Annabel said slowly. "That's why you see Josiah and Melinda the way you do."

"That's why I understand them so well," Gable amended.

"Did your parents die recently?" she asked hesitantly.

"No."

"How—"

Gable interrupted her by taking her glass from her hands and putting it down. He seized her hands in his. His eyes were intense, his voice strained. "I don't want to talk about the past anymore, Annabel. I'm free of it. It took me years, but I am. I want to be here, right now, with you. Tonight—tonight it seems to me that we're the only people in the world. You're the only woman in the world, the only woman I want, the woman I desire more than I'd ever dreamed it was possible to desire someone. And the miracle is," he said, his words liquid and hypnotic, "that you're here beside me." His hands slid up her bare arms and rested on her shoulders.

At that simple touch, she felt a wave of inevitability rise up and crash down on her, sweeping her into a warm, sweet sea of surrender. Here was the man she wanted. His quicksilver eyes were glittering with the hard edges of his desire, and his face looked taut with his need. With all its sharp lines, its irregularities, it was immeasurably, impossibly beautiful to her.

For, Annabel realized, her hands trembling as she placed them on his cheeks, it was the face of the man she loved.

Chapter Seven

It was a quiet revelation; Annabel felt no need to sing or shout her sudden knowledge. She didn't feel faint or dizzy. She felt, she realized, bringing Gable's face closer to hers, incredibly strong.

The force of her desire fired his need, and they exploded into a kiss that brought them to shuddering, exultant life. He took her in his arms against the sparkling backdrop of the night, and the intensity of the embrace brought the stars and the dark sky down around them like an enveloping velvet cloak. It cosseted them, they were part of it, and they ceased to belong to the world outside its borders. They were a world unto themselves.

With every caress, Annabel knew that she was being led further and further from her control, and she didn't care. Now that she knew that she loved, some straining dam had finally burst, and she let the sweet, swift liberating force race through.

She was changing tonight, already *had* changed; she had become that most fierce and irrational of creatures, a woman in love. Every inch of Gable was dear to her now, and she cherished each tiny line radiating from the corners of his eyes; she traced all the ridges of muscle and bone in his strong back. She held nothing back, and her ardor fueled his. He loosened her hair so that it spilled onto her shoulders, and he buried his face in it, cradling her against him.

When he realized her legs were trembling, he swept her up into his arms. He looked down at her, with the silver sea and cobalt sky behind him and the moon illuminating his glittering gaze. The meaning of his wild look needed no words; no question needed to pass his hard mouth.

Annabel's arms were around his neck, and she tightened them, bringing his mouth down to hers again. She let the kiss build and grow into as complete an expression of her love as she was able to convey. It was tender, passionate, lush with promise, and when Gable pulled away to look into her eyes again, he found the answer to his unasked question there. She knew her need was naked and blatant, that he did not have to wonder if it matched his own. *This is no surrender,* her eyes told him. *We will each conquer each other.*

Gable's mouth tightened, and he turned to stride across the living room with her in his arms. A small lamp was swept off a table and crashed as it hit the floor, but he kept on going. He kicked open the door to his bedroom, and then they were inside, on the bed, rolling over with the impetus of that fevered walk and their explosive feelings.

It was urgent lovemaking, ravenous, ferocious. They grasped and clutched each other's arms and shoulders, they held each other fiercely, using mouth and hands and knees and thighs to express something that was completely inexpressible. To speak would be to break the spell, and their lovemaking was silent except for the inarticulate sounds of their need. Soon their bodies were slick with perspiration; their hands slid down warm, damp skin, and they licked away the salty moisture.

When Gable moved over her, possessing her utterly, she felt as though she were at the pinnacle of her life, her being, to be so wholly part of this man. There was no turning back, nor did she wish for it. She wrapped her legs around him, hugging him to her, wanting to entrap him forever in her softness and her warmth. They moved together with a feverish intensity that left them gasping.

Afterward, they lay silent, still entwined. Gable smoothed away the damp curls on her forehead. He kissed the glistening tears on her flushed cheeks and moved on to her mouth with salt on his lips. Their kiss was silken and deep, quieter, but infused with the still insistent, voluptuous throb running through their bodies. It was slow and easy, and this time it spoke of the tenderness underlying their passion.

Then Gable drew down the spread and laid her against the cool white sheets. He got up to retrieve their brandies from the living room. They drank them slowly and silently, watching each other, and then wordlessly, carefully, their eyes open this time, they began all over again.

Annabel woke to find herself nestled into Gable's body. He was cradling her, one hand resting on her breast. His breath stirred a curl, tickling her ear. She snuggled closer, enjoying each unfamiliar sensation.

Outside, gulls were crying the beginning of the day. Pale gray light was spilling through the blinds. Raising her head slightly, she smelled the tang of the sea.

Eager to see the dawn, she eased out from Gable's arms, drew the pale peach summer blanket from the foot of the bed around her shoulders, carefully opened the French doors and slipped out onto the bedroom deck.

The horizon was a molten mercury line, the sky there a luminous pearly gray that gradually shaded into dark moleskin. Annabel hugged the blanket around her, feeling completely at peace. It felt good to be here watching the sun rise on a day full of promise, while Gable lay still asleep, warm in the bed they had rumpled last night and into the early hours of the morning.

So this was what it was like, she marveled, to *make love*. Never had the term held so much meaning for her. To create love out of a fusion of bodies, out of intimate touches and words. To worship with your body another person, to hold them so heartbreakingly dear, to feel an emotion so pure that it felt too big for her body to hold. She was surprised she could remain standing here so prosaically when she felt so transcendent.

She leaned her elbows on the wooden railing and watched the colors and the growing rosy light, totally entranced with the spectacle. It seemed a glorious continuation of the new world she had discovered last night.

She heard Gable stir in the bedroom. The bed creaked as he sat up; then she heard him leave it and the sound of his footsteps approaching. He came up behind her and helped her hold the blanket around her body. He kissed her neck softly.

"Good morning," he said, his voice rumbling lower than usual. "You look very beautiful out here."

She turned in his arms. "Thank you. You look beautiful, too." He grimaced, and she laughed. "I like you all tousled. Are you always so cranky when you wake up?"

"I am insufferably cheerful when I wake up. And today, I'm absolutely ecstatic. Do you want some breakfast?"

"How can you think of food at a time like this?"

"Because I'm hungry. And because," he said, rubbing his mouth against her cheek, "if I'm going to attack you again, I have to refuel."

"How about a rare sirloin, then?"

"Very amusing." He kissed her, cupping her face. "I'd better go before I lose my initiative and crawl back into bed with you." He drew out a deck chair with a flourish. "Have a seat and enjoy the morning. I'll throw something together."

"Let me help."

"No way. Sit. You don't often get to watch the morning begin on the beach. I'll only be a minute or two."

It was more like twenty, but Annabel was content to wait. After a bit she wandered back into the house, passing by the kitchen and hearing a mysterious rattling of pans, and went to her room to pull on a cotton robe, brush the tangles out of her hair and wash her face. When she emerged, Gable was looking for her, wearing a pair of white pants, no shirt and a pleased expression.

"Breakfast is waiting," he announced, "on the deck off the living room."

"I keep meaning to ask you," she said, walking with him across the sunny, wide room, "why you are living in this house and driving that Ferrari if you're so broke."

"Broke in Hollywood is a relative term. I certainly will be broke if the film flops—not that I want to put any pressure on you or anything. Anyway, they're leased."

"You don't own this house?"

"The only house I own is in Vermont. None of this stuff is mine, including the lamp we broke last night, which, incidentally, I won't make you pay for."

"I appreciate it."

"The place isn't bad, though, is it?"

"It's very nice," Annabel said weakly. And here she'd been peeking at books and scrutinizing furniture, trying to get a sense of him. Luckily, she hadn't been able to form any conclusions from the elegant but unremarkable furnishings in the house. "And are you going to tell me that it's necessary to present the image of a successful man, so it was imperative that you hire a Ferrari?"

"No. I just like fast cars."

Her laugh ended abruptly when she arrived on the deck. The table was laid out with dish after dish of aromatic foods and luscious fruits, champagne was icing in a cooler next to a frosty pitcher of orange juice, and silverware and crystal were sparkling in the pale morning sunshine. A vase of yellow tulips waved in the slight breeze.

"Is this what you call throwing things together?" Annabel said, circling the table. "Tell me what all this is. What's under the covered dishes?"

"Herbed cheese omelets and Canadian bacon. And here we have roasted potatoes with dill and sour cream on the side. Cantaloupe and raspberries. And mimosas to drink, of course."

"Of course," Annabel said, dazed. She sat down and watched as Gable removed the cover for her dish, shook out her napkin and handed her the fork. She took a bite of the omelet and found it light and fluffy and perfectly seasoned. "You really did learn to cook in Vermont," she said, chewing appreciatively.

He handed her a tall tulip-shaped glass filled with orange juice and champagne. He was beaming at her, the sun picking up the highlights in his hair and making the patch of gray shine against the dark chestnut. He looked as carefree as she had ever seen him look, and she felt an unexpected lump in her throat. Here was how he should look, sunny and happy, instead of drawn and intense, carrying around a knot of pride and anxiety and something else, something hidden, something too painful to touch, that Annabel still couldn't figure out.

But now it was a joy to see him laughing, helping her to sample the succulent cantaloupe. They had the kind of breakfast all lovers should have, Annabel decided, leaning back and luxuriating in the warmth of the sun and the fresh ocean breeze and the sensual beauty of the meal.

Eventually, they demolished the food and then cleared the table, stacking the dishes in the kitchen for the maid. Gable poured them a second cup of coffee, and they returned to their chairs to lean back and idly watch the waves on the beach.

Annabel tilted her face to the sun, which flitted behind a cloud temperamentally and then reappeared to warm her again. She hated to spoil the mood, but she couldn't stop herself from asking what she wanted to know. "Gable," she said softly, "what about Delia?"

He scowled. "What about her?"

"I'd like to know how things stand between you."

Gable took a sip of coffee and looked out at the ocean. "We were close to getting involved once. I was attracted to the image I read about, and I discovered fairly quickly that the woman behind it was nothing like it. So things became strictly business. That seemed to be fine for Delia. She certainly hasn't lacked for male company."

"What about the Delia in the screenplay? Is she the woman you thought Delia was?"

"You might say that. I had to create a compelling character to spin out the fiction. Delia is a rather rapacious character, really, not the heroine type. I assume you've picked that up."

"Why is she so possessive of you, then? Is she in love with you?" Dread settled in Annabel's stomach, but she had to ask the question.

"Certainly not. I don't know why she seems to appear whenever we're alone. I can't figure it out myself. It could be just coincidence." He turned to her. "But surely you know that I would never have allowed this to happen if I had any kind of ties to her."

"I know that."

"You're very important to me. What happens to us is very important."

"Well, that brings up the next question. What *is* going to happen?"

"We finish our coffee leisurely. Maybe take a shower or a swim, if the weather holds up. And then I propose we go back to bed, spend the rest of the day in it and catch the very last available flight to Mendocino."

"And then?" Annabel asked quietly.

There was a short pause. "That's not for only me to decide. What do you want, Annabel?"

"I want everything to be easy," she said, keeping her head tilted toward the hazy sun and her eyes closed.

"Does that mean you won't make love to me anymore?" he teased.

She opened her eyes and turned to him. "I don't think I could stand not being able to make love to you," she said seriously.

"Good." He reached across the table, and she grasped his hand. It was brown and strong, warm and comforting. "Because I wouldn't let you say no."

She smiled. "Good. But," she said more soberly, "I think we should be careful. I don't think it's a good idea to let it get around."

"Ah, a clandestine relationship. But only until the shooting stops, right?"

"Absolutely."

"Then I can take you out to the most chic restaurant in L.A. and lavish kisses upon your person?"

"Well, we needn't throw caution to the winds."

"Annabel," he said, leaning over and brushing his mouth across her palm, "I should tell you that I am incapable of caution at this point." He looked up, his eyes calm and steel-gray but lit with a glittering warmth. His voice was husky, full of emotion. "You intoxicate me beyond all reason."

"I know," she whispered, feeling his words burn into her like a brand, making her want him again. Her voice was slightly hoarse in a dry throat. She swallowed. "What do you say," she suggested, "we forgo the swim?"

"My thoughts exactly," Gable said. He rose and reached out his hand. Behind him, she noticed that dark clouds had begun to gather, obscuring the bright sun. A few raindrops pattered on the deck as they ran inside, hand in hand.

She must be living a charmed existence, Annabel decided. How else could she explain it? She was doing the best work of her career, and she knew it. Ben and Sasha were hopelessly in love, and their fire was contagious. Fanned by Annabel's enthusiasm and the producer's unaccountable good mood, the entire cast and crew caught the fever and worked the extra long hours cheerfully to make up for time they'd lost during the rain. The weather cooperated by turning sunny and dry, with only an occasional misty day.

It was exciting and exhilarating, and as Annabel felt the great lumbering weight of the film lift and fly, she felt as though she were soaring along with it.

Something strange was happening. There was an unfamiliar feeling in her chest, as light as the summer air, as shimmering as the emerald ocean. A word such as *happiness* or *contentment* didn't contain it; she'd felt those emotions before. It wasn't even the feeling she'd associated with *being in love.* It was as different in quality as a magazine cover was from a Vermeer—or a Josiah Crane. It was, she realized, hugging the knowledge to herself, the real thing.

She felt giddy and gleeful and full of life, and a bubble of laughter seemed to reside permanently in her throat, threatening to break loose at any moment. *Exultant* was the word she was looking for; she was exulting in her joy. And it seemed to fuel everything. She'd never worked better or with such concentration, knowing that Gable was watching, knowing that it was a project he loved as well as she, knowing that later they would be all alone, all night, until the early light prompted Gable to return reluctantly to his room.

It seemed the fates had conspired to smooth their path in every way. Even Delia did not intrude. She had called to say that she was staying at the Beverly Hills Hotel until further notice. She might come back to the set, she might not. Nobody noticed. Even Giselle seemed more carefree when Delia was gone.

Annabel was especially pleased that her differences with Gable about the tone of the film had seemed to dissipate and float away. There was a harder edge to the difficult scenes between Josiah and Melinda, fueled by the white-hot relationship of Ben and Sasha, that seemed to satisfy Gable. He read the diary or the poetry at night with a thoughtful frown that Annabel found endearing. He didn't comment, but his easygoing presence on the set and his wide grins told Annabel that he approved wholeheartedly of what she was doing.

At first he had maintained his habitual stern, forbidding manner on the set after their weekend in L.A., but when Annabel had teased him about it at night, saying that he didn't have to act like Louis B. Mayer to produce an effective smoke screen, he began, slowly, to relax around her during the day. After telling her that it was too obvious to share all their meals together, she'd find him waiting for her with a plate of food in his hands in order to make sure she ate. When she'd pointed out that they were, in fact, now eating all their meals together, he'd claimed neutrally that he just didn't want all the expensive food to go to waste. But later, when they were alone, Gable was not neutral at all.

The only disquieting element about the whole thing was that Annabel found herself, at odd times, thinking about the fact that they were both so careful never to use the loaded word *love*. For her there was no question, but she felt uneasy being the one to introduce the word and all it connoted. She wouldn't say it until he did. She had retained her initial impression of Gable, she knew instinctively that he was a man who did not love easily, so she bided her time. He was everything to her—lover, friend, confidant and colleague; how could she complain about the lack of one little word?

Chapter Eight

Annabel was curled up in the rocking chair in her room, ostensibly studying the schedule for the next day but actually wondering where Gable could be—he had been strangely elusive that day—when there came a knock at her door.

She bounded out of the chair, relieved, but drew back in disappointment when she saw it was Giselle. Luckily, Giselle was so flustered that she didn't notice.

"Oh, Annabel," she said, "I know I'm being an awful busybody, but I thought I should let you know what everyone else knows."

"About what?"

"About what's going on. I'm afraid there's a bit of a crisis brewing."

"What is it, Giselle?"

"Ben and Sasha. They've had a terrible argument. Ben left for town, and Sasha refuses to come out of her room.

She told me privately through her door that she doesn't think she can do the love scene tomorrow with Ben—she doesn't ever want to *look* at him again—and I just don't know what to do.''

"Oh, dear." Annabel sighed. Tomorrow they were shooting a climactic love scene between Josiah and Melinda, where they make love out of desperate emotion. Melinda has discovered that her husband will never grant her a divorce and that her church and her family have disowned her, and she gives herself to Josiah out of guilt and rage and pain, knowing that he will be her only world from now on. It was a turning point in the relationship and a crucial scene in the script.

"I'll see if I can talk to her," Annabel said. She quickly left her room and went upstairs. She knocked softly on Sasha's door. There was no answer.

"Sasha, it's Annabel. Please let me in."

The door slowly opened, and Sasha peeked out. Her eyes were swollen and her face puffy from her tears. She sighed and opened the door wider for Annabel to enter.

"The only reason I'm letting you in," she said, walking back toward a box of tissues on the floor, "is because you also know what a bastard Ben Hall is." She sank down on the floor next to the tissue box, took a handful out and blew her nose vigorously.

Annabel crossed the room to sit beside her. "What happened?"

"Oh, not much. I just made the colossal mistake of assuming I had a future with him. Can you imagine my unmitigated gall to suggest we would be continuing this relationship after we finish filming?''

"What exactly did Ben say?"

"It wasn't what he said, exactly, Annabel, it was the look on his face. You might know it. That hunted-animal look as he tries to squirm out of the trap. I'm surprised he didn't start gnawing on his leg." Sasha burst into tears. Annabel handed her another bunch of tissues, and she buried her face in it and rocked back and forth. "I hate him," she managed to gasp. She wiped her eyes fiercely and then continued. "I had made some innocent remark about the future, about what we'd do after the film was over, and he started to stammer about his commitments to other projects and a new film. Then he practically ran out of here with a terrified look on his face. I threw my shoes after him. And a huge glass ashtray." Sasha giggled. "Unfortunately, I missed." Her expression sobered, and she looked at Annabel bleakly. "You have to know what I'm talking about. After all, you were involved with him once."

"Not really," Annabel said softly. "He was never in love with me, Sasha. Maybe he's afraid that this is the real thing."

"Oh, come on, Annabel," Sasha said scornfully. "You're talking about the biggest skirt chaser in Hollywood. I just didn't play by the rules, that's all. I should have known better. God, how I hate him." She started to cry again. "It's just that I love him so much. He's been so good for me. He's taught me about having fun—he acts as if the world is here for his pleasure, he *enjoys* things so. And he knows me so well." She blew her nose. "And I know him so well. I don't know why I keep thinking he'll change and settle down with one woman."

Annabel sighed and took Sasha by the shoulders. "Sasha, all is not lost. Ben is acting like a child, but we all have a tendency to do that when we're in love. And he's in love with you." Sasha looked at her gloomily. "He *is*. We're going to find him, bring him back, and you two are going to talk this out. Then if he still acts like a jerk, I'll help you throw things at him. Okay?''

"I don't know," Sasha said. "I never should have gotten involved with an actor. Not to mention a sex symbol. I must be crazy."

"Maybe if I talked to him . . ."

"I don't think that would work. Sometime when I was screaming at him he yelled back that no woman could possibly understand him. Cripes, he's an idiot."

Annabel got up and started for the door. "Think of it as temporary insanity. Everything can still work out."

"No, it can't," Sasha sniffed. "Actors never work things out. They just go on to the next person. Annabel, I don't want to be difficult, but you're going to have to tie me up to get me to crawl into bed with that rat tomorrow."

"I'll do whatever I have to," Annabel responded grimly, and she headed out the door.

She closed it after her and paused a moment, thinking. If Ben was in town, he was probably sitting in a bar, like any self-respecting lover after a quarrel. Sasha was probably right; he'd never listen to Annabel, and it seemed rather inappropriate for her to go after him. She knew who the best candidate would be.

Gable's room was only a few steps away. She went back down the stairs swiftly and knocked on his door.

He opened it. His face looked strained and tired. He looked like the old Gable, she thought suddenly. His face didn't light up with a grin at the sight of her, and she realized how much she'd come to depend on that.

"Annabel." He passed a hand through his hair wearily. "I'm sorry I haven't come by yet. I'm rather tired tonight—"

"That's not why I came," Annabel said, looking at the lines of fatigue in his face. "Are you all right?"

"I'm fine."

"Is there something bothering you? I'd be happy to—"

"I'm fine," he repeated tersely. He stood holding the door, waiting.

"Well," Annabel said nervously, confused by his abrupt manner, "I came because we seem to have a problem. Sasha and Ben have had a major battle, and things won't go too well tomorrow if we don't somehow persuade Ben to come back and talk to her. He's in town—at a bar, I imagine."

"What would you like me to do?" Gable asked patiently.

"I thought maybe you could drive into town and talk to Ben a bit. You know, man to man, and all that."

"Annabel, I don't think I'm the best person—"

"Why not?" Her question seemed to muddle him for a moment. "He needs to talk to another man, Gable," she went on.

There was a slight struggle visible in his features; then he sighed. "All right. I'll go. Just give me a minute."

"Whenever. Gable?" Annabel said as he began to close the door. He looked at her, waiting. "Are you sure you're okay?"

He looked impatient, then controlled himself, and his expression softened. "Stop worrying. I promise I'm fine. Now I'd better get going if any of us is going to get any sleep."

"All right. Thank you, Gable," she said again. "I know you're not in the mood for this."

He smiled again and closed the door.

Annabel started down the hall back toward Sasha and heard someone calling her name. It was the script girl, yelling from the bottom of the stairs. Annabel leaned over the railing.

"What is it, Sandy?"

"Telephone call for you."

"Thanks." She reversed direction and headed back to her room. She picked up the phone and heard the hum of long distance.

"Hello?"

"Annabel? Hi, it's Gish McCrea." The voice sounded high and nervous.

"Gish, hello. How are you?"

"I'm fine. Listen, I've been trying to get hold of Gable. He's left a message that he's not to be disturbed. Is he, uh, all right?"

"He seems fine," Annabel said. "I just spoke to him. A little subdued, maybe. Is everything all right?"

"Oh, yes, I'm sure. I probably shouldn't have called and bothered you. I'm sorry. I know you probably have a terribly early call."

"That's all right. I don't think I'll be getting to sleep for a couple of hours. Gish, is something wrong? Please don't say 'nothing,' like Gable. I don't like to pry, but he doesn't look well. Is he okay? Is he sick?" Annabel's voice rose as she began to get anxious.

"He's fine—don't worry." There was a sigh, and then a long pause. Annabel clutched the receiver, waiting. When Gish spoke again, she had to strain to catch her words. "Today is the anniversary of our parents' death. For various reasons, it's always a difficult day for Gable and me, and usually we make an effort to be together. That's why I've been calling him and why I was worried when I couldn't get through. So you see, it really is nothing, in a way, but—"

"I understand," Annabel said quickly. "Why don't I go and tell Gable that you've called, and that if he wants to reach you he can call you back?"

"Please don't mention that I told you—"

"I won't. Don't worry. He seemed fine, just a bit down."

"Okay. I'm sorry to bother you. And Annabel?"

"Yes?"

"I'm glad you're up there."

"Thank you," Annabel said quietly. They said good-bye and hung up.

Annabel hurried out the door and raced down the hallway to Gable's room. She wanted to catch him to give him Gish's message, and she also had to find a tactful way of excusing him from the trip to town. She was sure it was the last thing in the world he wanted to do tonight. She would just have to go herself. She knocked on the door and, relieved, heard him tell her to come in.

Gable was leaning down to lace up his walking shoes. "I'm gone," he said, standing up. "Cavalry to the rescue."

"Listen, Gable, I thought about it, and I think you're right. You don't know Ben that well. I'll go. Maybe he'll want to talk to a woman after all."

"Annabel, I don't want you to go out this late. You need your rest more than I do. Go to bed. I'll take care of it."

"No, really, I insist."

"I'm all ready to go. No problem." He started out of the room.

Annabel sighed and surrendered. "All right, then. Oh, Gable, Gish has been trying to reach you, so she gave me a call. If you want to call her, she'll be up late."

"Okay."

"You could call her now, and I could go to town," Annabel suggested.

"I'm already out the door, Annabel. Why are you—"

He stopped, and Annabel backed up a step as realization dawned in his eyes. "And did she tell you," he said tightly, "why she wanted to talk to me?"

"Gable, I understand. Naturally you feel depressed. I—"

"Don't." His voice was curt. "You couldn't possibly understand."

Hot anger flowed through her, feeling righteous and strong. "Maybe I could if you'd open your mouth and confide in me, talk with me, instead of treating me like a stranger. Gable, I—" Annabel closed her eyes and struggled to retract what she was about to say. The forbidden words, the words she would never say until she heard them from him. *I love you.*

"We're lovers," she continued in a calmer tone. "Why can't you trust me? It's a difficult day for you to get through—I understand that—but if you'd only talk—"

"You don't know what you're talking about." His words lashed across the room at her.

"Then tell me!" She was practically shouting. "Tell me what's torturing you! Why can't you tell me?"

He stood in the doorway, not moving, his eyes as gray and bleak as a frozen pond. "Fine," he said. "What would you like to know?"

"How did your parents die?" she asked huskily. "They died on the same day. How did it happen?"

"They died on the same day three years apart," he said. "My mother died six years ago. She was on a vacation with my father in Mexico, a trip I had given them for a wedding anniversary. They had their usual screaming match in the bar. My father went back to the room. My mother went for a swim. She disappeared. My father hoped she had done it deliberately, that she would be gone for a few hours to cool off and then turn up, but she didn't. Her body washed up two days later. She'd drowned."

"Oh, Gable. That must have been awful for you and Gish. Two days of waiting..."

"We didn't know," he said flatly. "My father didn't see fit to inform us. He buried her there in Mexico, at sea. Then he came home and told us she had died."

Annabel's blood ran cold. "But why? Why didn't he want you at the funeral?"

"Because for my father, her death was tragic for *him*, was the most traumatic thing in *his* life, because he was so destroyed he had to do it *his* way. It never occurred to him until later that Gish and I might have wanted to be there."

"That's incredible."

Gable laughed hollowly. "Incredible." He stopped, looking at the floor.

"What happened then?" Annabel prodded.

"Gish and I—it's so hard to describe how we felt. Amid all the grief, there was so much anger. We were furious at him. We weren't even allowed to share her death with him—he had to monopolize even that. But how can you be angry at a completely broken man?" He sighed. "We got through it somehow. We had a memorial service for her in L.A. My father went off the deep end for a while. We visited him often, we moved him to a new apartment on the beach, but he was never the same. He was just ... lost. Three years went by. And then—''

"Yes?"

"Gish got sick. She has diabetes, and she was going through a difficult period with her work—some big agency was making a pitch for her clients, and she was fighting like hell to stay afloat. She got more and more run down, and one day she collapsed. I was so afraid—'' He stopped again and shook his head. "I was at the hospital day and night. Then she turned the corner. She began to get better, slowly. Her spirits were still very low, though. One day my father came to see me at the hospital. He told me he wanted to go down to Mexico on the anniversary of my mother's death and float a wreath on the water. And he wanted me to come with him. I said no.''

Gable looked up at her. His eyes were full of a sadness she couldn't begin to understand. "I said no," he said painfully, "even though it was probably the only thing he'd ever asked me to do with him. And I was furious. Suddenly all the anger I'd suppressed when she'd died came out. I asked him how he could consider the trip when his daughter was so sick, when she needed him. I accused him of still putting his wife before everything, even when she was dead. He just said he had to go. He said goodbye to Gish, and he went. I wouldn't say goodbye to him.''

Annabel didn't prod this time; there was no stopping Gable now. She knew the ending of the story without his telling her, and she wished with all her heart it wouldn't be the ending she imagined. But it was.

"My mother died in the waters of a beautiful beach in Mexico," Gable said tonelessly. "The road that winds down to it is very high; it twists and turns along the cliffs.

Someone was on the beach the day my father drove down that road. They saw the car stop at a place overlooking the water. The sun was very bright that day, and it was glinting off the windshield. The car stayed there for many minutes. Then it backed up along the road. Then it accelerated forward, faster and faster. It didn't turn. It drove straight off the cliff, heading into the sun, and crashed into the water below.''

Gable's eyes were suddenly empty; she had never seen them so devoid of emotion.

''Is that what you wanted to know, Annabel?'' he asked her, his voice now full of bitterness, taunting her. ''Is that what you had to pull out of me? Are you satisfied now? Do you feel that you *understand* me now? Are we closer now?''

He looked at her as if he despised her, as though her need to know had forced him to tell her and he had been destroyed in the telling. Annabel felt pain twist through her like a knife. But despite her hurt at his tone, she longed to go to him. She knew his pain was infinitely greater than hers.

She took two steps, no more, with tears in her eyes that no longer sprang from hurt but compassion.

Gable's eyes were like flint. Her compassion seemed to anger him even more. The lines of his face were hard as he looked at her.

A small gasp escaped her at the cruelty in his expression. Then his face seemed to crumple, the anger dissolving, and she saw all the raging pain return.

She started toward him, but before she could move more than a step, he was gone.

Gable drove as fast as he dared down the dark, twisting road. He wished he were on an open straightaway so

that he could press the pedal to the floor and blow all his
churning emotions straight back into the wind. Instead
he had to carefully follow the winding curves so that he
wouldn't end up in the Pacific.

The thought provoked a grim smile. Rather a ghoul-
ish coincidence that would be, to wind it all up the same
way his parents had, after giving such scrupulous care to
living his life completely opposite from theirs.

The lights of Mendocino rose up out of the mist ahead
of him, a miniature New England village tossed onto the
rugged headlands. Gable sped up as he hit a straight
stretch of road. The thought of his own recent behavior
drove him to push himself to the limit.

Annabel was the only one he had ever told about his
parents' death. He'd never even told Adelaide, though
that wasn't so surprising. In three years with Adelaide he
hadn't begun to touch the emotions he'd experienced in
just three minutes with Annabel.

That's what had scared him tonight: the *desire* to tell
Annabel. He had wanted her to know, and he didn't even
know why. It hadn't been easy to get the story out, but he
had wanted to tell it.

And he didn't want to begin to consider the reason he
wanted to in the first place.

That's why he had gotten so angry with her, he supposed. She had looked at him as though a barrier had
broken, as if they were suddenly closer, and he'd known
it was true, and it had terrified him. Compassion and
understanding had made her face so beautiful to him.
And because of that, he had suddenly hated her.

Gable swore as he turned off the main road into town.
He'd thought that the three years he'd spent in Vermont
had taught him something. He'd come to terms with his
father's suicide; he'd learned to forgive himself for not

going on that last trip with him and preventing something that was probably inevitable.

But had he, Gable wondered, spotting Ben's Jeep and pulling in beside it, learned anything at all? He certainly hadn't learned anything about women. Annabel defied any notions he'd held so smugly before. She was infinitely more complex and mysterious than any woman he'd known. He felt a kinship with her, and that irritated him. He didn't want it to be there. But he couldn't walk away.

He'd been with Adelaide Anders for three years. She was beautiful, but that wasn't what had held him. She was kind, she was intelligent, she was an excellent hostess and she had taught him about good food and wine. She was smooth, polished and organized. She had filled his nights with an acceptable level of passion and a satisfactory level of good conversation. He hoped he had done the same for her.

That had been what their relationship was all about: the nights. The social functions, the company at dinner, the quiet evening at home, the basic human need not to spend every night alone. His time with Adelaide was neatly compartmentalized. His life was made up of his nights and his days, which were clearly separate. The day was for work. The night was for a relationship. It was simple and clean, never messy, never complicated.

Perhaps that was why, when she left him for the director on the film they had been working on together, he hadn't been surprised. Perhaps that was why he didn't miss her very much in Vermont. He had walked through the editing studio he had built for her and marveled at the absence of pain.

Gable got out of the car and leaned against it. He looked up through the mist, searching for stars, thinking of Annabel.

Annabel...Annabel wasn't simple. Things with her weren't clear; they were a jumbling, tumbling, scrambling muddle. He never knew what he was doing, and half the time he went around wearing an idiotic grin for no reason at all.

She filled his nights, but she also invaded his days, and he couldn't forgive her for that. She spilled over into them; she tantalized and teased him all during the day by the mere fact of her presence in the world. Just by *being*, she drove him mad.

And the nights... The lower the sun went in the sky, the more lighthearted he became. The end of shooting for the day made him want to celebrate. Each quarter hour brought him closer to having her in his arms.

Gable had never really been one for sex in the morning. He had always preferred darkness—for its mystery and romance, he had told himself. But with Annabel, he wanted to bring their lovemaking into the light. He wanted to make love with the lights on, in the mornings, in the afternoons, in sunrise and sunset, to watch the light illuminate each changing expression on her lovely face.

Gable's fist suddenly snaked out and punched the car roof, almost of its own accord. He cursed.

It had happened, then, the thing he had thought could never happen to him. He was obsessed with a woman. And now he was constantly teetering too close to the edges of his control. Too damn close.

But he wasn't in love. At least, Gable congratulated himself hollowly, he was spared that particular indignity. He wasn't capable of love.

So he was probably the last man who could help Ben Hall right now. Gable sighed and headed toward the entrance to the bar. He felt bruised and battered by the memories he was fighting and by his scene with Annabel, and he was sure that he'd be completely ineffectual with Ben anyway. He was hardly the type to give advice to the lovelorn. But he had to try. He'd promised Annabel.

Annabel sat on the top step of the stairs, too weak to walk up them to see Sasha again. Her heart was pounding from her encounter with Gable. She could only guess at the emotions she'd aroused in him, but she knew he needed time to sort them out on his own. She could give him time, she could give him anything; she hoped that he would come to see that his revelation *had* brought them closer. He had finally given her a glimpse into his past, and that could only bind them more closely. She began to see how he'd come by that proud, solitary nature. She saw now the boy and the man he had been as well as the man he was now. And she loved him even more fiercely because of it.

Finally she sighed and got up. The night was far from over, and she had things to do. She climbed the stairs back to Sasha's room. She listened carefully, but there were no sobs or crashing glassware coming from behind the door, and the light was out. She tiptoed away, hoping that Sasha had been able to sleep.

As she reached the head of the stairs, she heard voices raised in argument. She paused for a moment and then recognized Delia's voice. She must have returned from L.A., then. Annabel hoped it wasn't a bad omen.

"But, Delia," she heard Giselle say, "I'm just doing what you said. You said I looked dowdy and twice my age. You said—"

"Will you stop telling me what I said! I know what I said! I said— What did I say, again?"

"You said I should get some new clothes. You said you'd pay for them. So I did."

"But, Mother, hasn't it ever occurred to you that I didn't realize you'd end up becoming a Delia clone? You're dressing exactly like me. Look at this! And this! And this!"

"Delia, I just folded those—"

"And your hair!" There was a pause, and then Delia's voice suddenly grew calmer, so low that Annabel could barely hear it. "I want you to do whatever you want. Spend whatever you want. God knows, I owe it to you."

"You don't *owe* me anything," Giselle said bitterly.

"But don't you think it looks bad if you start looking twenty years younger?" Delia's voice rose again. "It has to stop! Or else we can't stay together. You should go back to Canada."

"I don't want to go back to Canada. It's too cold."

"Just through the winter," Delia went on irrationally, her voice pitched lower again.

Annabel suddenly realized she was eavesdropping and that was rude, so despite the temptation to stay and make sure that Giselle wasn't upset, she continued down the stairs. It was a family argument, anyway, and not her concern. She was surprised at Delia, though. If Annabel's mother looked as happy and fit as Giselle, she certainly wouldn't complain. Maybe by looking so much like Delia, she made Delia feel old.

Annabel looked at her watch. It was barely ten—not too late to call Gish. She should explain why Gable wasn't calling her back. Gable, of course, might be furious at her for interfering, but she'd already faced his wrath once tonight, and she supposed she could do it again.

"In for a penny, in for a pound," she muttered as she punched out Gish's number. Gish answered on the first ring.

Annabel briefly explained that Gable had left the house but he seemed fine. He was probably out searching for Ben. Then she paused.

"He told me, Gish," she said.

"Told you what?" she asked cautiously.

"Everything—about your mother's drowning and your father's suicide. I'm so sorry."

A sigh floated over the line. "It happened. We'll probably never understand the whole thing really." Gish paused. "It's a good sign that Gable told you. I don't think he's ever told anyone. You must be very important to him, Annabel. But then, I suspected that already."

"I think he needed to tell someone."

"He needed to tell you. Look, Gable has come to terms with all this, as I have. We had to. He felt a terrible burden of guilt for a while, but he knows he isn't responsible for my father's instability. We talked about it endlessly in Vermont. It was like therapy."

"In Vermont?"

"I was one of the reasons we went there. I really broke down after I heard the news about my father. I was recovering from an illness, and it was too much on top of everything. Gable insisted on taking me away from Hollywood, and he was right. It was funny how both our lives fell apart at the same time. Gable was having trouble with his film, and, well, in his personal life."

"I know about Adelaide Anders."

"Oh, dear, who doesn't? She was nice, but God, were they boring together. It was all surface stuff, Annabel. I don't think Gable felt much remorse when it ended. Especially when Adelaide sided with the director and cut the film according to what he wanted. In a way, I was glad it was a bomb. Anyway, Vermont was the best cure in the world for both of us. When I was ready to go back, he decided to stay. He ended up staying for quite a while. He seems much happier now."

"Not tonight."

"He's fine. I don't know why we both feel this compulsion to remember how lousy everything was three years ago. As family rituals go, it's pretty grim." Gish sighed. "You know, I feel kind of torn about you and Gable."

"What do you mean?"

"Well, I like you, Annabel. And of course I love my brother. Strictly from a sisterly standpoint, I'd want to tell you to hang in there because you're the best thing for him. But then..."

"But then, what?"

"Have you ever wondered why two old fogies like Gable and me aren't married? He's forty, and I'm forty-two. I don't know if we're capable of falling in love—I mean *really* falling in love like you're supposed to. Giving up your control. Losing yourself in someone else. Committing to a lifetime. And Gable—he needs distance, even from me. It's part of his nature. Only his work drives him. It sounds awful, I know. It *is* awful, but he likes it that way. So..."

"So?" Annabel asked carefully.

Gish's answer came blunt and strong through the receiver. "So if I were your friend, and not Gable's sister wanting the best for him, I'd tell you that, if you were smart, you'd run like hell the other way."

Chapter Nine

You know me," Ben said to Gable. "Or, rather, maybe you don't, so I'll tell you. I'm the nicest guy in the world. I wouldn't hurt Sasha for anything."

"Then why are you?" Gable leaned back and took a long pull on his beer. They had discussed fly-fishing, Ferraris and Buck Rogers movies, and finally Ben had brought up the subject they'd both been avoiding.

Ben leaned over the pitted Formica table. He waved away Gable's question. "You know what, Gable? I would say that I've fallen in love with every single leading lady I've ever had. And one director."

"Annabel," Gable said easily, smothering an irrational impulse to dump his beer on Ben's head. But Ben didn't know about Annabel and Gable. Nobody did, except for Gish. But he'd never been able to fool Gish.

"Annabel," Ben said, smiling. "I was terrified I'd be bloody awful in that picture, and then she'd look at me with those huge green eyes of hers and I'd do anything for her. Anything. She was so wonderful that I felt it would be the stupidest mistake of my life *not* to fall for her. So I did. Then I blew it. I always blow it. Luckily, there aren't many women around that it *matters* when you blow it, you know?''

Gable nodded. ''Then there comes a time when you find one where it does matter.''

''Aye, there's the rub,'' Ben agreed, taking a sip of beer.

''And Sasha?''

He shrugged. ''What can I say? I fall in love with all my leading ladies. It's an occupational hazard. She's great, but you know how it is. You get off the set and back to the real world, and suddenly it doesn't make sense. You see how she lives, or what she laughs at in the movies, or what books she reads, *if* she reads, and you wonder what the hell you have in common. Then there's another woman around the corner whispering how terrific you are. You know.''

Gable watched him over the rim of his glass. ''You've got to be kidding,'' he said.

''Huh?''

''You can't be that shallow.''

''Shallow?''

''Or dumb.'' Gable put his glass down deliberately and leaned forward. ''And I know you're not dumb. So what's the real problem, Ben? We all know you're crazy about Sasha. And we've all been around the block a few times.''

Ben suddenly slumped down, his head in his hands. ''She's the greatest thing that ever happened to me,'' he said despairingly. ''She's gorgeous. She's the sexiest thing I've ever seen, even at five-thirty in the morning. She's taught me more about acting than I've learned from a dozen directors. She's so smart, but she makes me laugh—"

"So what, man, is the problem?" Gable interrupted.

"I don't know. Yes, I do. I'm a bum." Ben raised his famous eyes at Gable; they looked washed out from weariness. "It doesn't matter how great they are, I just can't seem to stick around. I want it to be different this time—I do. But it's not just up to me. It's Sasha. She's so damn *smart*. She's going to come back to L.A. and look at my books and laugh. She's probably got shelves full of Stanislavsky and Flaubert and Tolstoy, and she's going to laugh at my Raymond Chandlers. She's going to think my taste in furniture is rotten. I don't even have a color scheme."

"I see. And you're going to laugh at something in a movie, and she's going to think you're stupid."

Ben reached out and grasped his arm. "You understand. Thank God."

"So what are you going to do?"

"What do you mean?"

Gable shrugged. "You going to dump her?"

"*Dump her?* How can you say that? What a horrible thing to say. She's not a disposable razor, you know!"

Gable put up his hand to calm Ben down. He wasn't in the mood to take one on the chin for trying to talk some sense into his head. "I'm just following your hypothesis to its logical conclusion."

Ben groaned. "Now you're talking like Sasha."

"Look, you're telling me that eventually it's not going to work out anyway, so why bother? Do I have all this correctly?"

"Well, I know it sounds stupid—"

"It *is* stupid. In fact, it's the stupidest thing I've ever heard in my life. Do you think all this is supposed to be *easy*? You say you love her. She's special in your life. You're the happiest you've ever been. You're going to walk away from that because *you don't have a color scheme*?"

"So what are you saying, exactly?" Ben growled into his beer.

"I'm saying that you're an idiot."

"Just give it to me straight, Gable."

"I'm saying," Gable said menacingly, leaning over the table and fixing his eyes on Ben, "that you're in this up to your neck, buddy, and if you think you can walk away scot-free, you're nuts. And if you think that you're going to feel any better by making Sasha miserable, you're even crazier than I thought. What are you going to do—tell her it's over and then shoot the rest of the film and shake hands at the wrap party? Can you imagine doing that?"

"I've always done it before," Ben pointed out.

"And you're leading a full, happy life, right? Don't drink too much or go out too often? Don't have to pay a whopping psychiatrist bill every month?"

"You sure know how to go for the jugular," Ben said, raising his beer and giving Gable and ironic salute.

He took a sip of beer, keeping his eyes on Ben. "Plus, I happen to know," he said carelessly, "that Sasha is a detective novel fan. She loves Raymond Chandler."

Ben brightened. "Well, that's something. Are you making that up?" he asked suspiciously.

Gable held up his hand. "God's truth. We talked about *The Big Sleep* over lunch one day."

Ben suddenly grinned an earsplitting, utterly charming grin at Gable. "Maybe I could do it. I could really change. God, I feel good. Let's sing."

"What?"

"Men always sing after they have a man-to-man talk. Something robust and stirring."

"I don't sing," Gable spat out. He'd go only so far for Annabel.

"Okay, let's have another beer," Ben suggested cheerfully. "I'll sing."

Annabel was making patterns out of the cracks in her ceiling, which were illuminated by a shaft of moonlight, when she heard two slightly off-key baritones singing what she finally recognized as "A Nightingale Sang in Berkeley Square." She grinned as they swung into the chorus, then shushed each other as they fumbled with the front door.

It sounded as though Ben was in a better mood, at least. She hoped he'd be waking up Sasha tomorrow morning with some kind of an apology.

She heard them padding silently up the stairs. They must be relatively sober if they could negotiate the dark hall without crashing into something. She heard Ben head up the final flight toward his room. Apparently Gable was hesitating.

Annabel stiffened with her longing to have him come to her. She hadn't been able to sleep from the unsettling emotions churning inside her. They didn't need to make love, or even to talk; they just needed to hold each other. Surely he felt that need as acutely as she. Things had ended so awkwardly.

His footsteps came slowly down the hall. She heard them stop outside her door. She wanted to bid him to come in, but some instinct stopped her. Gable needed to come to her this time. He needed to show her that he hadn't regretted the new ground their relationship had gained tonight.

Her hands were clenched into fists, and she was barely breathing. The moments seemed to spin out into an eternity while she waited, lying rigid, straining for the first tiny sound of the knob turning.

Instead, she heard a floorboard creak as he moved away. She heard him retreat down the hall. Her muscles relaxed, and with that relaxation a gush of emotion overwhelmed her. With tears running down her cheeks, she heard his door close.

The sky was an oppressive pewter, and it was cold, the first really cold morning they'd had. Vapor steamed out of the crew's mouths as they gave directions to set up the shot. They looked puffy and unrecognizable in their down jackets.

Annabel sipped her scalding coffee and watched them. Ben and Sasha strolled by, already made up for the first shot. They had obviously straightened out their differences. They were actually laughing, which seemed impossible at this hour of the morning. Apparently Gable had accomplished his mission and come back with a more mature Ben.

But where was Gable? Annabel had been delaying the start of the day, waiting for him to appear. She'd knocked at his door this morning, but there had been no answer.

And then she saw him striding across the wet grass in a leather bomber jacket and jeans. Her heart ached at the sight of him.

"Good morning." His voice was clipped.

"Good morning." Hers was wary. "Where have you been?"

"I've been walking around the grounds. I came to say goodbye. I'm leaving for L.A. this morning."

"Oh? Why?"

"Business."

Annabel stared back at him, refusing to look down, refusing to grant him any leniency. She wanted him to see the hurt in her eyes.

Gable looked away, over the top of her head. "Annabel, I really do have business there. But I also need some time."

"I see."

"Do you? Listen, I don't know when I'll be back. It could be Sunday, it could be later in the week."

"All right. Goodbye, Gable."

"Annabel, don't say goodbye like that. Hell, I wish I could kiss you." The words seemed to have been forced out of him. He looked away.

But he'd said them, and it finally made her smile ruefully. She tugged at the buttons on his jacket. "Button up. It's cold."

"I'll call you."

She nodded. "Are you all ready to go?"

"Just heading for the car. Jocko's going to drive us."

"Us?"

"Giselle's leaving, too. I get the feeling she's avoiding goodbyes. She wants to head for Canada and get back to life in the slow lane, she said."

Annabel frowned. "That sounds strange, Gable. I—"

"Gable!" Jocko, one of the production assistants, bellowed from the driveway. "You're cutting it awfully close."

"Right," he shouted, still holding Annabel's glance. "I have to go," he told her.

"Go." She wanted so much to hold him, to keep him there with her. A strange, unsettling feeling dropped into her chest.

"Goodbye, Annabel."

"Goodbye." It was silly, Annabel thought as she watched him walk across the lawn to the waiting car. Ridiculous. But why did she feel as though she were saying goodbye to him forever?

It was just as silly, Annabel told herself fourteen hours later, to wander around in his room, unable to sleep, wondering why he hadn't called her. She wasn't in high school, for heaven's sake; they weren't going steady. She touched a shirt thrown casually on the back of a chair and smoothed his pillow. The room seemed alive with his simmering, energetic presence.

She sat on the bed disconsolately. Then she reached over idly and picked up the bundle of papers on his nightstand. It was the poetry she had asked him to read, along with Melinda's diary. She knew he'd been reading them faithfully every night.

Annabel scanned through them again and frowned. She held them up to the light and squinted more closely at them. She could see tiny penciled markings opposite one of the poems. It was the one Melinda had titled "The Room and the Sky." In it she had described a "bleached" white room with an overhanging "sallow" sky, and somehow that room was mysteriously part of and led into another room, a room of color she did not describe, color that was agonizing for her eyes to absorb. It was one of Melinda's most confusing poems, and it was dated very close to the day of her suicide. She wondered why Gable had marked it. But at least he was thinking seriously about the poems.

She thumbed through the diary, curious, and found a few more light pencil marks indicating a passage here and there. Most of them had to do with Melinda's descriptions of the nursery that Gable had claimed existed only in her imagination. Was he changing his mind? One sentence was lightly underlined. "How like him to want to embrace the child so close to his heart by having him or her so near...."

Annabel yawned and decided she'd better get some sleep. Tomorrow was Saturday, and there was no shooting scheduled, so she'd be able to sleep in a bit. But she usually woke up at six no matter how tightly she pulled the curtains or how late she'd stayed up the night before. It took an enormous effort of will to force herself back to sleep. Unless Gable happened to be in bed with her, of course. She seemed to sleep so dreamlessly and well in his arms.

But she'd done enough thinking about Gable tonight, Annabel decided. She tucked the poems and diary under her arm and left his room.

She was heading toward her own room when she heard Delia speak to her nervously from the stairs.

"Annabel? Is that you?"

"It's me, Delia. I was just going to my room."

"I thought I heard a noise."

"Delia, there're plenty of people staying here. I don't think you have to worry about prowlers."

"I know I'm silly. But you know everyone disappears on the weekends. And there is a fortune of art in this house."

"We've finished with Josiah's paintings, and they've been sent back to the collector and his gallery in New York."

"Oh. Oh, I wasn't aware of that. Well, I'll sleep easier, then." Delia still lingered at the foot of the stairs.

"I'm sorry I didn't get a chance to see Giselle before she left this morning," Annabel said. "If you speak to her, could you tell her I said goodbye and that I'll miss her?"

"Of course. She'll like that. She was just dying to get back home."

"I see," Annabel said politely. "Well, good night."

"Good night." Delia started up the stairs slowly. She paused on the third step and nodded pleasantly at Annabel as she made her way to her room and went inside.

Annabel got back into bed with a few nagging suspicions that she couldn't pin down but couldn't dismiss. She sleepily reviewed the scene in the hall.

Why had Delia just lied to her about Giselle? Annabel knew that Giselle hadn't wanted to go. Was it merely embarrassment that had made Delia lie?

Sighing, she switched off the light and snuggled deeper under the covers, grateful for the warmth. She found herself drifting off to sleep with questions buzzing in her mind, still unanswered but now hazy and far-off, a puzzle from another time.

A puzzle from another time, she mused drowsily. Like Melinda Silver.

So many puzzles. Why had Giselle left? Why was there so much tension between the two women? Why was Delia always hanging about when Annabel was up late? Every single time Annabel couldn't sleep and wandered downstairs, she'd run into Delia. Let's see, Annabel catalogued sleepily, there was the time she was coming up from the kitchen and met her on the stairs.... No, that had been Giselle. But for a moment in that dim light, she had thought it was Delia.

Annabel's eyes snapped open. Giselle had looked just like Delia that night, and it wasn't the youthful, stylish clothes or the hairstyle. Neither had been visible in that light. It was something about the shape of her face, her body, that had led Annabel to assume that it was Delia, not Giselle, who was standing on the staircase.

Wasn't it strange, Annabel wondered slowly, that Delia looked so much like Giselle if she were her adopted daughter?

And taking that notion one logical step further, why did Delia resent it so much when Giselle dressed like her? Could it be because Delia didn't want anyone to see that resemblance? During the trial the similarity had been hard to see because of Giselle's gray hair and older appearance. But with the wealth came a new style—and a resemblance that hadn't been there before.

Annabel was now wide-awake. She shied away from the implications of her questions, because such a wild fancy would indicate that Delia had been lying, and that was impossible. There had to be another explanation. It was late. She was tired. She was imagining things.

But an insistent voice continued to hammer a question in her brain. Was Delia Worthington-Crane really Josiah Crane's daughter?

She swung her legs out of bed and paced back and forth as she tried to puzzle out what was disturbing her. If Delia was really Giselle's daughter, she had lied from start to finish. And so had Giselle.

Annabel stopped with that realization. She just couldn't imagine Giselle lying. She wasn't the criminal type. But what about that night on the stairs, when Giselle had said, *"At least good can come out of deception."* And what about Delia telling Giselle that she "owed" her? Suddenly every strange twist to their relationship could be seen in a new light.

"Annabel, calm down," she growled. "This is crazy." She suddenly wished that Gable were there to help her untangle all her silly suspicions and set her mind at rest. It was ridiculous to think that the two women—the vain, immature Delia and the friendly, vague Giselle—were pulling off the scam of the century.

Suddenly unable to remain in her room, Annabel slipped into her robe and headed out into the hall. She paused for a moment, listening for Delia, but the house was deathly still. She kept her flashlight turned off, however, and stealthily crept down the stairs.

She decided to sit in Josiah's studio for a while. Perhaps his spirit would help her examine her airy suspicions and dismiss them. She loved sitting in the room at night anyway, with the pale glow of the moon spilling through the skylight....

"The Room and the Sky," she repeated to herself, stopping on the stairs. Of course. Josiah's studio. What an idiot she was. Annabel giggled in relief. At least she'd figured out one mystery tonight. Melinda had been writing about the white studio in that poem. The sky seemed so much a part of the room. Perhaps the dreamlike room of vibrant color that it led to was a metaphor for his paintings, which Melinda had felt more and more alienated from as she sank deeper and deeper into despair. Annabel quickened her pace through the maze of rooms downstairs to the familiar oak door.

She didn't turn on the lights this time. She certainly wasn't in the mood to see Delia tonight, and heaven only knew how long Delia prowled around the mansion when everyone else was asleep. She shivered as she stepped farther into the studio. It was cold and drafty and dark.

The clouds were drifting across the moon, rarely allowing its silvery beams to shine through the skylight for illumination.

Annabel slowly lowered herself onto the red couch. A book of Josiah Crane's art had been left on the table in front of her, and she picked it up and leafed through it with one hand, holding the flashlight with the other. She wanted to push thoughts of Delia and her mother out of her mind and let whatever answers could possibly come to mind arrive naturally without her imagination inventing impossible Machiavellian plots.

But tonight must have been a night for mysteries, for she saw puzzles in the book as well. What secrets were concealed in these bold slashes of line and color? What emotions drove this artist? Why had Josiah stopped painting during Melinda's breakdown and for three years after her suicide? Had he been tortured by guilt as Melinda had?

This time Annabel passed over the color reproductions of Josiah's paintings and peered at his drawings, his pastels and watercolors, his studies for his paintings. Perhaps she would get more clues from the quick sketches, the half-formed ideas. What kind of a man was Josiah Crane? What kind of a man would give away his baby daughter and never, as far as anyone could tell, mention her again?

Annabel turned the pages slowly, absorbed. She examined each little reproduction of pages from his sketchbook and noted the dates. There was one pastel drawing, not dated, of a room whose walls were each painted a different vibrant color. There was a strangely configured turquoise chest in one corner. And there was an object to one side that looked like—Annabel squinted at it—a crib?

She shook her head. Impossible. How many art historians had pored over Josiah Crane's work? How many had scrutinized his paintings during the trial? And his style wasn't strictly representational. The furniture in the corner could be anything. She was letting the lateness of the hour, the silence of the huge mansion and Josiah Crane's own fanciful imagination influence her.

She looked carefully at the drawing again. No, it was just a room, a happy room, a sunny room, but just a room with an odd-looking turquoise chest of drawers. The chest did look familiar, however. As a matter of fact, it looked like the chest of drawers that was built into one wall of the studio. Annabel looked up. No, wrong again. It was similar, though. It was the same chest, only reversed—like a mirror image of the one in the drawing. And this chest of drawers was painted orange.

A mirror image. Annabel slowly walked over to the orange chest and shone the flashlight on it. She tried to remember what she knew about color theory. Weren't turquoise and orange opposite colors? She ran her hand quickly along the top of the dresser and then more carefully, not knowing why. Perhaps crafty Josiah had concealed another hidden drawer holding another enigmatic puzzle. She followed each carving of a leaf along the corners and the legs. She opened each drawer and felt around, and then went back and did it again.

And then she felt it. If she ran her hand along the top of the first drawer, her fingers touched a tiny lever at the very back of it.

Annabel's heart began to race. She pressed the lever carefully and stepped back a bit. Nothing happened. She pulled it. Nothing again. Frustrated, she shrugged and finally gave it a good yank. She drew out fingers covered in rust and sighed in disappointment. Her heartbeat returned to normal. It had turned out to be nothing, after all.

But then she froze as she heard a horrible groaning sound. Annabel stared, wide-eyed, as the built-in chest began to move, to tilt toward her. And the wall moved as well. Only a few inches, but it was moving forward, sliding on a kind of track. It stopped.

Annabel had to remind herself to breathe. She stepped forward cautiously and felt along the edge of the wall. She peered inside the crack. All she could glimpse was a black open space behind it, and she flashed the light inside. It appeared to be a closet of some kind, but she couldn't maneuver the light around enough to tell. The only thing to do was to somehow squeeze her way inside.

For the first time in her life, Annabel was grateful that she was so small. She looked at the opening again, gauging it. She could probably just make it.

She wiped her forehead and found a sheen of perspiration there. Gripping the flashlight tightly and mentally scolding her pounding heart to slow down, she shimmied her way into the crack and pushed. The wall moved slightly, allowing her to ease a bit farther. Then she took a deep breath for courage and squeezed inside the tiny opening to the blackness beyond.

Chapter Ten

Halfway through, she got stuck. Her nose was up against the side of the wall, her breasts flattened against it. If only she were flat chested!

A surge of panic gave her energy and strength, and Annabel pushed against the wall, moving it another fraction. She heaved herself forward with all her might and popped out of the crevice like a cork. She landed on her knees on what felt like a hardwood floor.

She was inside. And she was still gripping the flashlight, thank goodness. Annabel trained the light up, and it hit a wall.

Her heart seemed to stop beating. A pink bear was cavorting with a yellow giraffe, but it was no ordinary bear, no ordinary giraffe. That bold, individual stroke could have been made by only one hand.

She followed the bear and the giraffe with the beam of her flashlight and discovered a wall full of magic. There were birds flying over an emerald forest and friendly otters and sea lions in a blue, blue sea, all painted in the famous Crane palette of cerulean and cobalt, goldenrod and carmine.

She had found the nursery. Annabel sat back on her heels, bumping into a large object that was sticking out into the room. When she shone the light on it, she found the turquoise chest, which was simply the back side of the orange one in the studio.

Annabel felt a lump in her throat as she moved the flashlight slowly over the wall again. A father's love was in this room; Josiah had wanted the child as much as Melinda had. Why else would he have chosen to build the room off his studio, where he would be so constantly and so lovingly interrupted?

Annabel moved forward slowly, still entranced with the distinctive menagerie on the wall. She bumped into a chair, and she sank into it gratefully. It rocked back gently.

Here was where Melinda would have nursed her child. Here was where the child would have grown into a toddler, absorbed in paints and crayons like his or her father. No wonder, Annabel thought sorrowfully, Melinda couldn't face this room. Now she understood the meaning of her poem, "The Room and the Sky."

This was a room that danced and vibrated with color, that was so much a part of the studio behind the wall. It was a reminder of how Josiah had failed her, and of her own guilt at her acquiescence to that betrayal. They had committed a grievous sin: they had given away the child they had loved, all for the sake of their own passion. And the punishment was madness, not marriage—the annulment hadn't been granted, after all. Melinda had sacrificed her God and her family for nothing. She had been driven mad by it.

Annabel felt drained by the tragic memories in the room. She leaned her elbow on the small table beside her. Paper crackled underneath it.

She reached over and picked up the yellowing sheet. Shining her flashlight on the faded ink, she saw that it was an official document. She summoned up her French and translated it slowly. *Nom:* Tamara Silver Crane. *Mère:* Melinda Silver. *Père:* Josiah Crane. It was a birth certificate, then. How sad that they had given their child another name. Perhaps Giselle had named the baby Delia, the name she had already chosen for her baby, the one that had died.

Annabel's eyes slid up to the top of the document. She didn't see the expected word *Naissance*. Instead, the word that bombarded her with its stiff black formality was too easy to translate.

Mort-né. Stillborn.

The baby born to Josiah Crane and Melinda Silver had died. Thirty-five years ago.

A chill so profound it made her gasp ran through her body. She stood up, and the flashlight crashed to the floor. Darkness fell like a slippery satin cloak over her eyes.

Annabel felt an unreasonable panic rise up and clutch her. The darkness seemed to have muffled all sound as well, and she felt as if she were utterly isolated in a secret place she had no right to be in. All she wanted to do now was to get out of this room and run back upstairs to light and warmth and the living. A sob escaped her, and she stumbled back toward where the opening had been.

It wasn't there. In her panic and the sudden blackness, she couldn't find it. Another sob floated out, sounding strange and disembodied in the stillness, and her fingers scrabbled along the wall, searching desperately for the crack. If it had closed again, Annabel realized with sudden horror, she might never be found again. The walls were thick. Would anyone be able to hear her screams?

Calm down, she told herself fiercely, taking deep breaths and still feeling along the wall. It wouldn't do her any good to panic; she'd already lost her bearings. She could be anywhere in the room. She'd find the opening eventually. All she had to do was follow the wall.

Her fingers hit something—not the crack, but some object raised from the smooth texture of the wall. It was rough, bumpy, irregular. It felt like...the surface of a painting.

Then blessed light streamed through the opening, which turned out to be not where she'd thought it would be at all. The moon must have come out from behind a cloud, illuminating the studio. The light was faint, but it enabled her to go back and find the flashlight. She turned it on and pointed it toward the painting she had felt with her fingers.

The light trembled in her fingers so badly she almost dropped it again. "Melinda!" she cried in a whisper.

She didn't think she was capable of being shocked profoundly again this night, but her hands were shaking as she slowly picked out the canvases on the far wall. She was so stunned that she actually felt weak, and she lowered herself to the floor while she drank in the sight of the canvases.

It was a treasure trove of Josiah Cranes. Paintings that hit the eye, that dazzled, that seemed to spring off the walls with the concentrated emotion in them.

They were all of Melinda. But it was a different Melinda, one so far removed from the sunny, sensual portraits hanging in museums that she could have been a different person. This woman's face was marked by tragedy. Deep lines were etched around the eyes and mouth. This Melinda was haunted, strained, grieving. Some were portraits, head on; in others she was the primary figure in landscapes that were almost garish. In the last paintings along the wall, she looked out with eyes that were totally empty.

And in each painting, sometimes so faint or blurred it faded into the background, a small shadow hovered.

And the color! It was discordant, harsh, even while it astonished with its brilliance. It collided with the deep, rich hues on the walls with such clashing ferocity that it was painful to the eyes. Was this the color that had tormented Melinda, made her gasp with pain? Were these the raw colors that had flayed her spirit in those last desperate weeks?

And had Josiah Crane *wanted* her to face them, to face what was happening to her?

Annabel backed away toward the door, unable to take her eyes off the paintings but suddenly wanting to close the door on them. She felt like an intruder in a room full of pain, closed off because its secrets were too wrenching for anyone to face. Here was the record of a man watching his love disintegrate before his eyes. Guilt and rage were present in each stroke of the brush; love and pain radiated out from the surface.

Josiah Crane *had* painted during those three years, extraordinary portraits of a beloved woman who, in the end, could not support all she had to bear. The artist was clearly a part of these paintings; they were intensely, frighteningly personal. In them, Annabel had the sense that Josiah had almost gone mad as well.

His earlier portraits of Melinda were sumptuous celebrations of her beauty, of her luminous skin, her harmony, her wild grace. Here he was not interested in the aesthetic challenge of painting light on translucent skin. His brush strokes were not the generous, sensual ones he'd once lavished on the canvas.

In these paintings, everything was harsh, constricted, brutal with honesty. The movements of the brush were more slashes than strokes. Somehow he was trying to arrest Melinda's disintegration by capturing it. Through his talent and his energy, he would bring her back before she hurled herself off the cliff.

But Josiah Crane, that powerful, masculine, exuberant man, had been impotent, helpless. He had tried to save her the only way he knew how. But he had failed.

Annabel's cheeks were wet with tears. She turned away from the paintings. She couldn't begin to digest all she had learned; she could only grieve for these two tragic people.

This time, she slipped through the opening with ease. Using all her strength, she managed to push the chest back, and the wall slid across. She felt as though she was sealing up a tomb.

She wiped the tears from her cheeks with hands that still trembled and headed upstairs to her room, feeling numb. There was no more she could do tonight. It had all been too much, and tomorrow would be soon enough to face the implications of her discoveries.

Annabel woke up with a start. For a moment she couldn't remember what was so urgent. Was she shooting today? Then awareness roared through her brain, and she whipped the covers aside and sprang out of bed. How could she have slept until eight o'clock? She'd been positive she wouldn't be able to sleep a wink, so she hadn't set her alarm.

She splashed cold water on her face while she considered what to do. The first thing, of course, was to call Gable. No, the first thing had to be a cup of very strong coffee. Then she would call Gable.

She dressed quickly in jeans and a sweater while she went over the implications of what she'd found last night. All of them were disagreeable.

Of course, she'd have to confront Delia, a prospect she certainly didn't relish. Or perhaps she should contact the police. Actually, the best thing to do would be to talk it all over with Gable.

She could only guess at the shock and upheaval this would cause in the media and with the Crane estate. And, most immediately, of course, the film would have to be shut down. Today.

The story they were telling no longer applied. The focus of the film was the daughter of the famous liaison; the film began and ended with the grown-up Delia tracing her past. The tone of the film was infused with the obsession of two people and how it had marked the life of the daughter they had given up. At least they had filmed the flashbacks first; they had yet to film any scenes with the actress playing Delia. She would be arriving next week, as a matter of fact, and then the rest of her scenes were supposed to be shot in a Hollywood studio.

But the fortunate way the production schedule worked out was only a small blessing in the nightmare of shutting down the production. Cast and crew would have to be paid in full. No matter what, Gable would be ruined.

He would lose everything. How would she be able to break the news to him?

Obviously, she would have to find a way. Annabel sighed and picked up the phone. Gable should know as soon as possible. She listened, dismayed, as the phone rang and rang. Finally, his service picked up and she left a message, telling them it was urgent.

She started down the grand oak staircase, frowning worriedly. She would feel uneasy until she had talked to Gable, she knew. She longed for him now, for the reassuring sharpness of his mind, for the way, whenever she felt like disaster was around the corner, he would flash her a what-the-hell grin and her muscles would suddenly relax. They were partners, and they should work this mess out together.

She paused at the bottom of the staircase. Coffee could wait. She was longing to see the nursery—and the paintings—in daylight. Quickly she headed for the studio.

The room looked so innocuous this morning, with none of the moonlit mystery of the night before. She crossed to the orange chest and pressed the lever again. The wall opened more easily than it had last night. Annabel slipped inside and drew it almost closed behind her, careful to leave it open a crack. She certainly didn't want last night's fears about being locked inside to come true.

Aside from the shock and upset her discoveries would cause, Annabel had been guiltily hugging a thrilling secret to herself this morning—the canvases. They were the one redeeming factor in all the bleak consequences of finding the nursery. The images had swum continually before her eyes as she'd tried to fall asleep last night, and she was anxious to see them. She was no expert, but she imagined that the dazzling hoard would set the art world on its ear.

She was spellbound as she stood, once again drinking in the sight of them. The light allowed her to examine the surfaces of the paintings and see the colors more truly. They were even more extraordinary than she'd imagined. They froze the heart.

Annabel sank into the chair and rocked. Melinda stared back at her with her haunting eyes. *The soundless, spiraling cry I cry*... she seemed to say. Behind her, the small shadowy figure played on a rocky crimson beach. Rocks jutted up, alarming sentinels in a thick chartreuse sky.

"Tamara," Annabel murmured. She reached over for the death certificate to examine it again. It was gone.

She stared down in disbelief. It couldn't be gone. She clearly remembered leaving it on the table. She slowly stopped the soothing motion of the chair and rose.

Perhaps, she reassured herself, it had blown off the table when she's slid the wall back last night. She searched under the empty crib, along the baseboards, even under the turquoise chest. But it had disappeared, as completely as if she'd only imagined it in the first place.

"It can't be," Annabel muttered as she worked her way along the far wall. She carefully examined the opening. She pushed the wall open a bit. A small button on the floor winked up at her. It lay near the opening, as though it had been pulled off as someone had scraped through the narrow space.

Annabel bent and picked it up. Had it been there last night? It would have been easy to overlook. She turned it over in her hand, examining it, and a pounding began in her head and her eyes misted over so that she could barely see for a moment.

For she had recognized it. It was Gable's. It belonged to his leather bomber jacket, she was certain of it.

Had he been here, then, sometime this morning or late last night? In that case, where was he now? And where was the death certificate? Had he taken it?

She stiffened as she heard the wall begin to move. She had been so sure that no one would disturb her this early. The only one who ever came into the studio was Delia, and no one had ever seen her emerge from her bedroom before eleven.

But when she turned around, there was Delia in an apricot silk robe, yawning with a puffy-eyed look of complete boredom as she took in the sight of Annabel standing in the middle of the nursery.

Delia finished the luxurious yawn. "You're up rather early," she said dryly.

Annabel said nothing. She was watching Delia warily, trying to figure out how she could seem so unmoved when her world was crumbling around her.

"I have the distinct feeling," Delia said, walking casually into the room, "that you're going to want to do something about this."

"How long have you known about the nursery?"

Delia shrugged and sat down in the rocking chair. She rocked back and forth, examining her satin slipper. "Since last night. I followed you. I've been prowling around after you and Gable like some demented private eye ever since you found those papers in your headboard. I don't mind telling you that threw me for a loop. Thank God it was nothing specific, only more of Melinda's whining. But it kept me on my toes—I had to make sure that nobody was going to find anything else. But then you had to go poking around down here." She looked around idly. "How about this place? You put this in your film and nobody would believe it."

"So you're not Josiah Crane's daughter," Annabel said slowly. Even though she'd known it, she still had to hear it from Delia.

She smiled slightly. "Bingo."

Annabel couldn't resist. "Why did you do it, Delia?"

She laughed a brittle laugh. "For the money, of course. Why else?"

"*How* did you do it, then? How did you fool everyone?"

"It wasn't easy. Endless research and digging. But you know, the hardest part was convincing Giselle to lie in court. She's awfully squeamish."

"She *is* your real mother, then."

"Of course. I'm surprised the whole world didn't guess, these past few months, with her sticking so close, borrowing my clothes. It wasn't exactly a picnic to see what I'm going to look like in another twenty years. I had to make her go back to Canada."

"Did she really know Melinda Silver? And Josiah Crane?"

Delia nodded. "Didn't know who they were, of course—Mother can be rather dim when it comes to the cultural arena. It wasn't until he died and his life was splashed all over the news that she recognized him. That part was true enough. Then she told me the story of how the two of them were at the same nursing home in France, where she had me. When we started reading more about Crane, we realized that we just might be the only ones who knew that Melinda had been pregnant at all. It was the most amazing luck that the records of the nursing home had been destroyed in that fire. Now don't look at me, I had nothing to do with it—I was only two years old at the time. So, there were no records. No doctors still alive to tell the tale. Melinda had been secluded on the grounds—no one had met her except for Giselle, who was taking walks constantly out of anxiety. She wasn't married, you see, and she was scared to death. They used to talk a lot. Giselle learned quite a bit about her without knowing who she was."

"So how did you do it?"

"All it really took was nerve. I very discreetly investigated Melinda's family. I bribed the caretaker of this place and got inside, I went through everything with a fine-tooth comb. I found the diary hidden in the room you're staying in—that was the day I knew I could do it. It was the proof that Melinda had been pregnant. I left it there, of course. I knew they'd find it eventually once I turned up. And every single step I took only reinforced my story: I was the daughter desperately trying to ascertain whether the story my adoptive mother told me was true. Then I just brazened it out. It was the lack of information, you see, that helped me. I didn't forge any materials or anything. I just substituted one baby for another."

"What about the death certificate?"

"It was never officially filed—can you believe it? I can only assume that Josiah fixed it so that there'd be no record of Melinda's ever giving birth. I had to fly to France to find that out. The certificate you found isn't official. It's from the nursing home, not city hall. I really don't know how they did it. They must have resorted to a very large bribe. Maybe the doctor was an art lover, I don't know. I guess Josiah figured it was worth a try—he was still hoping for the annulment then. He probably thought it would make everything come out all right. You know, halfway through this, I started to feel sorry for the guy."

"Speaking of the death certificate, Delia, where is it?"

"I guess Gable has it."

"Gable?" Annabel practically squeaked the word. "He's here?"

Delia nodded and stretched. "I got up at five—it's not easy to get up before you, Annabel—and came down here. Gable was here with the certificate in his hand."

"Yes, I thought he'd been here. I found this." Annabel held out the button.

Delia looked at the button and began to nod. "Oh, yes, I saw it last night—I didn't know it was Gable's."

"You saw it last night?"

She nodded. "You see, Gable's known about the nursery for a while. He told me this morning that he started to get nervous about somebody finding the room. That's why he went to L.A."

"Why?" Annabel asked cautiously.

"Because he wanted to rearrange the production schedule so that you could do the rest of the shooting down there. He didn't want anyone to be in the house anymore. It was too big a risk. Let's face it, if you could find this room, anybody could."

"But we have to shut down the production, obviously."

"Not if you keep your mouth shut."

"You must be joking."

"I assure you, I'm not." Delia rose languidly and moved over to the crib. She rocked it with her little finger. "Although there's no reason, really, to pack up and leave the house. Finding the nursery won't mean anything. It doesn't prove the baby died. Gable's destroyed the death certificate, and now all we have to do is destroy the paintings.''

Annabel gasped. ''You must be mad. You couldn't destroy these paintings.''

Delia looked over at them carelessly. ''It would be a shame, I know. I don't know much about art, though I've been learning since I've become the daughter of a great painter, but these seem very good. Really, Annabel, again I'm no expert, but it's clear even to me that death is all over these paintings.'' She shuddered. ''They're too...*obvious*. I just couldn't stand listening to art critics analyze them and have all those speculations start again. Who knows what other loose ends are floating around?''

''And what does Gable think of this?''

She shrugged. ''He agrees.''

Annabel shook her head, sickened. ''I don't believe you. You can't do it.''

Suddenly rage tightened Delia's face. She looked haggard. ''Of course we can. Don't you realize that Gable is ruined if this gets out, just as I am? I'll go to prison. Do you think we could possibly let that happen? You'll go on to another film—you all will—but Gable doesn't have that luxury. Surely you know that he has everything sunk into this.''

''He woudn't do it,'' Annabel said hollowly. Then, as she heard the words, she realized that she believed them. ''He wouldn't do it,'' she repeated more firmly. ''You're lying. He didn't destroy the death certificate.''

''Tell me this, then,'' Delia said. ''Why did he let you keep shooting the film when he knew about the nursery already? I saw that button last night, you know. And wasn't Gable wearing that leather jacket yesterday?''

''I don't know what's going on, but I trust him.''

"Then you're a fool," Delia said lightly. "Maybe you should just head on back to New York. Gable hasn't been happy with the job you're doing anyway. And we patched up our little lover's quarrel this morning, so I don't think he'll be knocking at your door anymore at night. He'll be in my room."

"I doubt it, Delia," Annabel answered coolly. "Because very soon, your room is going to have little bars on the windows." She turned on her heel and walked out. She was sorry for Delia, in the end. Did she really imagine that Annabel would believe such obvious lies and, cringing with Gable's imagined betrayal, turn tail and run back to New York? Her scornful words were the last, pathetic attempt of a desperate woman to save her skin.

Sighing, she went straight to Gable's room and knocked on his door.

"Come in."

When she entered he was hanging up the phone. He looked at her face. "Do you know?" he asked wearily.

She nodded. "I've been talking to Delia. She's saying that you've destroyed the death certificate, that you've known about the nursery for some time, that you went to L.A. to try to get production moved up so that we don't have to shoot in the house anymore."

"And what do you think?" he asked cautiously.

Annabel flopped onto the bed wearily. "Well, I know she's lying, of course, but what are we going to do now? We don't know how far she's prepared to go with this."

Gable looked startled for a split second, and then his expression was even more forbidding than before. His mouth was a thin, rigid line. His words were sharp, glittering like broken glass on pavement. "Why are you so sure she's lying?"

Annabel looked at him, puzzled. "Because I know you." He said nothing, and she tried to smile. "Though it doesn't help when you leave clues behind," she said, holding out the button. "Delia tried to tell me you'd left the button yesterday morning, before you left for L.A."

Gable's mouth curled into a sardonic smile Annabel had never seen before. It made her uneasy to see it now. "So that's when you knew she was lying."

"What do you mean?"

"Because you remembered telling me to button up yesterday before I left for L.A. You remembered I had all my buttons then."

Annabel laughed. "I'm not that observant. No, I knew you wouldn't shoot for even one more day if you knew that Delia was a phony. That's a lot of time and money to waste."

"So why did you trust me?" Gable bit out. "Why didn't you believe Delia? She convinced a whole nation of her honesty—why couldn't she convince you that I was in on it with her?"

Puzzled at Gable's concentration on what she felt to be a minor issue at the point, Annabel scrutinized him carefully. The lines of strain in his face weren't there from just the discovery of Delia's fraud. He was desperately trying to understand something about her, about them. And then, with a sickened rush, Annabel realized what it was.

The breath seemed to go out of her, but she managed to get out the words. "I trusted you for no concrete reason at all," she said evenly. "And you can't understand that. You think I would listen to another person's lies about you rather than have faith in you, a faith that I didn't need to question. And now you're going crazy because you can't figure out why."

She saw in his eyes that she was right, and rage began somewhere in her body and spread out to her limbs. Her legs and hands began to tremble. She had never felt such rage before. The words did not exist for what she wanted to tell this man, this man with his granite gaze and his face that was so closed to her, his hands clenched into fists by his sides. She had loved those hands, those eyes, that rigid face, loved them with everything she possessed. And she had given her heart and her soul so freely, not expecting anything back, only what he could give her without her asking.

She stood up. "I've made such a mistake," she said numbly. "I trusted you." She spoke more to herself than Gable, but he looked up, his expression suddenly keen. He looked, she realized with a sick feeling in her stomach, relieved.

"Then you believe Delia now? What happened to your faith in me?" he taunted. "Is it shaken now because I haven't told you that Delia is a liar? All right, then, Annabel, I won't keep you hanging by that slender thread of your faith. She called me last night and told me everything. She tried to cut a deal. I flew up here early this morning to see for myself. I didn't even speak to her—it's incredible that she would believe that I'd go along with that sickening scheme. Anyway, I've already contacted my lawyer and the authorities. I've already closed down the film. Are you satisfied now? You haven't made a mistake. My integrity is intact."

Boiling rage made her explode. "How *dare* you insult me like this!" she shouted at him suddenly. "My only crime was trusting you. Why is that so hard for you to bear? What kind of twisted soul do you possess?"

"I don't want your trust!" Gable forced out the words and turned away. "I never asked for it. I never asked for anything from you, and I never wanted you to ask for anything from me."

She grabbed his arm fiercely, forcing him to turn back and look at her. "You're a liar. You did ask for my trust. Every time you came to my room, every time we made love, you asked for it, and you know it. You *know* that trust was in that room with us, dammit! Why can't you face that now?"

"No, *you* face it, Annabel. I told you from the beginning that our affair had nothing to do with our professional collaboration. I told you I could separate it, and I did. It's not my fault if you misunderstood that. You didn't understand the rules, Annabel. I don't *expect* anything from you."

She dropped his arm, stunned at the venom in his words. She was seeing a new side of Gable, and his cruelty shattered her. How foolish she had been, Annabel realized now. *"Gable needs distance,"* she remembered Gish saying. How true that was, and how it galled her that she could have been so naive to ignore what she'd known about this man from the very first: he didn't know how to love. Not the way she needed to be loved.

His love was as insubstantial as moonlight on the ocean, seducing by its brilliance, not its depth. It was an insult to her and her feeling for him. It skittered along the surfaces of her personality; it never counted on her character.

And it was a love, Annabel realized in rage and grief, that she could not live with.

With an enormous effort of will, she drew her composure around her. "It wasn't a game, Gable," she said quietly. "I didn't know there were rules. And I didn't know we were having an 'affair.'"

"What did you think then?" he asked sardonically. "That it was the love of the century?"

A sob rose in her throat like bile and she choked it down. She was sorely tempted to lie, to taunt him, to tell him airily that she had never loved him, never felt very much at all. That it had been lust, not love. Nothing but a stray temptation in an isolated town, to wile away the weeks of shooting, to ease the tensions of her work. To say that she had never imagined a future with him.

But she couldn't lie. If she lied about her love for him, he would win.

She said the words she had dreamed of saying, that she had choked back every time they had made love—words she'd once thought she would say joyously. Now they were words of bitter pain, and they were ashes in her mouth.

"I only thought I loved you," she said. Then she turned and walked out. She closed the door softly behind her and went to her room to pack.

Gable clamped down on the emotion as he watched her walk out. His body felt strange—brittle, dry, bloodless. It was as though a million tiny cracks had radiated out from some central source. Any moment now, he would crumble into dust.

Don't be absurd. He stood for a moment, eyes closed, gathering his strength and his will back to him; they had been flung from him so far he didn't know if he could retrieve them.

That was what Annabel had the power to do to him.

Gable had thought he'd been at the end of his rope before, but now he realized what the term meant. His fingertips were desperately hanging on to the last fibrous thread, and he was close to spiraling down into darkness, into a profound despair he'd never even touched before.

And it wasn't the film. There was a certain comfort one could take when one had been ruined before. The situation held no unfamiliar perils. It would take some doing, but Gable knew he wasn't ruined forever. He'd climb his way back again.

It wasn't that Delia might lie and say he'd been in on the scam with her, or that people might believe her.

A sharp, unbearable pain pierced him. He remembered the words he had heard coming out of his mouth. He had called the past weeks an "affair," knowing how much it would hurt her. How could he have used that word to describe the shimmering, deep, languid loving that had been between him and Annabel?

I only thought I loved you.

Gable slammed his fist against the wall, welcoming the pain. He wanted to feel physical pain, to ache in such a pure, uncomplicated way. Anything was better than this messy, unfamiliar torment.

It wasn't the prospect of scandal and ruin and bankruptcy that was causing him such unaccountable suffering.

It was a woman. It wasn't just any woman. It was Annabel.

It was the knowledge that she loved him. Loved him in a way he'd never expected, never wanted to be loved: completely. Sweetly. Trustingly. Wholly.

All the things that every sane man wanted in this world. Except Gable.

But, oh, how that love tantalized him with a promise that whispered enticingly, brushing against his ear, murmuring, *"Take me, and you'll be safe forever. You'll never be lonely. You'll never want for company, or ten-*

derness, or understanding. You'll have sweet nights and sunny days for the rest of your long, happy life."

And if he said yes to that voice, if he yielded, he would drown in its sweetness, it would stop up his nose and his ears and his eyes until all he could see was love, all he could hear was love. He would withdraw from the world, he would consume and be consumed.

Gable's eyes were open now. He stared at the closed door. He hadn't disintegrated with the force of his passion, with the agony of his regret. He was still here.

He had hurt her, though, and he would never forgive himself for that. Her eyes would haunt him forever. But wasn't it better, he told himself angrily, that she should know the kind of man he was, that she should be awakened to all his deficiencies? All he could give her was his honesty, and he had done that. It was brutal, but it was necessary.

It was better for Annabel, Gable told himself again heavily, sitting down on the bed where she had plopped squarely with such a worried, trustful expression. She deserved a man who would love her the way she was meant to be loved.

Gable gave himself a brisk mental shake. Now that he had organized his feelings and made sense of them, he had to begin the complicated process of shutting down a film; there were a million details to attend to.

He got up and reached for the phone, but the receiver dangled in his hand and he forgot whom he'd been about to call.

Something was missing, he realized. Something essential, something important.

Then he realized what it was. Always, when he'd come to terms with the fact that a liaison was over, he would feel, with a twinge of embarrassed shame, the sense of the blessed lightening of a burden. A gust of pleasant relief.

Now he gripped the phone and searched for the feeling he'd so often known and welcomed. He couldn't find it.

But, Gable promised himself, it would come. It had to.

Chapter Eleven

Sally Porter swung into the parking lot of the train station exactly four minutes late, the amount of time she always insisted, despite the evidence, that the train would be behind schedule. "Hi, honey," she called cheerfully out the car window to Annabel. "You look awful. Train just get in?"

"Four minutes ago, Mom. And thanks for the compliment. I can always count on you to cheer me up." Annabel swung her weekend bag into the car and slid into the passenger seat after it. She smiled weakly at her mother, who kissed her soundly and then sat back and peered at her. Sally appeared tanned and healthy after her latest golfing vacation, her short ash-blond hair a tumble of stray curls in the breeze. At sixty, her mother looked a lot better than she did, Annabel reflected.

Sally shifted gears and quickly peeled her prize possession, an old yellow Jaguar, out of the parking lot. "Have you been sleeping at all?"

Annabel grabbed at the seat for balance. "Not much," she admitted.

"That's terrible. Geez, Annabel, I admit I don't know anything about the movie business, but I'm sure there's no need to worry. You'll get another film. It's not your fault that Delia Worthington-Crane turned out to be just plain Delia Worthington—and a crook."

Annabel squinted out the window at the suburban landscape, searching for comfort in its familiarity. "I know."

"You're still a talented director. I'm sure projects will be flooding in."

"I know." The truth was that Annabel already had a half-dozen projects she could choose from. None of them interested her, but that wasn't the problem. It wasn't the film shutting down, either. It wasn't that she had squandered six months of her life on a project that would never come to fruition. It wasn't even that hordes of journalists were driving her crazy with their constant bombardment, trying to get the "inside story" on Delia.

It was, of course, Gable. That was why there were dark circles engraved permanently below her eyes. That was why she'd been waking up these past two weeks at two, at three, at four in the morning, sweating and shaken, disoriented from a nightmare in which she found herself in Josiah Crane's loveless landscapes, searching for something that both frightened and eluded her.

But during the day she wasn't doing any wistful sighing over her broken romance—far from it. She was still at a rolling boil. Every time she thought of Gable's bewildering reaction to a simple act of trust on her part, of the cruelty of his hard words, her heart would pound and her face would flush. It had demeaned her, it had demeaned what they'd had together, and she could not forgive him for it.

There hadn't been much for her to do after production shut down. Gable had handled the multitude of details, and her agent had followed through on her financial interests. She hadn't had much contact with him at all, and what contact they still had, had been icily polite. She'd left that afternoon for Los Angeles, spent a day saying goodbye to Sasha and Ben and some of the crew members, and then flown back to New York. She hadn't heard from Gable since.

She imagined that her anger would fade; it had to. But meanwhile she had to endure the sleepless nights that she couldn't quite account for. She had wanted so desperately for everything to return to normal, for her life to go on as it had. But something was holding it up, and she didn't know what. In some subtle way she had been altered by the summer in Mendocino, and she felt slightly off kilter, slightly removed from things around her. Even in the dynamic, rushing phenomenon of living in New York again, she felt sluggish.

A weekend at her parents' home in New Jersey would be the perfect cure, she'd decided, and for once they'd be in town to receive her. Perhaps a couple of mornings waking up in her old bedroom would restore her perspective. Then she could return to the city and start reading those scripts and treatments her agent kept sending over by courier. Perhaps the quiet rhythms of suburbia would slow the furious drumbeats in her head whenever she thought of Gable McCrea. Perhaps she could forget about him altogether, Annabel thought wildly. She couldn't wait for the day he was a dim memory, merely a mistake from her past.

Her mother broke into her thoughts. "Want to go to the driving range and hit a few? I've got the clubs in the trunk."

"What a surprise," Annabel said dryly. "Mom, you know I don't like golf."

"It might do you good to smash something. You look like you could use an outlet." Sally reached over and picked up Annabel's hand, which had unconsciously curled into a fist in her lap. "What's going on, Annabel?" she asked, concern in her hazel eyes as she shot her a quick look. "Is there anything else wrong besides this film? Something more personal than work—like love, maybe?"

Annabel's laugh sounded uncharacteristically hollow. "Love? Hardly. I'm fine, Mom." When her mother shot her another anxious glance, she decided diversionary tactics were in order. She didn't feel ready to discuss Gable. She didn't think she ever would. "Really, I'm okay. Let's go hit a few at the driving range." Maybe, Annabel decided sourly, she could pretend the little white ball was Gable's head.

Sally brightened and made a fast, tight right turn that made Annabel clutch the door handle. "Oh, good. Your father will be so jealous." She patted her knee. "And I guarantee you'll feel better."

With Sally's driving, it took them only ten minutes to reach the range. It was a perfect crisp September day, and Annabel couldn't help but be cheered by the weather and the brisk exercise. Perhaps her mother had been right, she mused, as she slammed a crooked drive down the range. She was starting to forget Gable McCrea already.

"Tell me about that producer of yours," Sally said, picking a ball out of the bucket. "Gable McCrea."

Annabel's backswing halted halfway through. Then she tried to recover and followed through, but the ball rolled casually off the tee, dribbled a few inches and stopped. She winced and took another ball. "What about him?"

"Keep your eye on the ball, dear, and that won't happen. Well, I was reading in *Personalities* magazine that he's broke now. He had all his money tied up in your movie. And he's been fighting rumors that he was in cahoots with that Delia."

"Oh, he'll be okay. People will forget soon enough. And producers are broke all the time." Annabel kept her eye on the ball and swung the club back.

"He's a handsome devil, I'll say that for him."

This time the club slammed down on the Astroturf, barely missing the toe of Annabel's sneaker.

"Eye on the—"

"—ball, I know. Yes, I guess some people would think he was handsome." Annabel determinedly reset the ball on the tee. She gritted her teeth and this time drove it far down the green.

"Good shot, hon. Well, I think he got a raw deal. You, too, of course. And that poor Giselle Worthington."

"I think the courts will be lenient with Giselle."

"So after all that, do you think it would have been a good film?"

"It would have been a great film," Annabel said regretfully, leaning on her club. "I've never seen Ben Hall better. And Sasha Durant would have been a big star. There were some really incredible scenes between them. A director prays for that kind of combustion on camera. It was almost as if they'd explode out of the frame."

"I can't remember the last time I saw one of those sweeping love stories, you know, with people larger than life. A passion that destroys them. What we used to call a three-hankie picture. I'm sorry it didn't get made."

"Well, if it had gotten made, it wouldn't have been that kind of film. It was really Delia's story; we'd only filmed the flashback. It was her story that drove it—it gave a perspective on Josiah and Melinda. They really weren't larger than life. Life was too much for them."

"Oh," Sally said philosophically. She swung and hit a clean drive. "Too bad."

"Yes," Annabel said, "it is too bad." She took up her club thoughtfully and hit another ball, which arced crazily. She hardly noticed. "It *is* too bad," she repeated. "Why didn't that ever occur to us?" She stared off into the distance, then suddenly whirled around and checked Sally's swing with a hand on her wrist. "We have to go."

"Go? We've got half a bucket of balls left."

"Please, Mom," Annabel pleaded. She was already tugging her jacket back on.

Sally shrugged and gathered the clubs. "All right," she grumbled. "But you have to tell me what's going on."

"The film, Mom. I think I can save it." Annabel headed toward the car, with Sally trotting beside her to keep up. "Gable and I were so wrapped up in the fact that we couldn't use Delia's story that we forgot what a great story we had just with Josiah and Melinda. It's so obvious! The flashback can be the main story. We just need a little more juice, a little more plot. It could work," Annabel said, starting to run. "It could work!"

"Sounds good to me," Sally said, jogging companionably beside her. "Do you think Gable McCrea will go for it?"

Annabel stopped in her tracks. Sally, who had continued with her loping stride, found herself jogging next to empty air. She halted with a jerk and turned around. She cocked her head inquisitively at Annabel.

"You don't think he will?" she asked.

When Annabel looked up, her green eyes were fierce. "He will," she promised savagely.

"Uh-oh," Sally said, heading for the car. "I know that look. And I think I feel sorry for Gable McCrea."

Annabel had three important phone calls to make before she tackled Gable. It took less time than she'd expected, and when she sat staring at the phone, ready to punch out his number, she found her palms were damp.

"Just *do* it, Annabel," she chided herself. She didn't know if she was ready to hear that sardonic voice, with its low, vibrant pitch and its uniquely accented consonants. But it didn't matter if she was ready or not; she had to do it. Annabel gritted her teeth and dialed his number in Malibu. She hung on, her heart pounding, for seven rings, but there was no answer. It was anticlimactic, to say the least.

And there was no answer at one, at two, or for the rest of the afternoon and evening. Finally, she steeled herself and called Gish. She didn't want to hear sympathy in Gish's voice; she didn't think she could stand it. But Gish was friendly and businesslike. She didn't say "I was so sorry to hear..." or "I tried to warn you." She blessedly acted as though Annabel and Gable were only professional colleagues. And she gave Annabel Gable's number and address in Vermont. Annabel stared at the paper for long minutes and then decided to put it off until the next day.

For the first time in weeks, she slept like a baby. She awoke like a shot, her decision made. She sang in the shower and raced downstairs for her breakfast. Her mother found her squeezing fresh orange juice and whistling cheerfully.

"I forgot how obnoxious you are in the morning," Sally said as she blearily grabbed at the cup of coffee Annabel handed her. "Did you get good news from Gable?"

"I haven't talked to him yet," Annabel said around a mouthful of scrambled eggs. "And I'm not going to call him. I think I need to pitch this in person."

"You're going to fly to California?"

"I'm going to drive to Vermont."

"Oh. Well, at least the drive will be nice this time of year. What are you going to—" Sally stopped abruptly. She looked over the rim of her cup at Annabel, who innocently took a sip of her orange juice. "No," Sally said. "Not my baby. Not my Jag. You don't want to take it."

Annabel nodded.

Sally sighed and took a deep gulp of coffee. "Just make sure the RPMs are up there when you shift," she said, snitching a piece of Annabel's toast.

Annabel finished breakfast and was ready to go by ten, but she got a late start owing to Sally's insistence on crawling under the hood and making sure the car was in perfect running order. She didn't cross the New York–Vermont border until four o'clock. When she pulled over and checked the map, she saw that she should reach Gable's house within the hour.

She chewed thoughtfully on a ham and cheese sandwich and realized that she still hadn't completely formulated what she was going to say to him. It might be a bit of a shock for him, to find her tooling up to his retreat and bursting in on him with a crazy proposal to save their film. Especially considering how things had ended between them. And would she be able to control her still percolating anger at him for the good of the film?

Annabel sighed and crumpled up her paper bag. She'd have to. She'd fight for this idea with everything she had. She wouldn't let a disastrous ending to a petty love affair stand in her way. She could handle it.

From his kitchen window, Gable saw the yellow sports car zoom around the last curve, heading for the private lane to his house. It couldn't be one of his neighbors; not many Vermont natives drove cars like that. It had to be some tourist searching for the famous fall foliage, not realizing he was at least a month too early. He'd need directions to Brattleboro and the highway.

He sighed and turned down the flame on his simmering pot of soup. Wiping his hands on a dish towel, he headed for the front of the house.

He opened the door and stopped dead. The lush curve of a very familiar backside was his first sight, as Annabel reached into the yellow car for something in the front seat. A plume of light brown hair spilled down a green sweater.

Pain stabbed Gable, pain and sudden, surprising desire, and his eyes misted over at the sight. He didn't have time to wonder why she was here; he could only clutch the door handle, staggering with her presence in his life again, tumbling back down into the extravagant, urgent need he felt as his eyes took in every familiar, wonderful curve of her body, the glorious fall of hair, the line of one beautiful leg as she strained to reach over to the passenger seat.

She extricated herself from the car, dragging out a huge purse. She turned around, and their eyes met.

How could he have forgotten how penetrating her gaze could be? The emerald-green eyes were like a clear mountain pool dappled with sunlight and shade. They snapped him to attention, paralyzing him for a moment so that he couldn't summon up his manners or his poise.

Annabel seemed to have no difficulty. "You're probably surprised to see me."

"I am."

"I should have called, but—"

"It's all right. Come on in." Reeling from her nonchalance, Gable unconsciously led the way to the kitchen.

Annabel trailed behind Gable's broad back, feeling confused and unsteady. His manner was brusque, but she had expected that. What she hadn't expected was this view of Gable, in a faded blue flannel shirt with the tail hanging out, a dish towel slung over his shoulder, looking completely at ease in a home gleaming with wood she knew he had milled and finished himself.

She got even more flustered when she walked into a bright, open kitchen with a wood stove in one corner and a state-of-the-art industrial stove along one wall. The air was laced with the delicious aroma coming from a simmering pot on a burner, and Annabel could swear bread had recently been baked in the oven.

Who was this man? Was this the glimpse of the "real Gable," the one she had hoped to see in Malibu? She sank down into a seat at the refectory table and ran her hand along the wood. Funny that he should choose such a big table. It cried out to be crammed with relatives and friends for Thanksgivings and Christmases, not for a solitary man to eat his soup.

"What are you thinking?" Gable asked curiously.

"I was thinking what a wonderful table this was," Annabel answered honestly. "I was picturing it filled with food and guests at Thanksgiving. It's kind of huge for one person."

Gable's mouth twisted in a wry smile. "Do you see me as that friendless and isolated?"

Suddenly uncomfortable, Annabel nodded. "Well, isolated—yes, I suppose I do."

Gable sat astride a chair. "There *are* other people in Vermont," he pointed out. "I have them over for dinner, even. I'm not a hermit, Annabel, and contrary to what you may think, I do enjoy the company of friends. I don't eat a solitary TV dinner at Thanksgiving, you'll be pleased to learn."

Annabel could find nothing to say to that; she felt a little embarrassed. "That soup smells good," she tried.

Gable was smiling at her faintly. "Thanks." Then his smile faded, and he looked grave. He held her gaze for a long moment. "Annabel, I'm sorry," he said softly.

"For what?"

"For being such a failure at loving."

The expression in his eyes was so sweetly honest, so sad, that she felt a lump rise in her throat. *I will not relent,* she thought fiercely, choking back the sob. She closed a tight mental fist around the hard nut of her anger. It was so easy to be sorry, she reminded herself. Was it so difficult to change?

"Don't mention it," she said curtly. "Now, I should get to the reason I'm here. I've got a long drive ahead of me."

"Surely you'll stay the night. I have plenty of room."

"No." The word came out stronger than she intended. She didn't want him to think she was afraid to stay under the same roof with him. "I'd prefer to drive back," she added in a more reasonable tone.

He nodded. "All right," he said carefully. "Now, what was it you wanted to talk to me about?"

"First, just grant me one request. Hear me out. Don't say no right away."

"When requests start out this way, I know it means trouble."

"Come on, Gable, be a sport."

He nodded, and Annabel took a deep breath and began. "We still have a film we can make, Gable. It's not the film we wanted to make. It's not the film you wrote. It's better. It's not the story of a woman tracing her roots. It's a love story."

He grimaced. "Don't you think I thought of trying to salvage what we had? There's no story, really. No drive, no tension. And the story's too depressing."

"You promised not to interrupt. It's not too depressing, Gable. Not if we add something we didn't have before—*the beginning of the affair*. Do you remember how Josiah and Melinda met?"

"I'm not allowed to interrupt."

"They met in Boston, on VJ Day. Melinda had run out of her parents' home. She was torn between joy that the war was over and guilty depression because her husband was coming back. She couldn't bear her parents' satisfaction that at last she would have a 'real' marriage, start having children, settle down. She couldn't bear to live with the husband she didn't love. She walked and walked, trying to feel as celebratory as the crowds around her, but instead, she started to cry and couldn't stop. And then a soldier who'd been watching her came over and sat next to her. He didn't have anywhere to go after the war was over, so he was feeling displaced himself. And that was the beginning. I think it's a good one for a film, don't you?"

"Not really. Kind of trite."

"Then you can think of something better. We have to thresh it out, Gable, come up with a different structure. But we have the meat of the film already. We can't let those scenes between Ben and Sasha vanish forever! There's a story there, I know it."

"It's not the story I wanted to tell."

"So what? You did tell me that you wanted a human story, a personal story. Well, this is it." Annabel leaned forward. "We just have to dust off Fortuna's word processor."

"I can't write this, Annabel. It's a love story."

"You *can* write it. You've written most of it already."

"You don't understand. It doesn't interest me. The obsessive quality to the relationship isn't there anymore. They don't make any mistakes."

Annabel stood up stiffly and paced across the floor. "I don't agree. They make a lot of mistakes. And the obsession is still there—what's not there is the destructiveness, the neurotic element that you treasured so much. The one that led them to give their child away." Her voice was bitter. "You can't understand the kind of love that isn't unhealthy, destructive, that's all. You wanted to relive your parents' marriage, you wanted to justify how you felt about it and that you were right about it, but you can't do that now, so 'it doesn't interest' you." She spun around. "You can't graft your concerns onto Josiah and Melinda, Gable. If you want to work out your own problems, go to a therapist. Don't bore us by putting it on the screen."

"So you think my script was boring?" Gable asked with casual menace.

She sat down wearily. "No, of course I don't. But your insistence that you can't change it *is*. You don't have to be a cowboy to write a Western, Gable. And you don't have to be good at loving to write a love story. You can do it. Or rather, Fortuna can. 'Fortune favors the daring,' remember?"

He got up to stir the soup. "It opens up a ton of legal questions. We could be getting into trouble."

"That's what lawyers are for. I already called one. And you've dealt with the Crane foundation all along. You know they'd want you to finish the film. We can even show them the footage we already have. Look, as long as we don't use any of Delia's material, we're fine. And Gable, just think—we could probably get those paintings! You could talk the foundation into it. I'm sure you could."

Gable shook his head. "Even if we could, there's a ton of other problems. Logistically, it would be hard—"

"But not impossible—"

"Ben and Sasha are probably working on new projects—"

"Ben isn't slated for a new film for four months. He's taking time off to be with Sasha. She's in an off-Broadway play that's already talking about closing. By the time it does, the rewrite will be finished. We could be shooting in as soon as two weeks. I already called them—they'd be thrilled if we could pull it together."

"I see. And did you call anyone else besides the lawyer and Ben and Sasha?"

"I called Randy Scott. We do need the same director of photography, I think. He can do it if we finish shooting by the first week in October."

"The crew..."

"We'll get them. Come on, Gable. It's not a question of getting a crew. If you want to do it, you can do it. You know that."

Gable stared down into his soup, hoping to find answers there. All he could see, however, were the vegetables from his garden. Why did this wildcat of a woman have to come barging into his life again?

And why was he playing devil's advocate with her? Why couldn't he admit that just the notion of salvaging the film had caused the adrenaline in his body to pump as it hadn't in weeks? It was true that he was vaguely terrified of revising the script; it wasn't his kind of story, of course, but he also wasn't the most cheerful, industrious writer. Pounding out that first script had been an exercise in self-torture. Despite the immense satisfaction he had gotten out of the finished project, he didn't know if he wanted to go through that again. But if that were true, Gable asked himself honestly, why was every cell in his body singing out that he should?

Annabel watched Gable's back carefully. She knew the instant he had made the decision. Something about the way his muscles relaxed told her that he had decided to go ahead.

He turned around and nodded brusquely. "Let's do it."

Annabel sprang up from the table. She almost threw her arms around him, but the thought of his body against hers was so disturbing she quickly restrained herself. She stuck out her hand.

Gable shook it. His palm felt rough and warm against hers. Annabel had an uncomfortable and totally unwanted sensation of weakness in the knees. *It's not fair,* her mind screamed. It wasn't fair that the fates had saddled her with this irrational attraction that pulsed, steady and strong, no matter what this man did or said.

"I wish," Gable said softly, not letting go of her hand, "that you had followed through on your original inclination."

Annabel moistened dry lips. "What was that?"

He gently drew her body against his. "This, Annabel." He kept her there with only light pressure, letting her get used to the feel of him against her again.

And it took only a few seconds for her to remember with heart-stopping clarity how wonderful it had been, how right he had felt, how his hands and his mouth had coaxed responses from her that she'd never dreamed she could experience.

Gable rested his chin on the top of Annabel's head and closed his eyes as memory invaded him slowly, bit by tantalizing bit. The kitchen had darkened with the dusk, and he remembered those evenings in Mendocino that had seemed to go on forever, until the night brought her into his arms again. How every moment seemed charged with Annabel; how he had never felt so alive, so at the center of his existence, as on those heady, endless nights of love.

They stood in the middle of the floor, unwilling to move. To increase the contact would raise questions and consequences; to let go would be unbearable.

But an undercurrent of reluctance was there in Annabel's mind, in her body, and it was too insistent to ignore. She remembered all too clearly how this man had betrayed her, simply by being who he was. Her serious romantic nature could not survive another bout with him.

She could not be totally swept away by him as she had been once. Her mind would always be working; she would always be wary. And that wariness would be the death knell for any kind of true connection between them, which would be the only connection worth having.

It wasn't only that Gable wasn't capable of giving himself completely. She was no longer capable of it either.

Gable pulled away as he felt her withdraw. Her eyes had lost their seductive sparkle, he noted, and despair filled him. He had destroyed something precious in her feelings for him, and he realized with a shock what it was.

Trust. It had been trust that had made her expression so beautiful, her loving so giving, so inspired. Annabel had told him that once, but he hadn't known how to listen.

Now for the first time in his life, standing in his kitchen afraid to hold this woman even a tiny bit more closely, Gable knew why trust was so crucial in love, and why the loss of it was so irrevocable. He could never have Annabel again the way he'd once had her. Her eyes would always be measuring; her body would never again yield to him so willingly, so purely.

"I can't," she said simply.

"I know."

"I can't work with you and continue to be angry with you, Gable," she continued quietly, turning away. "But neither can I work with you and have this happen again. I think you'll agree that it's best to leave it alone now. Better for both of us."

"Yes, I suppose it is."

"Perhaps there will always be this...attraction between us. But we're not children. We can ignore it."

"Of course."

"I'd better go."

"Are you sure you won't stay—"

Annabel looked at him tiredly, her expression telling him to back off.

"—for supper," Gable amended.

"No, thank you. I'll call you tomorrow and we can talk about what we need to do. You'll have to check with the foundation, of course. We should resume shooting as soon as possible. When do you think you can have the revised script ready?"

"A couple of weeks."

"Fine." Annabel picked up her purse and Gable walked her to the door. She said goodbye quickly and walked out into a sunset splendid with the colors of pumpkin and maize. Gable stood in the doorway and watched her start up the car.

She leaned out the window. A ghost of a smile flitted across her face. "I'm glad you agreed to go ahead. So long, partner."

"So long." Gable raised a hand in farewell, but she was already backing up and didn't see it. She drove away without looking back. He squinted down the lane until the yellow Jaguar was swallowed up by the dusky twilight. He stood looking after her even after she had been long gone, until the streaks of orange and gold had faded and the wind had picked up, ruffling his shirttail and reminding him that it was time to go back into the house.

Chapter Twelve

Annabel? Gable. Well, one roadblock has been cleared, anyway. I've got the foundation's blessing to go ahead with the film. And I'm working out a different distribution deal—I want to open this version of the film in January. It's going to be smaller, quieter; it just might get swallowed up if we open Christmas as we'd planned, and anyway, we'd never make it a December release. You'll be under the gun as it is.''

"I agree. Listen, I have some bad news. Raleigh Briggs took another editing assignment.''

"Oh, no.''

"But I talked to Jessie Allan and showed her the footage we have and she's interested in taking over and working with me. *If* everything's in the can by late October and she's got some very sharp assistants.''

"Great.''

"Okay.''

"Well..." He paused for a moment.

"Uh, is that all, Gable?"

"Yes, I guess so. Well, good work, Annabel."

"Thanks. You too. Bye."

"Annabel, we've got Dorothy Halloran and Maxwell Douglas for Melinda's parents. And they'll both work for scale and percentages."

"Wow! How'd you do it?"

"I cooked Dorothy dinner in her apartment and Max worked with my father on *The Pirate and the Lady*."

"Your father was in that movie?"

"He was the first mate. I think it was his biggest role. My mother's in a crowd scene. It helps if you have a freeze-frame on your VCR, or else she's just a blur."

"I'll have to rent it sometime. Well..."

"Well..."

"Talk to you soon."

"Right."

"Gable, I loved the pages you sent me."

"But?"

"But I have a problem with the scene where they exchange vows after they find out Melinda's husband won't give her a divorce. Frankly, I think it's a bit corny."

"Corny? *Corny?* It's romantic. Sensual. Touching."

"I don't know..."

"Trust me, Annabel. With you filming it, it won't be corny."

"Hey, maybe we can do it on an exterior location—on a really cold day. That should be a good counterpoint to the mush. You know, a bleak landscape, bare trees, their hands all red and chapped and their eyes tearing..."

"You're a hard-hearted woman, but I like it."

"Great. Gable, do you have a cold or something?"

"Just a little one."

"Oh. Well, take care of yourself, will you? Don't work yourself to a frazzle. Keep warm, and all that."

"Sure."

"Update on locations."

"What is it this time, Gable?"

"We've got a great Boston location for Melinda's house—some musty old institute on Beacon Hill that used to be a mansion. But we just can't make it work in Mendocino. The budget won't stand it, and the foundation's dragging their heels about shooting on the Crane estate now."

"We don't have to shoot there. We've already filmed the important stuff. We can use the Boston locations and some New England exteriors."

"That's what I figured. I've already revised the new outline. Actually, I think it will tighten up the film. Gish suggested a great scene where Josiah bursts into the mansion—"

"You showed your script to Gish?"

"I figured it was about time."

"And?"

"I thought I was incapable of shocking my sister at this point. But I did."

"And?"

"And she loved it. She wants to represent me."

"I'm glad to hear that, Gable."

"Well, I'll talk to you soon. And Annabel? Thanks for the advice you gave me after the party in Malibu. I should have told her a long time ago."

"Don't mention it."

* * *

"Annabel, I've yet another brilliant notion."

"What now?"

"I want to edit the film at my house in Vermont. I have complete editing facilities here. The original design of the house called for it because a, uh, friend of mine was interested in working up here. Anyway, it would save a lot of time and money. You could move in for the duration."

"I don't know, Gable."

"I've already spoken to Jessie. She's thrilled. She'll come up in mid-September and start editing footage as you shoot. She loves to ski, and she's going to pack her whole family up here until Christmas. What do you say?"

"All right. We'll be working around the clock for quite a while, so it's not a bad idea."

"I've lined up your assistants, too."

"How's the script coming? You must be exhausted."

"Delirious. Okay, we're all set for the first day of shooting next week. I'll have to send you the rewrites for the last scenes in Boston. And Annabel—"

"Yes?"

"You know, I think this is going to work."

"Wow, did I just hear some cautious optimism there?"

"It takes me a while, but I do wise up eventually. Remember that."

It was hysterical, exhilarating madness, but they did it. They shot the rest of the film in three and a half weeks. The weather cooperated, the actors did their work beautifully, and the production designer somehow managed to pull together period sets in half the time usually allotted for them.

Annabel was rarely found stationary. She seemed to be everywhere. If there was equipment to be moved, she was hustling with the crew to move it; she fetched her own coffee and doled out the aspirins on long days. The crew couldn't help but follow her lead, and there was a spirit of cooperation and a feeling of family as they all worked as hard as they'd ever worked to get the rest of the film shot.

And then it was over, and they had come in on time. They were even a bit under budget. At the wrap party Annabel, Sasha and Ben slumped in a corner, drinking from a bottle of very good champagne since nobody had the energy to get up for glasses.

Ben lifted the bottle. "Here's to the best role of my career."

"Hear, hear," said Sasha, grabbing for the bottle to join in the toast. "And here's hoping the damn picture is as good as we think it is." She handed the bottle to Annabel.

"And here's to the smoothest, sunniest, luckiest, most trouble-free production—the second half, that is—that I've been involved with or even heard about or imagined in my wildest dreams."

"And," Ben said sagely, "we will never see its like again."

They all bowed their heads with the truth of the remark, and then solemnly passed the bottle around again.

"Well, Sash," Ben said after a particularly long sip of champagne, "should we tell her?"

Sasha smiled and nodded.

"Tell me what?"

"First of all," Ben began, "do you know that our producer, who has forged a friendship with me in the fire of romantic agony and off-key barroom singing, has invited us to Vermont for Thanksgiving dinner?''

Annabel shook her head. ''No, I did not. But I hear he's a great cook. At least, I hear it from Gable.''

''You'll be there, of course, probably still editing around the clock. So, Sasha and I thought we'd seize the opportunity, and—'' Ben paused for another sip.

''And?'' Annabel prodded.

''And get married.''

''What?''

Ben shrugged. ''Well, she asked me, and—''

Sasha punched him. ''Hey! You asked me!''

''Well, congratulations! I'm delighted.'' Annabel reached over exuberantly to hug them both. ''When did you decide?''

''Two days ago,'' Sasha said, her creamy skin flushed with excitement. ''We thought we'd wait until the wrap party to announce it. Hey! I think this calls for more champagne.'' Grinning, she jumped up and headed for the bar.

Ben watched her go. ''God, she's beautiful.''

Annabel watched Sasha as well. She felt churlish questioning Ben, but she had to. ''Are you sure, Ben?'' she asked softly.

''Ah, Annie, you worrywart, why wouldn't I be? I'm a changed man. Sasha makes me deliriously happy. She's astonishingly beautiful. She's amazingly intelligent. She loves me.''

''And you love her?''

''And I love her.'' Ben nodded vigorously.

Sasha came up with another bottle of champagne. ''So will you and Gable stand up for us?'' she asked Annabel.

''Of course. Have you asked him yet?''

"Yes," Ben answered. "He's thrilled."

Thrilled? That didn't sound like the Gable McCrea she knew. But then Ben was always prone to exaggeration.

"He's insisted on taking care of everything," Ben continued. "Does that man ever take off his producer hat?"

Sasha grinned. "He even promised us snow. Do you think he can pull it off?"

Annabel took another sip of champagne. "I wouldn't be a bit surprised," she said.

The snow began lightly on Thanksgiving morning. It was a gentle dusting, just enough to make the lovely Vermont landscape look like fairyland, but not enough to snarl the roads and slow traffic. It twinkled down against a white sky all morning long.

"Perfect," Annabel declared from the living-room window of Gable's house. "A perfect day for a wedding."

Gable got up to poke the fire. "All we need is the groom."

"Maybe he got delayed by the snow."

"It's not snowing in New York."

"Well, you know Ben: he's always late. And he's still got plenty of time. Sasha hasn't even started dressing yet."

"Speaking of dressing, I'd better check on the turkey."

"Are you sure I can't help? Even you can't put this feast on all alone, Gable."

"You can help later."

"Oh, good. I make a mean turkey gravy."

"No, I meant with the dishes."

Sasha came into the room, looking pale in a white velour robe. "Any word from Ben?"

Annabel shook her head. "No. I'm sure he'll be here soon."

"Come on to the kitchen with me, Sasha," Gable said. "I'll give you a piece of the bread I baked this morning. You've got to have some breakfast."

"Are you kidding? I could barely choke down a cup of tea this morning. I'm too terrified to eat," Sasha said, but she obediently followed Gable.

Annabel stayed at the window, watching the lacy flakes fall. She felt a curious but not unpleasant mixture of tiredness and exhilaration. For one thing, it felt good to be standing, not hunched over a moviola. She'd watched the sequences of *A Family of Two* so many times that it seemed to continually play on the backs of her eyelids.

Staying in Gable's house was amazingly easy. As a matter of fact, she rarely saw him outside of the editing studio. Jessie Allan had taken a house nearby with her two children and her screenwriter husband, and the assistants scattered to other lodgings nearby, so at night she was alone in the house with Gable. But Annabel had accepted the fact that though he could still be a nagging temptation, Gable was part of her past. She'd thought she had tasted true love for the first time in her life, with all the pure force of inevitability behind it, but she'd been wrong. That was hardly news. She'd been wrong before.

She had to admit that there were times she would lie awake in bed, every pore of her skin alive to the fact that Gable was only yards away, but she always ended up falling asleep almost immediately. One thing Vermont had done for her was to cure her insomnia.

"Annabel!" Gable bellowed from the kitchen. "I need a taster for the cranberry relish. Sasha went upstairs."

"All right!" Annabel yelled back. She'd noticed lately that she and Gable always seemed to be having conversations in separate rooms. Yesterday they'd discussed the pacing of an entire scene while he was in the study and she was in the kitchen having lunch. Maybe they were taking this avoiding each other business a bit too far.

She'd better get an apron before she tasted any cranberry relish, Annabel decided, heading through the living room toward the kitchen. She didn't want to stain her gown. It was a beautiful thick black velvet, rather an unorthodox choice for a maid of honor, but Sasha had envisioned a black and white wedding against the snow, and they'd all agreed it would be very dramatic and quite a fitting scene for two actors.

As she entered the hall, there was a knock at the front door. Annabel crossed quickly, ready to scold Ben for his tardiness. Instead, a uniformed man stood there with a long white box for Sasha Durant.

Annabel signed the slip and brought the box inside. She thought all the flowers for the wedding had already arrived. Perhaps Ben was sending an extra bouquet for Sasha.

When she opened the box and saw two dozen long-stemmed white roses nestled among the greens, an uneasy feeling snaked through her. Annabel stared at the little white envelope, telling herself she was being silly.

"Annabel?" Gable came up behind her. "What's the matter? You look as though you'd seen a ghost."

She shook off the mood. "These flowers came for Sasha."

"Oh. I think she's dressing. Why don't you bring them up and then come back down and taste the relish? I'm going to get into my tux."

"All right." Annabel went up the stairs slowly, with a feeling of foreboding she couldn't shake. She knocked softly on Sasha's door and went in.

Sasha was at her dressing table, putting the finishing touches on her makeup. She turned around and smiled weakly. She still looked a bit pale beneath the expertly applied blusher, Annabel saw, but even so, Sasha looked the epitome of the ravishing bride.

"I'm glad you came up. I think I'll need some help with the dress. My hands are shaking so badly."

"These came for you," Annabel said, holding out the box.

"How lovely," Sasha said, touching the perfect white blooms. "Oh, here's the card. They're from Ben! How sweet!" Annabel watched with her heart in her mouth as Sasha's face slowly changed. She became dead white beneath the rosy swath of color on each cheekbone. "Oh, my God," Sasha breathed. She stumbled backward and landed on the bed, right on top of her creamy velvet gown.

"Sasha—" Annabel sat next to her quickly. "What is it?"

Sasha was hyperventilating in quick shallow breaths, somehow unable to fill her lungs properly.

"Easy," Annabel said. "Just take deep breaths."

Sasha nodded, her eyes huge, and handed Annabel the small white card.

"I will love you forever..." it began.

Annabel closed her eyes. How could he have done this, she thought, enraged. If Ben had been anywhere within a hundred miles she would have hunted him down and gone after him with a lethal weapon. She put her arms around Sasha and held her tightly while she burst into a storm of agonized weeping. Annabel rocked her fiercely, feeling helpless, knowing that there were no words she could say, nothing she could do. She began to cry with Sasha from sheer rage, and their mingled tears soaked the elegant black gown and dripped down to stain the satin trimming on the wedding dress, now crumpled under them, forgotten.

She had never seen Gable so angry. Rage made his eyes the color of a stormy sky and his mouth a thin line.

"That bastard!" he exploded. He got up from the kitchen table and went to stand at the sink. He stared out at the snow, looking stern and implacable in his elegant tux. "How's Sasha?"

"About how you'd expect. He said in the note that he just couldn't go through with it. He couldn't bear to hurt her. He was trying to be strong for both of them," Annabel said numbly.

"He's a weasel," Gable said, his voice tight with his rage. "A coward. He should have done this in person, at least. Except that I would have broken every bone in his body."

"He's a child," Annabel said wearily. "He falls in love and then thinks he's being noble when he breaks it off. He doesn't like himself very much, and I don't think he's able to trust someone's love for him."

"That's a very charitable description, Annabel, for a man who just destroyed someone's life."

"I don't mean to be charitable," she answered. "I'd like to kill him. But I do understand what makes him such a cad. I had this awful feeling when I saw the white roses. That seems to be his method for delivering the coup de grace."

"Ah, that's right, you had experience with this before," Gable said, a note of bitterness creeping into his voice. "Too bad you didn't warn Sasha."

"Come on, Gable, you can't blame me. You can't warn someone when they're already in love. You can just cross your fingers and pray. I really did think that Ben was serious this time, that he was smart enough to see that Sasha could make a difference in his life."

Gable stalked back to the table and sat down. "You're right," he said, scowling. "I'm sorry I blamed you. I'm the one who patched up that stupid quarrel. I told Ben he couldn't possibly be as superficial as he appeared. Apparently I was mistaken. It's my fault."

"It's nobody's fault." Sasha stood in the doorway, fully dressed, her hair now combed neatly off her face. She looked strained and exhausted, but her eyes were clear. "Except mine. I knew what I was getting into with Ben Hall. I'd heard all the rumors. And Annabel, I saw the concern in your eyes all along." She came over and sat down with them. Gable got up and poured a cup of coffee, then handed it to her. She took it gratefully. "Being in this business can be pretty rotten sometimes. All you meet are actors. I'm going to have to rustle myself up some nice accountant." She smiled weakly at them.

"I'm so sorry, Sasha," Gable said softly.

She shrugged. "I know that eventually I'll feel it's for the best. Right now I feel like hell. But you know, I was so nervous this morning—I mean, really scared. Probably more scared than I should have been if I'd felt that this was the right thing to do."

"I suppose that you can take consolation from the fact that if he's this much of a louse, you would have been miserable with him anyway," Annabel said.

Sasha nodded and took another sip of coffee. "This tastes like the best cup of coffee I ever had," she said, smiling at Gable.

He put his hand on her arm. "Just wait until you taste the turkey."

"Gable," Sasha said hesitantly, "I don't think I'll stay."

"You have to!" Annabel cried. "You can't go back to New York alone."

"Actually, I thought I'd go home to my folks in Idaho. I can fly out of Boston if I leave here now—I just called. I suppose there's some kind of limousine service to the airport. I'll spend a few weeks at home, getting some perspective. I love you guys, and I know it sounds corny, but I just feel like going home."

"It sounds smart," Annabel said, then added lightly, "And besides, maybe you'll meet that accountant."

Sasha's expression darkened, and her eyes filled with tears. "I'm not ready to meet anyone for a long, long time," she said.

Annabel reached for Sasha's hand and looked across the table at Gable. His knuckles were white around his coffee cup, his expression furious. But he spoke in a gentle tone to Sasha. "Finish your coffee," he said. "Annabel and I will drive you to Boston and get you on that plane to your family. We're going to salvage this Thanksgiving for you somehow."

Annabel and Gable sat on opposite sides of the fire, silently sipping their wine. Their dinner had been equally as silent, as they picked at the turkey and corn bread dressing and cranberry relish that Gable had prepared. It had been hard to eat more than a few bites of the delicious meal; even the excellence of the robust California Zinfandel seemed out of place.

They had bundled Sasha on the plane with fervent bear hugs and earnest directions to call any time, day or night. They had driven back to Vermont and remarked only on the weather. It had been a strange, halting atmosphere for Thanksgiving. They had sat across from each other at the candlelit table, still dressed formally in their wedding clothes, both thinking their own solitary thoughts.

Annabel drew comfort from the fire, the wine, the snow that had begun to fall again, and, if she were honest, from Gable. He hadn't tried to inject a false note of jocularity into the evening; he had accepted the fact that she was distressed. The funny thing was that he seemed more upset than she about Ben's desertion.

"Annabel." Gable's voice rumbled from the depths of the couch. "Do you have to sit all the way over there?"

She got up and sat next to him. "Better?"

He reached out and draped his fingers over her shoulder. Then he sighed. "Yes. I felt the need for some human contact."

They sat together peacefully, sipping their wine, watching the fire as the night stole around them. Gable suddenly seemed less like a dangerous seducer and more like a friend. It was perhaps the first time she'd felt totally comfortable with him since Mendocino. And now it seemed quite natural to stretch out on the couch and rest her head against his chest.

Gable felt Annabel's soft hair brush against his chin. When he looked down he could see the curve of her cheek and the tip of one small ear. He remembered how dreamy her eyes had looked as she'd gazed at the fire. Slowly, as though he were a teenager sneaking his arm around his date in a movie theater, afraid she would bolt, he brought his hand across to rest along her arm. His fingers brushed hers.

When he reached over with his other hand to put his wineglass down, he saw his hand was slightly unsteady. It was having her so near, trusting enough to be able to rest against him.

He knew he should accept that one tiny step and be grateful enough not to push it. He should be able to hold her and watch the fire without desire flaming up in him. He should be able to accept the fact that she could be friends with him, finally. Wasn't that what he had been wishing for since she'd come to edit the film?

But he couldn't. He had held his desire in so long. He struggled to control the need that made his lower body ache and shifted position slightly. He looked at the fire instead of Annabel. But he wanted her so badly it was all he could do not to cup her face and lift it to his. Not to slide his hands along the black velvet and feel the material rub against her skin, soft against soft. Not to feel her beneath him as she used to be, straining, her body slick with sweat, winding her legs and arms around him, tugging his head to her mouth, to her breast. Urging him on with the extent of her passion. Making him crazy with her need.

Gable got up abruptly, causing Annabel's head to flop down on the couch.

She looked up at him. "What's the matter?"

The firelight caught the ends of her hair and the deep green of her eyes, lighting her with red and gold, softening her face. She had gotten thinner, he realized, since he'd met her almost a year ago. Her face didn't seem quite so softly rounded. Her classic cheekbones were more prominent now, but he'd liked her full, healthy glow. Now she seemed paler, and there were tiny lines of fatigue around her eyes that even the low light couldn't disguise.

And never before had she seemed so beautiful to him.

"Gable, what is it?"

"I was just thinking..."

"Yes?"

He took a deep breath. "How very beautiful you are." And then he couldn't stop himself. He crossed back to the couch and took her wondering face in his, cupping it as he'd wanted to so badly a moment before. "Annabel, I want to kiss you very much. I don't think I can stand not kissing you anymore."

Her breath caught, and then he felt it rush out past his fingertips. Her eyes held that caution he so despised now, but did he also see a warmth, a willingness, she couldn't disguise?

Her lips parted, and he kissed her.

He had known it would be dangerous, and it was. Immediately his body responded, and he was lost in her softness and his own hard need. He held himself in check, letting the kiss build slowly, letting her wariness dissolve under the heat. And then with a sigh she was lost as well, rubbing up against him like a cat, trailing her lips across his face, wanting him as much as he wanted her.

The events of the day had somehow left them open to each other in a way that they had never been before. The anguish of a friend, the long ride through a snowy landscape, the silent Thanksgiving dinner, had all wrapped a mood of magic around them, had made them yearn for each other in a basic human way. It had nothing to do with their past, or their future; for the first time since Mendocino, they were able to exist only in the now. All that was important was in that room.

It was lovemaking born out of desperation, a need to touch, to possess something that could not be possessed. With every caress, every kiss, Gable wanted to grind his need as deeply into her as he could, to brand her with all he felt but could not give without reluctance.

And her giving was reluctant as well. Together, the paradox of their fear and their passion fueled a duel, a battle, more than a coupling, that began slowly and then grew in a startling, leaping, flagrant progression to a height they'd never reached before.

It was a fierce, hard, aching kind of loving. Naked in front of the fire, flushed with its heat, they coiled around each other, their mouths sealed together. Annabel hadn't forgotten her anger at Gable, but it seemed to make her passion stronger. She was all raw nerves, agonizingly sensitive to every touch. She wanted him, and she hated the intensity of that wanting. She wanted to be free of him, but she was bound to him; with every touch he showed her just how piercingly vulnerable she was.

They were feverish, inspired, the fire making them see red and gold behind closed eyes. Annabel struggled with the intensity of her need, but it overpowered her, making her cry out a ragged, harsh surrender while she clutched him to her, digging her fingers into his back. And Gable cried out as well with his own release, his mouth against her flushed, dewy skin, breathing in her scent.

They rolled apart, gasping. Annabel felt tears on her cheeks that she quickly dashed away.

As her body quieted and her mind regained its focus, she felt again that hard knot of fear that still remained deep inside her. Now it grew and flourished into an instinct for flight. Suddenly she needed to be alone to sort it all out. She couldn't imagine what Gable would say, how he would respond to her now that this had happened, and she didn't think she could bear to hear it or see it.

She stood up quickly and went to gather her clothes. She slipped into the black gown and crumpled her underclothes and panty hose into a ball. She held on to the silky mass as a talisman; they were only garments, but they were wholly hers, and they reminded her of who she was and brought her back to a reality of sorts.

Clutching her underwear in one perspiring hand, she finally faced Gable. He had risen to a sitting position, and the firelight flickered on his long, lean muscular brownness, burnishing his still-glistening skin. Shadows obscured his face, but she could see that his brow was furrowed quizzically.

"Gable, I can't—" Annabel paused and tried to breathe normally. She was panting, as if she were being pursued. "I want to be alone," she said simply, her voice shaking. "I didn't want this to happen."

"Why not?"

"You know why."

"Annabel, I—"

She held up her hand. "Don't! Don't speak, please. There's really nothing to say." He was still watching her, and he looked so beautiful in the firelight, such pure coiled masculine power, that it was all she could do not to run across the room to him.

"I don't want to want you!" she burst out suddenly, emotion choking her voice. "I can't be happy with you! I can't—" Her voice broke as tears began to fall, silently and steadily, down her cheeks, "I can't stand this. Please..."

The word was a plea, for forgiveness and for restraint, as Gable began to rise to come toward her. He ignored it, rising naked and strong to come to her side, and she panicked. She backed away.

"No!" Now her voice was strong and resolute, halting him in his tracks. "Nothing's changed," she said. "We're still the same people. No, Gable," she said gently. It took every ounce of strength and will in her body, but she walked out of the room, leaving him standing there, still poised to comfort her.

Chapter Thirteen

Gable rose early and went for a walk. Gray was giving way to a pale pink that brushed the spidery tops of the trees as he walked underneath them, the snow crunching pleasantly underneath his boots. It was a hushed, silent world, crystalline and beautiful, and it held no answers for him.

He had hoped that the coming of the day would bring rationality. Surely the fevered, burning night he'd spent would be quenched by the cold light. But his body was still raging, straining to disobey her wishes, her pleas, and go to her. Just the thought of her in her warm bed, her hair a tangled, glorious mass on the pillow, the blanket drawn up so far that the only thing visible was the end of her nose, made him feel like running and diving onto that bed with her like the crazed, irrational, sad creature that he was.

"We're still the same people," she had said, her eyes wild in the orange light, her hair streaming over her shoulders. She had stood barefoot in the black velvet gown, her skin as white and fragile as snow, and her honesty had halted him as nothing else could. It was what had kept him away from her; it was what held him here in the chill dawn, trying to walk off an emotion that he knew could only bring them disaster.

He was forty years old; he was no kid, wild with love, thinking that it could be enough to guarantee happiness. He knew how complex emotions could be; he knew the potential for ruin a consuming passion had. He knew himself so well, and as hard to take as the knowledge was on this particular morning, he knew he could never make Annabel happy. Their life would be made up of separations. He would constantly pull away, afraid of being engulfed. He would never be able to give as much to her as she so easily could give to him.

He was too old to change. But not, Gable thought bitterly, running his fingers along the pale bark of a birch, too old to hope.

Some people could luxuriate in love; they could take sensual pleasure in wallowing in it, in licking it off their fingers for every last drop of its sweetness. They could live for each moment. They could think that because they loved so much, their love would last forever.

Gable had never understood those people; often, he'd been scornful of them. He would always see consequences. He would always see implications. The future would begin to rush at him like a speeding train. Panic would constrict his throat, until the affair ended and he could breathe more easily again.

Now he breathed deeply, inhaling the cold air that was so sharp it felt as though it would cut his lungs. Gable suddenly thought of how warm it would be in L.A. now. Gish would be working twelve-hour days, a thought that comforted him. She was happy, as he had once been happy, consumed by work, making deals, maneuvering in the intricate world of actors and films and contracts. She understood him and what drove him—that fundamental lack in him that she knew so well because she possessed it herself.

He had to go. He had business there anyway, business he'd been putting off because of Annabel and because of Ben and Sasha's wedding. Gable grimaced when he thought of Sasha's wounded eyes. He had been so foolishly happy when they'd called with the news. He had really believed Ben when he'd said that Sasha had changed him. He had wanted so badly to believe it. Now he felt a fury at Ben Hall that he'd never felt for another man.

He wouldn't be the coward that Ben Hall had been. He wouldn't string a remarkable woman along just because it was so easy to love her. He would make the decision now, before he hurt her too badly.

L.A. it was, Gable decided, turning and heading back to the house. He would immerse himself in work, and he wouldn't return until the final cut was done. He'd do the right thing and leave Annabel alone.

But first, he thought, his footsteps suddenly slowing, dragging through the snow, he had to say goodbye to her.

"Goodbye? Where are you going?" Annabel paused with the coffee scoop poised over the beans. Here she'd been planning on what to say all night, how she would tell Gable that she just couldn't get involved with him again, and now there was no need for her calm, mature speech.

She didn't feel the expected relief, however; she felt a little bereft.

"L.A. I've been putting off a lot of work. We're going into that last crucial period for the film—marketing, publicity and so on. I shouldn't have stayed this long. You've already got a rough cut, we know how the film is going to look. I'll be back to look at the final cut."

"All right. Would you like some coffee?" Annabel kept her voice carefully neutral. Gable was deciding the ground rules: they were going to pretend that last night had never happened. That was fine with her.

"No thanks. I have to pack."

Annabel turned back to the coffee beans. She could feel Gable still behind her, standing at the entrance to the kitchen. She painstakingly measured out the beans and poured them into the grinder, making sure that each bean was securely inside, carefully replacing the scoop back in the glass jar of beans, plugging in the electric grinder. All through her deliberate motions, she felt him watching her. But she wouldn't turn around. What could she possibly say? *Gable, don't go. I can't be with you but suddenly I can't conceive of being without you.*

Finally she heard him leave. His footsteps went down the hall and around the curve to the staircase. Only when she heard him mount the stairs did she turn around and gaze at the spot where he had stood. She debated furiously with herself. Shouldn't she go after him, shouldn't they at least discuss what had happened? Was it fair to avoid a discussion because it would bring fresh pain?

She stood there staring, while the kettle began to boil and the phone began to ring. Annabel collected herself, turned off the kettle and crossed to the phone. She said hello absently, her eyes still on the doorway where Gable had been.

"Annie, thank heavens it's you."

"Ben?"

"I was praying you'd answer. God knows I didn't want to talk to Gable."

"Or Sasha?" Annabel asked icily.

A heavy sigh came through the phone. "How is she?"

"How do you expect she is, Ben? How could you do this to her?"

"Believe me, Annabel, she's better off not married to me. I just couldn't do that to her."

Anger boiled over inside Annabel. "Spare me your noble act, Ben. You expect me to applaud your act of cruelty? When are you going to grow up?"

"You're right. I was a heel." Ben sighed again. "What I need is a woman who won't put up with me."

"What you need is a good analyst."

"Hey, you think I should change mine?"

Annabel sighed and leaned her forehead against the wall. "Ben, what do you want?"

"I wanted to see how Sasha was. And, well, I feel so badly, Annabel. I want to make sure that you understand. That you'll forgive me eventually."

She spoke quietly. "Not this time, Ben."

"Well, the thing is, Annabel—not that I think you're not professional and all—but I hope that my, uh, behavior won't prejudice you in any way. In the cutting room, I mean."

Annabel stood bolt upright as his words sank in. He hadn't called out of genuine concern for Sasha; he just wanted to make sure Annabel wouldn't diminish his close-ups. All at once she burst through the thin shadowy scrim of Ben's personality into the true substance of character behind, and the sight sickened her. Now his voice, so full of insinuating charm, with those hesitations and that sincerity, was exposed to her in all its falseness. Ben would always be selfish in a way so pure it was frightening.

Ben seemed to grow nervous at her long silence. "Annabel? Listen, it's not just for myself that I'm concerned—it's really for the good of the film. Josiah has to be a strong character for it to work. It's for all of us, Sasha included. I do want the best for her," he concluded sincerely, a note of wistfulness in his voice.

Annabel could think of nothing to say to him. Perhaps the best response was none at all. "Goodbye, Ben," she said, disgust and finality clear in her tone.

"But Annabel, wait! Are you going to—"

She didn't wait to hear the rest, but quietly replaced the receiver. She walked back to the kettle and began to make coffee automatically, but she had to stop; she found that her hands were shaking. She sat down at the kitchen table.

She was sick at heart, sick and angry, too. Angry not just at Ben, but at Gable as well. Who were they, to think they were being so courageous, so honest, as to declare, *"I don't know how to love."* What a monumental act of selfishness, of cowardice, that was.

She put her head in her hands. She was better off without Ben Hall as a friend, she knew that now. And she was certainly better off without Gable. He was cut from the same cloth; his honesty was a thousand times more dangerous than the smoothest man's lies.

Finally, with only three shopping days left until Christmas, the film was completed. Jessie and Annabel sent it to the sound studio and treated the assistants to the fanciest dinner southern Vermont had to offer. Then they sleepily drove home together, compared plans for the normal life they could return to, and hugged goodbye.

Annabel walked into a cold, silent house. Shivering, she lit a fire in her bedroom, one of the delights of Gable's house. She felt strange being here after her work was completed, even for only one night. She could hardly wait to leave the next day.

She wrapped herself in a warm flannel robe and curled up with a book. It had been so long since she'd had the luxury of reading, Annabel thought. She would certainly enjoy a few weeks of leisure time. She dipped into the first chapter expectantly.

The phone shrilled by her bedside; she sighed and picked it up.

"Hello?"

"Hi, it's Sasha. Did I wake you?"

"No, not at all. I might not be coherent, but I'm awake. How are you, Sasha?"

"Pretty good, actually. I'm coming back to life. I have this method I developed in Idaho. I give myself a deadline when I have to stop feeling miserable. I tell myself I'll be all over Ben Hall by January fifteenth."

"Sounds good. But Sasha, I hate to ask this, but what happens if January fifteenth rolls around and you're not over him?"

"No sweat. I just extend the deadline. I work in the film business, remember? You know, Annabel, I've discovered that there are times in life when you just have to resort to tricking yourself."

Annabel laughed. "How's Hollywood these days?"

"Pretty grim. But I did have a high point three weeks ago—I saw Ben at Remember the Alamo."

"Where?"

"Really, Annabel, you must brush up on your restaurant IQ. It's the latest Mexican place. Anyway, he was there with Delia Worthington—"

"No!"

"Yes! She's still awaiting trial, you know. I was there with Gable—he was letting me cry on his shoulder. Anyway, we both choked on our margaritas when we saw Ben. Ben started waving at us and Gable ignored him. Can that man be frosty, or what? And he said Ben was lucky he didn't go over and punch him. I told him I felt like dumping my plate of enchiladas on Ben's head. He said it sounded like a very good idea to him. So I did."

"You didn't!"

"I did. It felt great. Not only that, a photographer was there from *Personalities* magazine. I was upset when the picture came out—tempestuous star loses control, you know—but my agent was thrilled. Anyway, James Fortinbras saw it and called me. He's been going crazy looking for a lead in the film he's making of *The Custom of the Country*. Do you know it?"

"Edith Wharton, of course. And Fortinbras is incredible—he produces the classics and the people actually go see the films. They're wonderful. That's great news, Sasha."

"Well, the reason I'm calling, besides the fact that I wanted to check and see if you were alive and kicking after all that frenzied editing—"

"Alive, maybe, but not kicking yet."

"—was because Anthony Burden-Jones was slated to direct, but Fortinbras fired him, and now he's looking for an American director, and I mentioned you. And Annabel, he's really interested. I mean, this is top secret, but he's going to be suggesting a meeting any day now."

Annabel sat up. "You're kidding."

"No! The only thing is that production is slated to start soon, the end of January. In France, Annabel! Won't it be great?"

"It'll be cold. That soon, huh?"

"I know you'd be stepping in at the last minute, but you can handle it. You pulled *A Family of Two* together."

"I don't know, Sasha. I consider preproduction as half my job, and somebody else has already done it. And I've just done a period film. Besides, I'm not finished with *A Family of Two* yet. I've still got to meet with the composer, and—"

"But Annabel, you're the best. I trust you so much. I'm dying to work with you again."

"I want to work with you, too, Sasha. But I don't know whether this is the project."

"Well, you can meet with Fortinbras, can't you?"

"Sure."

"He's flying in to New York Christmas week. Do you have any plans?"

"Not really. Tomorrow I'm getting on the parkway and driving straight to Bloomingdale's. I have to catch up on my Christmas shopping."

"Well, just leave some time for him. Listen, I have to go. I'll call you back really soon, all right? And think about it."

"I will." Annabel replaced the receiver slowly. She'd have to do a lot of thinking about this one. She was attracted to the material, but she didn't know if she wanted to step into the project immediately before filming. The main attraction, she realized, was that it would take her out of the country and immediately plunge her into work again. She wouldn't spend any time stewing about Gable. She was aware that she'd been able to push thoughts of him away because of work, and she'd have to deal with him eventually. But not yet.

Maybe Sasha's method would work. "I'll be over him by January 15th," she said aloud. Then she shrugged. "Heck, I'll be over him by Christmas," she tried. That sounded good.

The phone rang and she snatched it up. "I'm still thinking," she said.

"About what?"

No matter how often she heard his voice, it always stopped her breath for a moment. "Gable, hello. I was just discussing a new film project with Sasha."

"Oh, yes, *The Custom of the Country.*"

"Yes. What have you heard about it?"

"That it's been in trouble from the word go, although now that Burden-Jones has walked and they signed Sasha, the situation should improve. You thinking of stepping in?"

"Maybe."

"Awfully cold in Paris this time of year."

"I know. But Paris is always . . . Paris."

"I suppose," Gable said noncommittally. "Well, to return to your current project for a moment, I'm going to the studio tomorrow to see the film. I'm sorry I couldn't get to Vermont this week."

"That's okay. I did want you to see it with me before we sent it, though."

"I saw the rough cut. I'm not worried. And I always see the final alone anyway."

"Oh. Well, Gable, I guess this is it. Thanks for the use of your house, and for everything. You were a great producer."

"Thanks." His voice was gruff. "And thanks to you, too, Annabel. You were remarkable. You surprised me in a thousand ways."

She laughed, a short reluctant bark. "Not all of them pleasant, I'd bet."

"All of them pleasant," he said softly.

A pause spun out into an endless moment. Annabel gripped the receiver, barely daring to breathe, utterly incapable of saying the word that would sever her from Gable. Such a simple word, but it wouldn't pass her lips. *Goodbye.*

Oh, they would invariably meet again, at a party, or a restaurant, or a premiere. Perhaps they'd even work together again—someday. Would the magic still be there? Annabel wondered as her heart galloped frantically against her ribs. Would it still shimmer, would it still seduce, would it still ensnare? Would she continue to be cursed her whole life long with the memory of this impossible, magnetic man?

She opened her mouth, but no sound came. *Goodbye, Gable,* she silently practiced in her mind. *Goodbye forever, for the next time I see you, you will be a stranger to me. And you were never that, not even when I hated you.*

Then he spoke, so softly she had to hold her breath to hear the words.

"I'll never forget you, Annabel."

The click was faint, but it reverberated through her consciousness with an ominous, heavy reality.

Annabel replaced the receiver softly. "Goodbye," she said. Her voice sounded unnaturally high and thin in the silent house.

Gable swung the Ferrari to the front of the building and tossed his keys to the attendant. He was running late, as usual, but it hadn't been for lack of trying to get here; he couldn't remember ever feeling quite this expectant to see a film he had produced.

He had had a busy, exhausting time in Hollywood, his days crammed with meetings and decisions, exactly as he'd hoped. Gish had been busy too, with one thing or another, and he'd been surprisingly grateful that that was the case. All of a sudden he was reluctant to meet her shrewd eyes. He was aware that he was looking different these days; harassed and edgy, he prowled around town, looking for a peace that eluded him.

And last night...Gable paused on the third step, thinking of his conversation with Annabel. He hadn't expected it to be as hard as it was. When she'd told him she was thinking of doing the film in Paris he thought he'd have a heart attack. Suddenly he couldn't bear to think of her there, thousands of miles away, in his favorite city, for months. Paris, cold and gray, with its incredible, luminous light, would be such a backdrop for Annabel's exuberance, her lush, intelligent beauty....

He came to and discovered he was standing on the stairs while people streamed around him. He gave himself a brisk mental shake. Paris could do that to you, he supposed, make you dream for things you would never be able to capture.

He hurried into the projection room, settled into his seat, exactly dead center, and signaled to the projectionist to start the film. The first scene began to roll.

He'd seen the footage a thousand times at least, but somehow the break had refreshed him, and the film looked fresh and new. He'd been prepared to view it with a critical eye, but a strange thing happened; he began to feel moved by what he saw. It was as if somebody else had written these plain, harsh words, had crafted these poignant scenes. He could even laugh at the occasional humor.

Annabel had been right. She had been right every step of the way. The film had turned out to be a stunning display of her vision. She had taken his simple words and fashioned them into a film that shimmered with life and joy. As the plot grew more convoluted her images grew more dense, and their power, along with the complexities of the characters, twined around each other until the inevitable tragic outcome grew like a deadening weight in the chest.

He was lost in the crucial scene of Melinda's discovery of her pregnancy when he felt a tap on his shoulder. An assistant hunched over him.

Gable looked at him irritably. It was a rule of his that he was never to be disturbed in the projection room unless the building was on fire, and he was surprised, as he always was, when someone ignored his wishes.

"Sorry to interrupt, Mr. McCrea. It's your sister. She's on the phone. I told her you were in a screening, and then she put me on hold, so I wasn't sure what to do...."

"That's okay. Could you stop the film, please?"

The assistant nodded and scurried away. Gable picked up the phone by his chair. He said hello but was met with silence. He grunted impatiently and waited, drumming his fingers on his leg.

Finally, Gish came on. "Hello. Who's this?"

"Don't you know," Gable pointed out, "that when you call and interrupt someone, you're not supposed to put them on hold? I'm in a screening."

"What? A screening? Oh, *that's* what the guy said. Jeez, I'm sorry, Gable. I went to get another box of tissues. Look, you can call me back—"

"Don't be silly. What's with the tissues? Do you have a cold?"

"No." Gable held the phone away from his ear as Gish blew her nose like a trumpet into the receiver.

"Are you upset?" he asked, the truth finally dawning on him.

"Something terrible has happened."

"What? For God's sake, Gish—"

"David asked me to marry him."

Gable's body sagged in relief. The first thing that had darted across his mind had been that something had happened to Annabel. Instead, it had been another semicomical episode in Gish's complicated love life. He tried to suppress a chuckle, but he couldn't. "This is terrible?"

"Don't laugh. You know it is."

"Why don't you just say no like you do with all your other proposals?" Silence met this question, and Gable realized with a start that he hadn't grasped this situation after all. "You want to?" he asked cautiously.

"Do you think I'm crazy?" Gish asked wildly, blowing her nose again. "I've gone for forty-two years without marrying. How can I marry now? How could I make him happy? How could it possibly last? What if he completely swallows me up? He may look like a pussycat, Gabe, but let me tell you, he's a firecracker."

Gable smiled at the image of the rumpled, mild-mannered David being a firecracker. "You're mixing your metaphors."

"Oh, so now that you're a writer with a hit film you can split hairs?"

"I don't know if it's a hit film. I haven't been able to watch it yet."

"And, Gable," Gish went on, her voice dipping low in foreboding, "he has *kids*. Three of them!"

"Do you hate them?"

"Are you kidding? I *adore* them! They're delightful, and fun—did you know that kids could be fun, Gable? We were such horrors. Anyway, the whole deal is just so overwhelming. I mean, what if I start baking cookies? Wearing aprons? *Vacuuming?*"

"I can't imagine you doing any of those things," Gable answered truthfully. "For heaven's sake, you both have enough money, you don't have to do them."

"That's not the point, and you know it. Gable, you know what's terrifying me, you know it more than anybody could."

"I know, Gish," he answered quietly. "Do you love him?"

"I love him so much I feel sick," Gish sniffed. "He's the best man I know. I think of being without him and I simply can't imagine it. For once, I think I would probably die. I think of anybody hurting him and I want to kill them. Not that David can't take care of himself, but—you know."

"I know," he said, frowning. For once, he *did* know.

"But I have to make a decision about this," she continued frantically. "I have to."

"I don't think so," Gable said slowly.

That stopped Gish in her tracks. "What?"

"I think that when it comes to love, you never really make a decision at all. You don't have to. I think you know what you want, and you just called me so that I'd tell you that you won't fail, you won't be swallowed up, that David isn't the kind of person who would want you to be anything less than what you are. You want me to tell you what you already know—your marriage will be long and happy, and you won't change, either—except that you won't call me in the middle of a screening when you're upset, you'll call David instead.''

"So what are you waiting for?" Gish demanded. "Tell me."

"Gish, you won't be swallowed up. Your marriage will be long and happy," Gable answered obediently.

"Since when did you get so wise?"

"Go call David and make him a happy man. And congratulations."

"I love you," Gish said, sounding teary. "I really do."

"Me, too," Gable said quietly, and they hung up.

The projectionist saw him replace the receiver, and started the film again. It took him some time to realize he wasn't concentrating on it, and then he watched it with a heightened sense brought on by the warm feeling he'd gotten from Gish's happiness. He'd seen her happy before, but it had been a different kind of happiness that had colored her voice today. It was as though she would burst from it.

The combined weight of Gish's happiness and the pain of Josiah and Melinda, Sasha and Ben, made the film gain a strength and power that hit Gable in the stomach. When it ended, he was limp with emotion. He thanked the projectionist with a wave and headed out the door quickly. To his surprise, he bumped into Jessie Allan.

"I thought you were staying in Vermont for Christmas," he said, giving her a quick hug hello.

"Believe it or not, I got tired of the snow. Just see the film?"

"You've done a great job, Jessie. I'm prouder of this than anything I've done."

"I learned a lot from Annabel. If you knew me a little better, you'd know how unusual it is for me to say this.

She's such a tight director, she's a joy. And it was your script, of course. I hope you come out of the closet and do more, Gable. It was poignant and lovely. I haven't seen many films that really capture that kind of love. You're very good.''

"Well, thanks. I consider that high praise.''

"You'd better. Did you see how we tightened the scene in the field, by the way? It was one of those one-o'clock-in-the-morning breakthroughs.''

"I must have missed it,'' Gable admitted. "My sister called in the middle, and I was a little distracted when I got back to the film.''

"You took the call?'' Jessie's warm brown eyes were wide with amazement. "That doesn't sound like the Gable McCrea I know. Well, I've got to get moving. Happy holidays.''

"You too,'' Gable said automatically. He walked out, blinking when the sunshine hit his eyes. He felt dazed all of a sudden; his legs were like jelly. His thoughts were whirling in a bright confused mass. Jessie's words revolved in his head, though she had certainly said nothing revelatory. What was it that had given him such a start, as if he'd been lashed with an electric current? *"That doesn't sound like the Gable McCrea I know...."*

He handed his keys to the attendant and started down the stairs. He couldn't make sense of his thoughts, couldn't puzzle it all out. His brain was revealing some obvious message, like a patient teacher pointing out the alphabet to a child. And he was staring at the letters, but not connecting them with the words that could open up a whole new world.

And then he stopped.

Revelation almost tipped him backward. It was beautiful, dazzling, pouring over him like the light and warmth of the sun.

Jessie Allan had casually pointed out to him what he should have known already. It *was* unusual that he had taken that call from Gish. Once he would have had no scruples about instructing the assistant that he would call her back. It was the kind of relationship they'd always had; they'd always understood each other's priorities.

But today he had taken that call unthinkingly, instinctively. It was his sister. She was on the phone. She needed him.

And he had been secretly, delightedly pleased that she wanted to marry David. He had told her to go ahead and do it without a second's hesitation.

He had just seen a film he'd written, and it was a love story. He had captured that feeling. Not only that, but he had enjoyed writing it. It had worked because he had understood the characters, had loved them.

Even looking back on the making of the film, Gable barely recognized himself. He had counseled an actor on his romantic troubles, no matter how ineffectively. He hadn't for one moment worried about how it would affect his film; he hadn't for one moment passed it off as just another broken romance, pedestrian and common as swimming pools in Beverly Hills. He had considered it important enough to fight for, and he had been happy when he'd thought that Ben and Sasha had worked out their problems.

Now he understood his rage at Ben, for what was Ben Hall but his own double? Heedless of everything but their own fear, reckless of anything but their own need, they sped through life, roaring around its corners, while in their wake people smashed up and were broken. Gable had looked into a mirror when he'd looked at Ben that Thanksgiving Day, and it had sickened him. He had seen a crippled, pathetic spirit. He hadn't been able to accept it, so he had run away.

But he'd been wrong. The image he'd been running away from facing was no longer his.

He had changed. He was a different man. He was a better man. And he knew now, with such stunning clarity he thought his heart would burst with the knowledge, why he had been changed.

He loved.

And now at the age of forty, damn stupid fool that he was, he was just beginning to understand what that meant.

Love didn't diminish, he knew now; it expanded. It didn't engulf; it broadened.

He had been fighting so hard against Annabel's hold on him, insisting so hard he would never, could never change, that he hadn't begun to see how changed he was already. Through loving Annabel he had been given a gift. She had given him the capacity to love better, wider, more deeply. His love for Gish was clearer than it had ever been; through writing the story of Melinda and Josiah, the *second* story, the one that Annabel had urged him to do, he had understood his parents' compulsions enough to be touched by them.

He had cared enough about Ben and Sasha's troubles to try to bring them together, and when that had failed, he had felt an empathy for Sasha he'd never been capable of before. He had wanted to reach out to her as one human being to another, while he'd watched the beautiful compassion soften Annabel's eyes.

It was as though Annabel's love were a stone dropped into a pond, disturbing its stillness, but the concentric rings of caring she'd created spread out to embrace everyone who was close to him. Through loving Annabel, he had expanded; through loving her, the world was open to him in a way it never had been before.

Now he understood so many things he had scorned, so many things, banal and sublime, he had never comprehended. Amazing, that love could bring such exhilaration, such a sense of newness to life. It was wonderful, Gable thought suddenly, and then he smiled. He was acting like the first man who had ever been in love, he realized, and it was utterly delightful.

He had been so terrified that love would overwhelm him. Now he was overwhelmed, and he welcomed it. Love made a new family in all good ways—for in a family, Gable realized now, life became worth living.

There was no mystery to life; it was all too abundantly clear. And he had almost missed it. It was a miracle that he had not; a bigger miracle if he could somehow remedy his mistakes. It gave him an immense confidence to realize that he was about to make a fool of himself, and he didn't care.

He laughed aloud, not minding who heard him; he had never felt so free. Some heavy burden had dislodged and floated away some time ago, and he had never noticed. Suddenly, the world looked new.

When the parking attendant approached with his car, he pumped his hand joyously. As he slid behind the wheel, he tossed him a twenty-dollar tip. Then he turned the dial until the radio hummed with Christmas carols, the same songs he used to shudder to hear.

He roared out of the parking lot, singing. He had no idea where he was going, but he didn't have much time. Even that contradiction delighted him.

Chapter Fourteen

Annabel took a deep breath of the cold winter air. Snow was falling lightly in the bright noon light of Third Avenue as last-minute shoppers swirled around her. She was poked with umbrellas and shopping bags, but she remained motionless an extra moment, gathering her courage. Then she swept into the pandemonium of Bloomingdale's on Christmas Eve.

Years of Manhattan living had taught Annabel survival tactics, and she threaded through the crowds lightly, knowing that grace was more important than brute force against these odds. She had already decided what her purchases would be, and she proceeded directly to the departments where they would be found.

What luxury, Annabel thought as she selected the beautifully cut wool suit her mother had wanted but had hesitated to buy, to be able to purchase what she'd always wanted for her family. It had taken a phone call to her accountant to reassure herself that *Writing Off Craig* was still indeed a hit, and now Christmas shopping was a joy to do.

She picked up a Harris tweed jacket for her father and wild sport watches for her nieces and a portable cassette player for her nephew and chose the sexiest satin robe she could find for her sister-in-law, all the while congratulating herself that she was able to do her shopping so cheerfully, so unconscious of the heavy weight that had oppressed her for months. Gable McCrea was as far from her thoughts, she sang to herself, as if she'd never known him at all.

New York and Christmas had returned her to her priorities. Mendocino and Vermont were other worlds; Gable had no place in this one. Annabel spied a pair of cobalt kid gloves that her sister-in-law would love and she slapped down her credit card. She was having a marvelous time.

She was already weighted down with shopping bags when she headed for the men's department on the first floor. It was packed densely with shoppers as they scrambled through the shirts and sweaters on various tables in the aisles. Annabel found a relatively deserted glass counter with an array of cashmere sweaters. She hesitated over them for her brother, telling herself it would be madness to buy the heathery lilac one when she knew he would rather die than wear it.

Gray was certainly more appropriate for an investment counselor, she told herself, and scrutinized the many shades in the case. She signaled for the salesman, who, remarkably enough, came to her aid immediately and spread out a charcoal gray she supposed her brother would appreciate. Then next to it he tossed an extraordinary pearly gray, a color she had always associated with Gable's eyes.

Her hand snaked out tremulously to touch the soft wool. She closed her eyes and imagined Gable in the sweater, stoking up the fire on a cold winter night.

When she opened her eyes again she saw that she was gripping the sweater, crumpling the material, and she smoothed it out as the salesman came back and looked at her oddly.

"Can I help you?"

"I'll take it," Annabel said, her voice thick.

"Which one, ma'am?"

Tears began to slip out of the corner of her eyes, and Annabel lowered her head. "I—I don't know. Both of them," she said, panicked.

She signed the charge slip without seeing it and shoved the bulky package under her arm. She started to walk blindly to the exit, horrified at her tears, which kept sliding down her face no matter how sternly she told herself to stop.

She spied a chair, miraculously unoccupied and partially hidden by racks of fisherman sweaters. Annabel sank into it, her purchases falling at her feet. She fished into the pocket of her tweed overcoat for a handkerchief, feeling foolish. This had never happened to her before. She was utterly incapable of controlling herself.

The tears kept coming, now mingled with muffled sobs, and Annabel was grateful for the serious concentration of the shoppers and the busyness of the clerks. Nobody would notice her as she sat here, quietly having a nervous breakdown.

I've lost control of myself in Bloomingdale's on Christmas Eve, she thought wildly. And on the heels of that realization came another, one more profoundly shocking and certainly more terrifying.

I really must be in love.

Annabel had never been overly emotional. When a cashmere sweater reduced her to uncontrollable tears, she had to stop and examine the situation. But as she sat there, crying as though her heart was broken, she realized that she couldn't begin to examine it. Logic didn't enter into this at all; love swirled in her brain, so messy and so overwhelming it left no room for anything else but its object.

She couldn't forget him. He was as potent a force in her life as the ability to draw breath. There really was such a thing as one true, unforgettable love, and she had found it. She would probably never get over it. She wouldn't forget him by Christmas, or by January fifteenth; she would never forget him, and that would be her impossible burden to somehow bear.

The tears ran swifter now, and her handkerchief was a sodden crumpled mess. She couldn't imagine any worse fate than to love like this and to be alone. To want and not to have.

It was Gable's fault, that damned cool man, with his twisted half smile and his burning practiced fingertips. She had fallen in love so deeply she was unable to climb out. He had never, not for one moment, been fair. He had loved and withdrawn, loved and withdrawn, until she had felt bruised beyond repair.

And as she sat there, huddled in the chair, miserable and aching, she had to ask herself if *she* had been fair. Somehow it was a question that hadn't occurred to her before. All along she had reacted to him, to his needs, to his misconceptions. Had she ever stood up proudly, unafraid of her feelings, and to hell with the consequences? Or had she, Annabel thought with increasing horror, merely been too afraid to make a fool of herself?

What was the matter with her? When it came to her work, she had the determination of a bull and an ability to clamp down on any fear. She put one foot in front of the other without worrying too much if ground would be there to meet them. She had learned early on that to be a woman director meant that she had to work longer and harder than anyone else, that she had to hang on and take blow after blow until she got what she wanted.

So why was she so fierce when it came to her work, and so timid when it came to love, the thing that so supremely mattered?

How could she have been such a—Annabel mentally sputtered with indignation—a *wimp*?

She resolutely wiped the tears from her cheeks with her palms. She was done with tears, with whining. It was time for action.

Gable had pushed her away because of some misguided notion about love, and she had let him do it. What did she expect, for Gable to come riding up on a white horse and sweep her away? For him to be the strong one to dictate how their love would go? She had seen love in his eyes, she had felt it in his touch, she had sensed his hesitation and his need, but she had been afraid of laying herself on the line and so she had simply withdrawn.

How could she have let him push her around that way?

Annabel stood up. She picked up her red and green shopping bags and the bag of cashmere sweaters. She pushed her way through the crowd, suddenly anxious to feel the cold air on her face. She had no idea where this burst of energy was taking her, but she knew one thing: all she wanted to do right now was pick up Gable by his lapels and shout at him, to let him know he was being a complete idiot and she wasn't going to stand for it.

But how? she wondered as she pushed out onto Third Avenue and searched for a cab in the crush. What should she do? Phone him? Incur her parents' wrath and fly to California tonight?

Just then she saw a yellow cab heading for the curb, and she rushed toward it, praying no other intrepid New Yorker had noticed it.

But she stopped short when she saw Gable fly out of it, tossing a bundle of bills exuberantly at the driver and shouting a "Merry Christmas" at him. She stood paralyzed, her bags heavy in her gloved fists. What was he doing here on Third Avenue when he should be floating in a pool in Malibu?

Then her earlier wrath galvanized her into action. She covered the distance between them in a quick bound that sailed her past a Salvation Army Santa. The light coating of snow was slippery, and her boots slid along it. Her arms windmilling as much as possible while weighted down with her bags, she slid unceremoniously into Gable. Her cold nose hit his camel overcoat.

Annabel dropped her bags on the wet sidewalk and grabbed the perfectly tailored lapels. The expression in those same gray eyes that had made her weep so tragically was amused, but she ignored it.

"You're an idiot!" she shouted. "How can you be so blind and so stupid as to throw away what we have? You're holding on to some misguided notions about love for some cockamamy reason having to do with your parents and your father's death. Gable, I'm sorry you had a rotten childhood and you feel responsible for your father's death, I truly am, but enough already! It's interfering with your happiness, with *my* happiness, and I'm not going to stand for it! I simply won't have it, be-cause—'' Annabel stopped. Gable was grinning, a full, amused, dazzling grin. How dare he laugh at her!

"Because what?" he asked, straight-faced now and politely ignoring the fact that his lapels were up around his ears.

"Because I love you," Annabel said helplessly. She started to cry again. "You jerk," she added in a choked voice, searching for her wet handkerchief.

Gable threw back his head and laughed with pure exultation. He wiped her tears with his gloved thumbs and hugged her close to him. "You are such a romantic," he murmured. "It's one of the many reasons I love you."

Annabel pushed him away. "I will not be patronized, Gable McCrea—" she began with great formality, and then stiffened. She peered up into his face. It was the same angular face that she'd known and loved, but something was different. Were his eyes *dancing*? "What did you say?" she asked.

"I said, my darling Annabel," Gable said gravely, "that I love you. You're the most wonderful woman in the world, and I want to spend the rest of my life with you."

"You do?" she whispered.

He nodded. "I do." He held her head gently in his hands and let her look into his eyes. All traces of amusement were gone, and she had never seen a more honest, more beautiful expression, for she had never loved or been loved like this.

"I think we should get married," he said. "Will you?"

"Yes," she said clearly, but the Santa rang his bell vigorously behind her, and her voice was drowned out. She launched herself at Gable, and he caught her in his arms.

They kissed for a long time, a dizzying kiss that sent spiraling threads of magic around them, isolating them from the frenzied Christmas scene around them. Through it all, through the softness of Gable's mouth and the secrets it told her, Annabel heard bells and carols and felt the icy delicacy of snow against her cheek. She would always remember the joy of this moment when she saw snowflakes twinkling down against streetlamps, she decided when she pulled away.

"I hope you just said yes," Gable said. She nodded. "Well, I'm just warning you," he said suddenly, "that I'm not going to take up vacuuming!"

"Whatever you say, darling," Annabel said happily, having no idea what he was talking about.

"Come on, let's get your packages together and go somewhere warm and private," Gable said. "We'll never get a cab, so we'd better walk."

"Gable, my apartment is over forty blocks away."

"But the Waldorf is only ten." He reached down and gathered up the shopping bags, then put his arm snugly around her.

"By the way, are you taking that film assignment?" he asked as they began to walk.

"I haven't decided. I suppose we should talk about it."

"I'm so happy I don't care where I spend the next six months. And besides, it's never occurred to me before, but Paris would be rather wonderful for a honeymoon. Do you think anyone's ever thought of that?"

"I'm sure we'll be the first," Annabel said solemnly.

They walked down Third Avenue amid the Christmas Eve bustle, past flushed smiling faces and twinkling red and green lights, their arms intertwined, leaning against each other as the snow fell softly around them.

Gable looked at her and smiled. "A family of two," he said.

Annabel nodded. They walked a few more steps in the deepening twilight. "And what," she asked casually, "if that family gets expanded one day?"

Gable tucked her arm more securely in his. "Oh, I'm counting on that," he said tranquilly.

*   *   *   *   *

Silhouette Intimate Moments

COMING IN
OCTOBER

SEA GATE
by
MAURA SEGER

**Atlantis . . . land of the imagination.
Or is it real?**

Suppose a man of our world were to meet a
woman who might not be exactly what she
seemed. What if they found not only love, but
a way to cross bridges that had never before
been crossed?

Travel with them in SEA GATE, a very special
love story about two very special people.
Coming next month, only from Silhouette
Intimate Moments.

Don't miss it!

IM209-1

Silhouette Special Edition

COMING NEXT MONTH

AVAILABLE THIS MONTH:

Starting in October...

SHADOWS ON THE NILE

by

Heather Graham Pozzessere

A romantic short story in six installments from best-selling author Heather Graham Pozzessere.

The first chapter of this intriguing romance will appear in all Silhouette titles published in October. The remaining five chapters will appear, one per month, in Silhouette Intimate Moments' titles for November through March '88.

Don't miss "*Shadows on the Nile*"—a special treat, coming to you in October. Only from Silhouette Books.

Be There!

IMSS-1